Katherine Towler

# SNOW ISLAND

MacAdam/Cage Publishing
155 Sansome Street, Suite 620
San Francisco, CA 94104
www.macadamcage.com

Library of Congress Cataloging-in-Publication Data

Towler, Katherine, 1956 —
    Snow Island / by Katherine Towler.
        p. cm.
    ISBN 1-931561-01-X (alk. paper)
    1. World War, 1939-1945–New England–Fiction. 2. Teenage girls–Fiction.
    3. New England–Fiction. 4. Islands–Fiction. 5. Widows–Fiction.
    6. Grief–Fiction. I. Title.

    PS3620.O94 S66 2002
    813'.6–dc21

                                                                    2001058678

Manufactured in the United States of America.
10 9 8 7 6 5 4 3 2 1

Book design by Dorothy Carico Smith

Katherine Towler

# SNOW ISLAND

MacAdam/Cage Publishing

San Francisco ◆ Denver

*For Jim, with love*

# PART I
*The Summer Before the War*

## — 1941 —

George Tibbits stepped from the 4:03 with a small leather suitcase, the only passenger to disembark in Barton. A moment later the train pulled away and left him alone on the platform. Through the rain-streaked window of the station, he could see the attendant seated in the ticket booth. He envied people who had jobs that required a uniform. When you wore a uniform, people knew who you were without asking. They didn't study your face. George shifted the suitcase from one hand to the other, crossed the tracks, and headed for Front Street. He had not expected rain.

The narrow streets by the docks met him as they always did, with the smell of salt and fish. George passed lobster boats and quahog skiffs bobbing on their moorings, and the prim ferry waiting for the morning run. He passed Gilley's Bar and Morgan's Fish Market, and turned up the hill toward town.

He found Mrs. Santos where he had left her a year earlier, in the lobby of the Priscilla Alden Hotel, slumped in an armchair behind the desk with the Philco blaring at her side. Blinking her eyes as if emerging from a long rest, she produced the key to room twenty and set it on the tattered blotter. George climbed the wide stairs from the lobby, listening for footsteps overhead or the creak of a bedspring behind a closed door, some sign of life. The rough static of the radio, crackling when the station was lost, carried from down below, the only sound to be heard as he paused on the landing.

Cautiously turning the handle, he swept his gaze over the furniture and the faded wallpaper. Room twenty had not changed. The bed was in the same place against the wall, with the bedstand and small, bent rocking chair beside it. The oval mirror hung above the dresser. After setting his suitcase on the floor, he moved the rocking chair by the window, arranging the room exactly as he remembered it that night in 1919 when he came home from the war to sit in the dark without sleeping, staring out at the rooftops and the docks and the black surface of the bay.

George lowered himself into the rocking chair and watched a woman hurry past the pin factory across the street, a long brick building that took up the entire block on the back side of the hotel. The collar of her raincoat was turned up, and she walked with her arms folded over her chest, as though trying to keep warm. The last glimpse of the woman as she scurried around the corner only confirmed what he already knew: the world was not the place it had been in 1919. The streets of Barton were not the same streets. Yet, for a night, he could pretend.

He made the journey every year, and every year it followed the same pattern. He waited through April and May until the weather was right; then, on a day he recognized as the day he would leave only once it had arrived, he went to the station and boarded the train. This year the forecasters had let him down. George imagined waking to the bright morning he remembered, hovering expectantly between spring and summer. Instead there was the rain, turning the docks to thin, fluid lines in the distance. If the rain did not end, he would not follow his plan of spending one night at the Priscilla Alden and taking the morning ferry to Snow Island. He would stay at the hotel until he woke to a clear day.

George took his coat from the bed, where he had left it neatly folded, and closed the door to room twenty. He was halfway across the lobby when Mrs. Santos looked up from her magazine. "Lotta rain," she said, taking a toothpick from her mouth and rolling it between her fingers. "You might be staying more than one night, huh?"

George nodded and crossed to the door. Outside, he opened his umbrella and glanced at his watch. Five twenty-four. He turned up Front Street, away from the center of town. There was no one on the sidewalk. He took small steps, trying to keep his pants legs from getting wet, until he came to Nellie Worthington's door.

"Mr. Tibbits," she said, inclining her head as she stepped aside to let him pass. "Mrs. Santos called to tell me you were coming." She followed him down the hall and into the dining room. George took his place at the head of the table. Some years there were others boarding at Mrs. Worthington's, but this time he ate alone. He sat at the long table while she served ham, fried potatoes, and biscuits with last year's blackberry preserves.

Mrs. Worthington told him the news, how she had no one eating with her regularly now that Morris Barnes had passed away, poor man, and how the lilac festival was ruined this year with the terrible weather. George finished drinking his coffee. She brought his hat and umbrella from the stand and reluctantly ushered him to the door.

He was aware immediately of the stillness, drawn close to the bed like a watchful mourner, when he woke later that night. George lay there rubbing the worn sheet between his fingers. Something was missing. Then he realized: the rain. On the other side of the window, there was silence.

He pushed back the covers and stepped from the bed. The floor was cold against his bare feet. George raised the window a crack. In the morning, he would pull the door to, descend the stairs, and walk down to the docks where he would catch the ferry. He could feel the island out there in the bay, a tiny, unprotected slip of land underneath the clearing sky. It waited for him with its lonely pull, its terrible sameness. If he came back for anything, he came back for this, the remoteness, the vulnerability of the island, the strange quiet strength of the place. Everything else could change, but the island kept its solitary vigil from year to year.

The islanders who stared as he stepped from the ferry each spring believed he wanted to remember; yet just the opposite was true. He wanted to duplicate that first homecoming as precisely as possible because it was only then that he could forget, for a moment, what had waited for him on the island that day. It was only then that he could make himself believe it might have been different. The return to the island was a piece of his life he kept living over and over, until the day when he came home in 1919 had become like a rock along the shore, shaped into an even surface by the motion of the waves.

The bell in the church steeple chimed the hour. Four long, slow tolls hung in the air; the last echo faded, and quiet took its place. He would not have long to wait until morning.

# — CHAPTER 1 —

In the winter, the men left at dawn, walking out across the ice that circled Snow Island. They chopped holes in the surface and lowered their
quahog tongs into the water, and brought up wire baskets filled with
clams. Alice Daggett imagined she could see them now, still figures in the
early light, breath leaving their bodies like steam. One morning she had
gone out with her father, the two of them inching over the ice, her hand
circled tightly by his. When he pulled up the clams, she grasped the end
of the quahog tongs with him, feeling his strength. The quahogs live all
winter under the ice, he told her. Alice had wondered if the sand where
they burrowed was cold, and whether a clam could feel such things.

  This morning the men were out in boats, around the west side of the
island, and Alice had a clear view across the bay. She watched as the sun
rose into the sky, touching the rocks along the island's shore. She had
dreamed of her father again. He was rowing in after a day of work, steering the boat into a small cove. It might have been Gooseneck Cove,
except the place in the dream was different, a landscape she recognized
but did not quite know. He dropped the oars and raised his cap the way
he had so many times in life, as though she were a grown woman and
they were meeting on the streets of some town. She was about to call to
him when the foghorn had sounded, its long blast jerking her out of
sleep.

The foghorn continued to sound now, blanketing the island every sixty seconds, though the rain had finally ended. Alice made her way down the ferry dock and sat with her feet dangling over the water, trying to hold on to the memory of her father's face. He was alive again in the dreams, so real that she woke expecting to find him at the side of the bed. Sometimes the sense of his presence stayed with her all day.

Footsteps sounded on the dock's wood planks. Alice turned to find Owen Pierce shuffling toward her. He took his pipe from between his chapped lips and stared at it, as though the thing might remind him where he was headed. "Morning," he said gruffly. "Store open yet?"

"I was just on my way to open up." Alice got to her feet and, trying not to walk too much faster than Owen, turned back up the dock.

"Rain finally stopped. Ground ain't gonna dry out for planting for I don't know how long." Owen gripped the pipe in his mouth, so his words were muffled and his brown teeth showed. "One year we didn't plant till after the first of June – the year of the '96 blizzard. That was a storm now. We had snow up to the roofs. Didn't get the roads cleared for a week."

Alice forced herself to take small steps, matching his slow and awkward gait, as they walked the length of the dock. At eighty-two, Owen was the oldest person on Snow. He had gone out quahogging until his late seventies, when the arthritis curled up his hands so badly he couldn't work any longer. Now he spent most of his time seated by the stove at the store.

"We don't get winters like that anymore. My grandfather walked from here to Barton one time. Bay froze solid. Winter of 1857 that was. Ain't hardly anybody remembers winters like that now."

"The bay froze the year my father died."

"What's that?"

"The winter my father died. The bay froze that year."

Owen gave her a confused glance and moved his pipe from one side of his mouth to the other. "We don't get the snow like we used to anymore. I know that much."

Life had gotten soft, he said, what with having electricity since they
laid the cables from the mainland after the hurricane, and deliveries of
milk and meat, and even vegetables out of season. They didn't used to
have things like that on the island. Any milk they had came from their
own cows and meat from their own chickens, and that wasn't often. You
didn't just have a chicken every Sunday when he was growing up. Alice
listened to him go on and felt the sun on her face, like a miracle after the
days of rain. When they reached the store, a small shack-like structure
past the dock, she bounded up the porch steps and inserted the key in the
padlock.

"We didn't used to lock anything around here, neither," Owen said.

"My mother worries. I don't know why."

"I don't blame her. You never know who's getting off the ferry these
days." Owen followed her into the musty darkness.

Alice reached for the string hanging from a bare bulb over the
counter. Molly, the cat, let out a loud mew and emerged from the shelf
where she slept in the back, pressed against cans of cleanser. She rubbed
her head against Alice's bare leg. "Breakfast's coming," Alice said. Molly
cocked her head as though she understood and leapt up next to the cash
register.

Owen rested both hands on the counter and breathed heavily. "I'm
'bout out of tobacco."

Alice reached into the case beneath the cash register and removed a
pouch of tobacco. Molly followed her movements, ears erect.

"Mark that down now," Owen said as he slipped the pouch in his
shirt pocket.

Alice opened the ledger and wrote the price in a long line of figures
below Owen's name, though she knew he would never pay for it. He
leaned over the counter and squinted at the ledger. "I'll be good for it
come summer. We're getting a fair price for quahogs now, and it's bound
to go up when the summer people come. I'll be heading out soon, I
expect."

Rubbing the top of Molly's head, Alice shut the ledger. Owen kept up the fantasy, in his own mind, that he still went out quahogging and had money to pay for his tobacco. In those awkward moments when it was clear even to Owen that he was not out on a quahog skiff, he would offer a quick excuse. "Can't work as long a day as I used to, you know."

Alice watched as he walked haltingly toward the door. She thought of her father, who had always stopped to talk with Owen when they met on the road or down by his dock. Once her father told her that Owen Pierce knew more than anyone else on the island. "I didn't say he was smarter, mind you, but he knows more."

At the door, Owen stopped and turned to look at her. "You know quahogs can live longer than people. That's what the Indians said. Claimed quahogs could live more than a hundred years."

Alice smiled. Owen was famous on the island for ending conversations with this observation. He went out onto the porch. She listened to his slow footsteps move toward the bench. After a moment, the heavy scent of his pipe smoke came through the screen. Alice opened the door in the stove and tossed in some bits of driftwood and wadded newspaper. There was enough coal left that it might catch. She lit a match and held it to the paper. The cat mewed.

The fire had just caught when Alice's mother and her brother, Will, arrived. "Hot in here," Evelyn Daggett said as she took off her straw hat and set it on the counter.

"I thought you'd want breakfast." Alice shut the stove's door and reached down to pet Molly.

"Will, what do you have in that basket?" Evelyn asked.

Will peered beneath the bit of cloth that covered the basket hanging from his arm. "Three eggs."

"Three eggs. That's your breakfast. Those two hens still aren't laying."

"There's some bread left." Alice went to the back room and returned with a frying pan. She spooned a bit of grease from a can beneath the

12

counter and cracked the eggs into the pan.

"Fried?" Will whined. "I hate fried."

"There's not enough eggs for scrambled," Evelyn said.

The eggs sizzled in the pan, gradually crisping around the edges. Alice took three plates from the shelf under the counter, slid a cooked egg onto each one, and added a slice of bread. Before sitting down to eat with the others, she cut a couple of pieces from the white of her egg and set them in a bowl for Molly, who followed Alice to her shelf in the back.

"Why's that foghorn still howling?" Evelyn asked.

"I don't know." Alice pulled a stool up to the counter and reached for a fork.

"That Ethan Cunningham, staying up half the night and then not even bothering to shut off the horn. He's a poor excuse for a lighthouse keeper. His poor mother. I know she's got no choice now that Phil's gone, but I think that Ethan worries her sick, up there with his paintings all night long. He needs to get married."

Alice shot her mother an amused glance. "You think getting married will solve everyone's problems."

"It's a place to start. Will, stop playing with your food."

"I want cereal."

"You can't have cereal."

"Why not?" Will eyed the boxes of cereal on a shelf down the first aisle.

"Because we can't afford to eat any more of the stock. We don't hardly have enough money to order anything for the summer people."

"But that cereal's been here all winter."

"The boxes ain't been opened. There's nothing wrong with them."

"Except the ones the mice been nibbling on."

"Will Daggett, when was the last time you saw a mouse in here?"

"Yesterday."

Evelyn rolled her eyes at Alice. "I don't know what he's talking about."

Will shrugged. "I'm done."

"No, you're not. Finish that egg." Evelyn pointed to the yolk in the middle of his plate.

Will took his fork and smeared the yolk around.

"Will," Evelyn said in a warning tone. "Eat it, don't play with it." She pushed her plate away and lit a cigarette. "I still say one of those Cunningham girls should have come home to live with their mother. I don't know if that Ethan is even fit to be taking care of her. The way he neglects the lighthouse, you can only guess what he does with her. You know she can't get in and out of bed by herself."

"I know," Alice said, only half-listening. The story of Mrs. Cunningham's troubles was one her mother particularly relished since Mr. Cunningham had dropped dead of a heart attack back in January. Mrs. Cunningham, who had suffered from polio years earlier, could only walk with the help of leg braces and crutches. Ethan had come back from the mainland to take his father's place as the lighthouse keeper and to care for his mother.

After the 1938 hurricane the Coast Guard replaced the kerosene lamp with an electric one that simply needed to be turned on at night and off in the morning. The old keepers had slept fitfully or not at all, watching the kerosene flame to make sure it stayed lit. Now Ethan rolled out of bed whenever he pleased and flicked a switch. Sometimes he left the lighthouse lit and the foghorn braying until eight or nine o'clock in the morning, long after the fishermen had headed out. It was nothing short of a scandal on Snow.

"I bet he leaves her lying there for hours, just waiting for him to come get her up and fix breakfast," Evelyn went on smugly. "Not that Mrs. Cunningham would ever let on. She's too good for that. Never wants to say anything bad about anybody, especially that genius son of hers. But I can tell it's not all light and roses in that house these days. She came from money, just like Phoebe Shattuck. Spent it all on Ethan's education and look where it got her. Poor woman. Phil Cunningham was only fifty-eight, you know."

"I know," Alice repeated.

"You got anything to give Mr. Pierce?"

"Bread and butter."

"You better call him in."

"I already gave him some tobacco."

"Well, we can't let him starve."

Alice collected the dishes and took them to the sink in the back room. Threading her way back through the aisles, she gave the meager stock left on the shelves an appraising glance. They would need to order a great deal to be ready for the summer people. Out on the porch, Owen sat gazing off at the water, puffing on his pipe.

"Would you like some breakfast?" Alice called.

He turned his head slowly, as though he had never dreamed of receiving such an invitation. "That would be fine. A little something before I head out for the day. That is, if you can spare it."

Alice held the door open while he shuffled over the threshold.

* * *

Five boxes of safety matches, two balls of string, three boxes of clothespins. Alice marked them down on a pad of paper and went on to the next shelf, taking inventory. Through the screen, she could hear her mother out on the porch, talking to Owen, their voices rising and falling aimlessly. Will had gone off to mow a lawn at a summer house up the road.

Alice was sixteen now, and she had been managing the accounts since soon after her mother took over the store. When she went down the aisle, counting the cans of baked beans, she felt she had a personal stake in every last item on the shelves. Her mother had not been a likely candidate to run the store. It came about as an accident of timing and necessity. A week after Alice's father died, a delegation of islanders arrived at the house, led by Ernie Brovelli, the island's policeman and game warden. They had a proposition. Walter Johnson wanted to sell the store, and Evelyn needed to find some way to support herself now. She could use the money from the sale of her husband's boat as a down payment, and Walter would throw in the old Model T truck and the store's stock. Evelyn agreed in a whisper. She did not have the strength to refuse, and where was she going to go, what was she going to do, with two children to support?

Alice understood the situation only too well, though she was just eleven when her father died. Either they made a success with the store, or they starved. Her mother sat behind the counter in a stupor, gazing at the islanders who came through the door as though she had never met them and couldn't imagine what they wanted with her now. She left the mail sitting in the sack for hours without sorting it, unwilling to believe this was her job, too. Alice took to running as fast as she could from the schoolhouse in the afternoon, so she could sort the mail and put it in the wooden boxes lining the wall behind the counter before the islanders came looking for their letters. The hours at the schoolhouse dragged by while she stared out the window, wondering if her mother was giving the fishermen too much in exchange for their bartered catches or extending credit when she shouldn't. She could not get over to the store fast enough.

For the first year, Evelyn ignored Alice when she went through the books and made changes in the order forms, until one day she threw the ledger book across the counter and said, "All right, you do it. You run the store." Now it was understood. The islanders came to Alice with special requests or to settle their bills.

She had moved down the aisle and was counting the tins of soup when the door swung open. Nate Shattuck crossed the floor, whistling.

"Hey, sweetheart," he called. "Think you could get me some groceries?"

Alice took the list he handed her, which had been written out by his wife, Phoebe. She knew that Phoebe was ashamed to come down to the store herself because they had paid nothing on their bill for so long. Alice had sworn earlier that week that she was cutting off their credit. Now, glancing at the short list, she couldn't bring herself to do it. Nate Shattuck might be shiftless, as everyone said, but he had three children to feed.

Alice measured out five pounds of flour and took a bottle of milk from the cooler. She brought a bag of rice and a jar of molasses from the shelf. Nate watched her, whistling all the while.

"Nice day, huh?" he said. "I thought that rain would never end."

Alice nodded and set the groceries in a box on the counter.

"Guess you're looking forward to the summer people coming. Me, too. I've got a lot of work lined up." Nate gestured toward the parking lot beyond the porch, where the summer people left their cars for the winter. "Ain't none of those cars going to start."

Nate grinned as he slid the box from the counter. He could already hear all those engines turning over, dead. "You're a doll," he said. "Thanks, Alice."

Alice watched him go with a sense of misgiving. Like everyone else on the island, she couldn't say no to Nate.

The store filled up with people after that, in the fifteen minutes before the ferry was due to arrive. Miss Weeden, the schoolteacher, came in for her throat drops, and Rose Brovelli, Ernie's wife, bought penny candy for her grandsons.

When the ferry's horn sounded, Alice followed the customers out the door. Tony Mendoza, the captain, was just nosing the ferry alongside the dock. Evelyn had joined the islanders gathered by the parked cars. Alice paused at the end of the porch, where Owen stood leaning against the railing. "George Tibbits," he said, gazing at the deck of the boat.

For the people of Snow Island, spring did not begin when the last chunks of ice disappeared from the shore or the first summer people arrived to open their houses. The start of the season was marked by the morning George stepped from the ferry, blinking at the light. He came to Snow each year on a warm day when you could smell the water after the locked-in months of winter, when the air was thick with the clotted scent of mud and salt and dried seaweed.

This year George was late. It was well into May, past the days that ordinarily mark the start of spring. Owen Pierce and Ernie Brovelli had been speculating for weeks now about when Tibbits would show up, though they were not especially surprised he had not appeared. The winter of 1941 had been a hard one. The temperature fell below twenty degrees and stayed there for most of January, and patches of snow clung to the rocks in the woods until April.

Owen was right. The stooped figure standing at the railing in a brown suit was George Tibbits. Alice should have known this was the day he would come, but she had not thought of it once.

Captain Tony set the gangplank in place. George reached for the small leather suitcase at his feet, gave a quick nod of his head to no one in particular, and made his way down the plank. The people assembled by the dock parted to let him through. He did not look to the right or left. With his head bowed, he took the path past the store and up the hill to the road.

"I knew he'd come today. That man's a walking barometer," Owen said, watching with everyone else as George reached the road, shifted his suitcase from one hand to the other, and started for the far side of the island.

# — CHAPTER 2 —

At the top of the hill, Alice came to a stop and stood with the bicycle between her legs. The still, blue water stretched to the horizon, where the ridged line of the mainland looked like a tiny mountain range. The west side of the island had an eerie feel before the summer people came. The small places on the east side sat primly and expectantly with their boarded-over windows, but the larger houses in Snow Park, rambling places that dotted the hillside, appeared lost without their human inhabitants.

Alice's friend, Lydia, coasted to a stop beside her. "Any sign of George Tibbits?"

"Nope," Alice said.

"He must be still in the houses. What do you think he does in there?"

Lydia's twin brother, Pete, pulled up beside them on his bicycle. "Beats me," he said.

"Sometimes he mows the lawn," Alice offered.

"Yeah, but then he just stays in those houses. Creepy. Let's go see if we can find him." Without waiting to discover if they were in agreement, Lydia turned off the main road onto a narrower dirt road that skirted the top of the hill.

Alice and Pete exchanged a dubious look and followed her. They pushed their bicycles over the rutted road, still muddy from all the rain, past the Cheavings' and the Allertons' and the Lampreys'.

After the Lamprey place, there was a long gap before the road narrowed to a path, and they came to an overgrown field. Crouched together beyond the high grass, the twin houses stared impassively off at the water, mirror images of each other. Black shutters were closed over the windows in the two-story houses, and the walls were painted a shade of red so dark it might have been dried blood. Yellowed sheets of newspaper covered the glass panes in the front doors.

Alice had heard the story of the twin houses so many times she imagined she had known the two sisters George Tibbits found there when he came home from the war. She saw Sarah Tibbits as thin and pale with large black eyes, a little slip of a thing, and Bertie Tibbits as bigger, plump but stern, and always wearing an apron. Alice didn't know why she pictured Bertie in an apron, but she liked to think that Bertie did the cooking for the two households while Sarah, the dreamy one, spent her days crocheting or reading or sitting on the porch cooling herself with a paper fan. People said Sarah had been a little touched in the head.

Frank Tibbits had come to Snow with his two daughters at the turn of the century and bought more than fifty acres of shoreline on the west side. No one knew why he had come to the island, and his buying the land remained one of the more fantastic events that had ever occurred on Snow. There was nothing on the west side then but rocks and wind and a dense overgrowth of woods. The first settlers back in the 1700s had used the land for grazing sheep and goats, but the animals and their keepers had long since moved on and the fields filled in. Frank Tibbits built the twin houses atop the highest hill without explaining what he had in mind and died suddenly a year later, leaving his daughters alone with the wind blowing off the water and the nearest neighbor more than two miles away. Piece by piece, Bertie had sold off the land around the twin houses to vacationers from Connecticut and Massachusetts, people she never spoke to again once the sales were completed.

The islanders said that the Tibbits sisters were strange from the day they arrived on Snow. In the winter they lived together in one of the twin houses, but in the summer they divided up, one sister in each. When they made the trip around the island for provisions at the store, which wasn't often, Sarah said odd, disjointed things while Bertie glared at her and told her to shush. They did not attend the annual chicken supper or the quilting bees or the recitals at the schoolhouse, and they received little mail. When they brought their infant nephew, George, to live with them after his parents died in a fire in Maine — or maybe it was upstate New York, no one had ever been sure — they kept even more to themselves than before.

Owen Pierce claimed that for all the oddness of his upbringing, George Tibbits didn't turn out half bad. He went all the way through grade school and high school at the schoolhouse and stopped by the store regularly to trade talk about the weather and the price of quahogs like anyone else. When the Great War came, he was the first of the island boys to enlist.

On that day in May of 1919 when George Tibbits came home from the war, Owen Pierce was there at the dock, and he swore that George seemed perfectly normal as he stepped form the ferry. His limbs were intact and so were his wits, not like some of the other boys who returned with that crazed look in their eyes and never quite recovered. George made the long walk to the west side by himself because he wanted, he said, to get to know the island again.

When he reached the twin houses, he discovered the bodies. Sarah lay in an upstairs bedroom in one house, and Bertie was stretched on the sofa in the parlor of the other, wearing her best dress. Ernie Brovelli called in the coroner from the mainland to figure it out. It was finally determined that Bertie died of natural causes a week before George's return, and Sarah took her own life a few days later. A telegram on Sarah's bedside table, which arrived after Bertie's death, provided the only explanation for her action. It came from the Army and mistakenly informed her that George Tibbits had been killed in the last days of the war in France.

As soon as the sisters were buried in the cemetery, George left Snow without telling the islanders where he was going or what he intended to do. He had not spoken to anyone on the island since then, beyond conducting the barest necessities of business, and the twin houses had remained uninhabited. Yet each year George would return on a spring day very much like that day when he came home from the war. He would walk over to the west side, spend a few hours in the houses — doing no one knew what — and walk back to the Snow Inn to stay the night. The next morning he would board the ferry and return to New Jersey. Rumor had it he worked in a drugstore in Trenton.

Alice stopped behind Lydia and lowered her bike to the ground. She listened for sounds of life, but an uneasy silence hung over the spot. Even the insects were still. She could see the small white lines of the waves breaking down below on the rocks, but their sound did not carry.

"The lawn's been mowed," Lydia said, keeping her voice low.

The neat patch surrounding the houses made the rest of the field look even more wild. He must be inside, Alice realized, but there was no sign of George Tibbits' presence apart from the cut grass.

"I guess he's in there," Pete said. "He doesn't even open the shutters."

"Let's wait for him to come out," Lydia suggested.

"Here?"

"Sure. Why not?"

"He might never come out if he sees us. You know how he is."

"All right then, we'll sit on the Cheavings' porch and wait for him there. And then when he walks by, maybe we can get him to talk to us."

"He doesn't talk to anybody."

Lydia gave her brother a look of disgust. "That's because nobody tries to talk to him anymore. They've all given up."

Lydia rotated her bike and started back toward the road. Alice did not bother to climb onto her bike again, but walked it over the rough ground. Pete did the same, wheeling his alongside hers around the puddles.

There was no furniture on the Cheavings' porch, though they could see the wicker armchairs and loveseat through the front windows, draped with old sheets. They sat on the wide steps looking down on the water. Alice took off her shoes and socks and leaned back on her elbows. Her bare feet rested on the warm wood of the bottom step.

"Would you kill yourself if you thought the rest of your family was dead?" Lydia asked.

Pete took a stalk of grass from a clump at the base of the steps and put it in his mouth. "I don't think so."

"Alice?"

"No."

"It's awfully strange. And then how he comes back every year and won't talk to anyone. Did he come every year when you were a kid?"

"I guess he's never missed a year," Alice said. "My father used to wait to put the garden in until George Tibbits came. He said then he was sure there wouldn't be a frost."

"Did you and Hank ever get inside the twin houses that time?" Lydia asked Pete.

"No. We just pried the shutter loose and looked through the window."

"What'd you see?"

"Not much. Pretty dark in there. Some old furniture, an old couch and a couple of chairs. Nothing, really."

"You think he'll leave the doors unlocked when he goes over to the inn today?"

"Lydia."

"Well, I'm just curious."

"I doubt it."

"It must have stunk to high heaven when he found those bodies in there."

They kept their voices low, in case George Tibbits came along. Alice watched as a gull dropped a clam onto a rock down by the water, swooped

to retrieve it, and coasted off, into the light. She followed the bird's silhouette as long as she could, until it disappeared behind a stand of pines
over toward the sandy beach.

The Gibersons came to Snow the year after Alice's father died, so
they never knew him, a fact she found hard to believe. It seemed to her
that everyone in the world should have known her father. Alice was
twelve years old, in the seventh grade that fall, the only person in her
class at the one-room schoolhouse until Lydia and Pete joined her. To
have twins just her age move to Snow was too good to be true. The
Gibersons never intended to live on an island, but they had, as Mrs.
Giberson frequently remarked, no say in the matter. City people, they
came from a town outside New Haven, which they would not have left
except for the failure of Mr. Giberson's insurance business and the death
of Mrs. Giberson's great-aunt, who owned the old inn on Snow and left
it to her in her will.

Alice saw Snow and her life through new eyes after the Gibersons
came. From Lydia she learned about such things as silk stockings, and
getting your period, and the etiquette of dating. Much of the information
Lydia imparted was of little use on Snow (there was no one to date), but
it made Alice appreciate the fact that if she had grown up on the mainland, she might have been a different person entirely, something that had
never occurred to her before Lydia came and pronounced everything on
Snow small and backward. Alice forgave Lydia even this. At last she had
a friend, the first real friend she could claim as her own.

Though Lydia and Pete looked alike, they were complete opposites
in every other respect. He did not miss mainland life the way she did; he
did not care about going to the movies, or being able to buy the latest
styles of clothing, or having a telephone. Lydia had never recovered from
the loss of the telephone, even if she had been too young to make much
use of it when she lived in Connecticut. There were no phones on Snow.

The three of them had been sitting on the porch steps for close to
half an hour when George Tibbits finally did appear. Lydia was talking

about the first dance of the summer at the dance hall. Silas Mitchell had already scheduled it for the third week in June, right after school was out, and a band was coming down from Providence. When George Tibbits came silently out of the trees at the edge of the field with the suitcase in his hand, Lydia stopped in mid-sentence.

He paused, looked at them, and moved on, bowing his head. Lydia opened her mouth, as though she were going to say something, and shut it again. He filed past them without looking up, inching along in his brown suit. Men on Snow were seldom seen in suits, except on Sundays. They watched his back as he made his way slowly to the main road and turned up the hill. Alice caught a glimpse of the profile beneath his hat. His face was neither young nor old. Devoid of expression, it looked like the ageless, sexless face of one of the mannequins in the store windows in Barton.

No one spoke until he was out of sight for a few moments. "I thought you were going to get him to talk," Pete said.

"I couldn't think what to say. You two weren't any help."

"Don't you get a chance to talk to him over at the inn?" Alice asked.

"He eats up in his room, and Mom always takes his food up. She says she doesn't want us bothering him. I checked him in once, but he just nodded when I told him what room he was in. Didn't even smile. I don't think he knows how to smile anymore. Come on, let's go see if the doors are unlocked."

Pete waited while Alice pulled on her socks and shoes. They left their bikes in front of the Cheavings' and went after Lydia reluctantly. When they reached the edge of the field, Pete said, "Lydia, I don't think this is such a hot idea."

"Why not? Are you scared?"

"No, I am not scared. I just think we should leave George Tibbits alone."

"I am leaving him alone. What's it hurt him if I try the doors? You two are so boring." Lydia spoke the last word over her shoulder, making it sound as venomous as possible, and started across the field.

Pete shook his head. "I'm not going up there."

Alice agreed with Pete. Whatever George Tibbits did in the houses each year and whatever his reasons for not speaking to anyone, she thought it was his own business. But when Lydia glanced back, giving her an exasperated look, she went after her, running to catch up.

"God, he's such a drip," Lydia said when she reached her.

"No, he isn't."

"You don't have to live with him. Last year he only went to one dance all summer. It's ridiculous. What's the point of having a brother if he doesn't make himself useful? You know what he's saying now? He wants to be a quahogger. He wants to stay here and become a quahogger and not even go to college. My mother's ready to murder him."

When Alice glanced back, she saw Pete lying in the grass at the edge of the field, staring up at the sky. The fact that Pete did not act like her as well as look like her was a source of constant puzzlement and hurt to Lydia.

"I wish he'd at least get a girlfriend and act normal for a change."

"Where's he going to get a girlfriend?"

"This summer. There'll be lots of them. Meg Sibley, he could date her."

Alice found this unlikely. Meg came from one of the wealthiest summer families. They owned two boats and wouldn't be caught dead taking the ferry. People like that did not pay much attention to the islanders, though Lydia and Pete were in a somewhat different category, since they were not natives.

Lydia darted up the steps of the house on the left and crossed the porch.

"Padlock's on," Alice called from the grass.

"Yeah, I see." Lydia tugged on the padlock. She turned with a resigned look, descended the steps, and started back toward Pete. "I bet the bodies are still in there."

"No, they're not. They were buried in the cemetery."

"That doesn't mean anything. You could dig up the coffins and they might be empty."

Pete was still lying on his back. "No luck? Too bad. I know how you like trespassing on other people's property, Lydia."

Lydia kicked him gently on the foot. "You aren't even curious."

"Sure I'm curious, but I don't have to break into somebody's house to satisfy my curiosity."

"You and Hank tried to get into them."

Pete looked embarrassed. "That was Hank's idea."

Lydia was not impressed with this answer. "Come on, I'll race you over Schoolhouse Hill."

Without turning to see if they followed, she ran down the road toward the bikes.

Pete got to his feet slowly and laughed. "Guess we got no choice. Race you."

He didn't run, though. He walked beside Alice and slowly reached for his bike. Lydia had already crested the hill and disappeared down the main road.

"Watch," he said as he climbed onto the bicycle. "I bet I can catch her."

He pushed off, and Alice jumped on her bike and followed. Alice did not try to keep up as Pete gained on Lydia. She watched Lydia's braids bobbing up and down against her back, getting smaller and smaller in the distance. By the time the two of them disappeared, careening down the hill toward Bay Avenue, Alice had made her meandering way to the schoolhouse. A gull shrieked overhead. When she looked up, she found the bird perched on the schoolhouse roof, staring down at her with its head cocked, as though trying to remember a question it wanted to ask.

She saw George Tibbits when she reached the bottom of the hill and turned onto Bay Avenue. Lydia was in the lead. George Tibbits flinched as her bicycle went flying past. Pete followed moments later.

George was almost to the inn when Alice reached him. She pedaled slowly, staying to the edge of the road. He did not turn around as she approached. He appeared hot and tired in his suit, but he met her gaze as she wheeled past. "Hello," she said, keeping her voice low, as though she were speaking to a small child or an animal encountered in the woods.

He inclined his head to acknowledge her greeting, and she thought she saw the corners of his mouth twitch.

# — CHAPTER 3 —

Alice stood over the cookstove, stirring a pot of clam chowder. A few weeks earlier she had opened the trap door to the crawl space beneath the house and discovered there were no potatoes left. Without the potatoes, there was not much to the broth. She added another spoonful of flour and waited for it to thicken.

"Alice?" her mother said. "I don't know if I can make it to the table."

Alice turned to look at her mother, who lay on the sofa with a damp rag over her eyes. "Maybe if you sit up, you'll feel better. The biscuits are done, and the chowder's almost ready."

Evelyn raised the rag and squinted at her. "Today of all days to get one of these headaches, when we have so much to do."

The previous fall, Alice had insisted her mother visit a doctor on the mainland, but he could find nothing wrong, no "discernible cause" for the headaches that kept her stretched on the sofa for hours at a time.

"There's not so much left," Alice said. "We've only got four boxes to unpack."

"Only?"

"Will and I did the rest."

"You know how long four boxes will take me. It's the canned goods. My arms get worn right out. Tomorrow. We'll see if we can make a dent in it tomorrow. But not tonight. I'm just worn out."

Alice was not about to suggest they go back down to the store after supper. She filled the bowls with chowder, set them on the table, and called Will. He came racing in from the front yard, slingshot in hand.

"If I just had a little more energy." Evelyn draped the rag over the arm of the sofa and came to the table. "Everything goes black when I get one of these headaches. I feel like I can't even see."

"Will," Alice said, glaring at the slingshot.

"Don't!" He grabbed the slingshot before she could. "Don't touch it."

"I don't want to touch it. I just want it off the table."

Will tossed the slingshot across the room, toward the sofa. It landed on the floor. Ignoring them, Evelyn bowed her head and clasped her hands together. "Dear Lord, we ask you to bless this food and make us ever mindful of the needs of others. And keep us safe from harm this night. Amen."

Alice and Will mumbled "amen" and put the cloth napkins riddled with mended spots in their laps. Will slurped his chowder, but Alice said nothing. She was sick of the constant effort of correcting him, trying to get him to act like a civilized human being.

"I gave the Shattucks credit this morning," Alice said.

"I thought we were done with that," Evelyn answered.

"Nate came in with a list Phoebe made out. I couldn't say no."

"I didn't think we could cut off their credit. Honestly, I didn't. Didn't I tell you so? I know, Alice, you've got a better head for business than I do, but you have to remember what's right, what's the Christian thing to do."

"I did. I gave them credit."

"Yes, but was it really necessary to make Nate Shattuck think we were cutting them off? Scared him half to death. I don't like to make him beg, or anybody for that matter. That's a terrible thing to do to a man."

Alice did not think it was easy to scare Nate, especially over something he had so little regard for, like money.

Will aimed his biscuit at the bowl of chowder, making a whistling sound between his teeth. "Bam," he shouted as the biscuit crossed over the bowl. "Direct hit."

"Will, honestly." Evelyn put one hand over her ear.

"Rat-a-tat-tat. Take that, you Nazis." He continued to dive bomb the chowder to a full range of sound effects.

"Will, stop it. She has a headache. Are you going to eat that biscuit?" Alice asked.

"Yes." He popped it in his mouth. "What's for dessert?"

"Don't talk with your mouth full."

He chewed rapidly and swallowed the biscuit in one gulp.

"There is no dessert, Will honey," Evelyn said. "We're all out of fruit preserves. Maybe I'll make you some cookies tomorrow."

"I want a pie."

"We don't have anything to make a pie with. All the blueberries are gone."

Will frowned. "If we get in the war, I'm gonna join the Army."

Evelyn smiled and nodded blankly at him.

"I don't think they take eleven-year-olds," Alice said. "Besides, everyone says we're not getting in the war."

"Who's everyone?"

"Mr. Giberson, for one"

"What does he know?"

"More than you do." Alice cleared the bowls and took them to the sink. "There's some coffee left," she said to her mother. "You want me to reheat it?"

"No."

Sometimes her mother drank it cold. Alice poured the black, oily liquid into a cup and set it on the table. Supper was not over until Evelyn finished her coffee. Alice and Will sat watching her, waiting for the moment when she would set the cup down and peer into its empty depths. She did not seem to notice their intent looks.

"Do you really think we can make this delivery business work?"

Evelyn stared at the sink as she sipped her coffee. Her question was addressed to no one in particular.

"I don't think we have a choice," Alice answered.

"I can drive the truck," Will said.

"Will," Alice chided.

"I can. I drove it last summer."

"Delivering groceries around the island is different from driving once across the field."

"I don't see what difference it'll make," Evelyn said. "Why can't they just come and pick up their groceries like always?"

"Because." Alice had already explained this to her mother at least five times. "If Morton's over in Barton is going to deliver groceries from the mainland straight to people's docks, why is anybody gonna bother to drag a wagon all the way down to our store?"

"Oh, but to put in an order with Morton's, they've got to think ahead, send it over on the ferry. Who wants to be bothered with that, when they're on vacation?"

"Last year Morton was getting orders in the morning and filling them by the afternoon."

Evelyn sighed and took another sip of the coffee. "I still don't know why we have to do this."

"We can't be late with the mortgage payment again, Mom. I showed you that letter from the bank."

"Oh honestly, what do they care with a little shack of a store on an island they've never been to?"

"They don't care. That's just the point. All they want is their money."

Evelyn lowered her head to the table. "Don't they know I'm all alone over here trying to support you two?"

Alice slid the empty coffee cup from between her mother's folded arms and took it to the sink.

"Can I go down to the beach?" Will jumped from his chair and retrieved the slingshot.

"All right. But be back by dark."

He was gone before Evelyn had finished speaking, letting the screen door slam and racing across the front lawn.

Alice pumped water into a pot and set it on the stove to heat. "If this weather lasts, we won't need to get any more coal."

Evelyn raised her head, uncovering her eyes. "That's good, because we can't pay for it." She reached for a pouch of tobacco on the sideboard and, licking her lips in concentration, slowly rolled a cigarette and lit it.

Alice washed the dishes and set them in the drainer by the sink while her mother stared at the smoke she blew toward the ceiling.

"Do you want to go over to the Gibersons to listen to 'Your Hit Parade'?" Alice did not look at her mother as she spoke. She didn't want to encourage her to come, yet she felt she couldn't leave without asking her.

Evelyn studied the wet end of her cigarette. "No, sweetie, you go along. I'm honestly not up to it."

Alice squeezed the water out of the dish rag and draped it over the pump handle. "How's your headache?"

"A little better."

"Maybe you should rest your eyes again."

Evelyn beckoned Alice nearer, and Alice stood motionless, letting her mother reach up and smooth her hair back from her face. "Mom," she said finally, impatient.

Evelyn let her hand fall to the table. "I like your hair this length. It frames your face so nicely."

Alice hurried to the door. "See you," she called.

She took the back way to Lydia's, through the woods. Watching for puddles in the gray light, she followed the path through the thickets of blackberry bushes and came to the cemetery, a small plot surrounded by a broken-down stone wall. The nearest graves were the oldest, with dates from before the Revolutionary War. The gray stones tipped forward precariously, so thin they looked like they would snap in two if you touched them. Her father's grave was in the rear, next to the wall, an oblong marker set flat in the ground with his name and dates: William Eustis Daggett; December 3, 1903 — March 19, 1936. Her mother said at first she did not see how they could afford a stone, but Alice insisted. They saved the money, a quarter a week, until they had enough for the down payment. In the stone yard in Barton, there were beautiful marble slabs with carved ribbons around the edges and quotations cut in flowing letters. Alice would have put a quote about the sea on her father's marker, but there was not enough money for anything but his name and dates on the plainest stone they sold. "Your father will understand," Evelyn said when the stone arrived on the ferry. "We did what we could."

Alice paused by the rock wall, but did not go in to see his grave. The cemetery was the last place Alice thought to look for her father. He was everywhere on the island but here.

She followed the path out of the woods, down the hill past Our Lady of Snow Chapel, the island's Catholic church. The rest of the islanders worshipped at the Union Church, up the hill from the dock. Alice stopped by the statue of Mary in front of the chapel. The statue's blue eyes gazed out at the bay, and pink circles were painted on her cheeks, bright as a jawbreaker with a couple of layers of color sucked off. Mary held one hand in the air, fingers parted, as though testing for the direction of the wind. Alice gathered a fistful of the long stalks of grass and thrust them between the statue's fingers, making her look like she was scolding someone or taking a feather duster to the air. Once Lydia had left a paper airplane between her fingers and another time a cigarette butt. Alice patted the statue's shoulder and ran down the hill, sending the gravel flying. Lydia was waiting for her on the porch of the inn. She came down the steps two at a time as Alice approached, and motioned her toward the path to the lighthouse.

"What about 'Your Hit Parade'?"

"The president's speaking. We can come back. Come on — I've got something to show you." Lydia kept her voice low.

The white beam from the lighthouse swung above the path to the garden, swept toward the beach, and disappeared out on the inky black of the water. The air was thick with the scent of lilacs. Alice followed Lydia past the garden and onto the wide path to the lighthouse. Thick and lumpy, the sand shifted underfoot. Spiked strands of beach grass brushed her legs. When they reached the lighthouse, Lydia slumped against the concrete base, on the far side facing the water. Alice sat next to her.

"Look." Lydia reached into the pocket of her shorts and produced a rumpled pack of Chesterfield cigarettes. "I found them in Betty's top drawer, under some old panties. She must have left them here last time she was home."

"I didn't know Betty smoked."

"Of course she smokes. Everybody smokes. She just doesn't let my mother see. She'd kill her."

Lydia extracted a cigarette and jammed it between her lips. "There's four of them. You want your own or you want to try mine?"

"I'll try yours." Alice had never smoked a cigarette before. The smell of her mother's cigarette smoke first thing in the morning made her feel nauseous sometimes.

Lydia lit a match. She held the cigarette balanced between her fingers like a star in a movie, like she had been doing this all her life. She inhaled and, after a moment, began coughing.

"Here, you try," she sputtered.

Alice took the cigarette gingerly between her thumb and forefinger.

"No, no, no. Like this." Lydia slid it between her first two fingers.

Alice tried to keep a grip on the thin cylinder while making it look the way the movie stars did, as though the cigarette balanced in her hand were made of air. She brought it to her lips. The smoke made her dizzy. She held the cigarette there a moment and passed it back to Lydia.

"You didn't take any. Alice, by the time the summer people get here, we've gotta be good at this." Lydia inhaled again, this time more tentatively, and let the smoke go without coughing. "Not bad." She held the cigarette in front of her, studying it. "Tastes like —"

"Dirt?"

"No, it does not taste like dirt. I don't know. It tastes kind of cool."

Alice thought this description was a stretch. Lydia handed her the cigarette again. She tried to inhale this time, but her head felt suddenly light, like it was floating away from her body. Then she was coughing.

"Here. Give it to me," Lydia said. "You're not doing it right."

Lydia smoked the rest of the cigarette, throwing her head back and puffing the smoke up into the air. When it was down to the end, she stubbed it out in the sand.

"Look, Alice, we're gonna keep practicing, so you can smoke like a pro when we go to the dance hall this summer."

Alice nodded, not because she was in agreement with this plan, but because she knew Lydia would not give her a choice.

Lydia buried the butt in the sand. "All right, now we have to get rid of the smell."

Alice went down to the shore and stood next to Lydia while she skipped stones over the still water. "You think 'Your Hit Parade' is on?"

"Maybe. If they didn't cancel it altogether." Lydia waved her arms in the air and exhaled forcefully several times. "Here, smell." She moved close to Alice and breathed on her. "Can you smell it?"

"Yes."

"Shoot. What should we do?"

"I don't know."

"All right, come on. By the time we get back, it'll probably be gone."

When they reached the garden, Lydia waved Alice down a side path. "Look," she whispered, steering Alice around the vegetable beds to a row of lilac bushes and pointing to the corner window on the second floor.

The shade was raised and, though there was no light in the room, the silhouette of a man's head and shoulders filled the window, gazing toward the water. He leaned forward with his chin propped in his hand.

They were standing in the shadow of the lilacs. Even if George Tibbits turned his head, he was unlikely to see them. Still, Alice thought it was wrong to watch someone who wasn't aware of your presence, the same as spying.

"He sits there all night," Lydia whispered. "Doesn't even sleep."

"How do you know?"

"He's still there at ten at night, and I've seen him sitting there, fully dressed, at six in the morning."

Alice did not think this proved anything. "So he doesn't sleep."

"Or talk to anybody, or eat his meals in the dining room like anyone else, or act even remotely normal. The man's crazy."

Alice supposed George Tibbits was crazy, and his aunts before him, but she thought she knew what made them crazy — people like Lydia and the rest of the islanders. Sarah and Bertie Tibbits were just trying to live the way they wanted, as George was now, but that wasn't good enough for the islanders. No, you had to attend the chicken suppers and stop by the store for the latest gossip and behave just like everyone else.

They made their way toward the inn. At the back door, Lydia stopped. "How do I smell?"

"Not too bad."

Mrs. Giberson barely acknowledged their entrance, she was so absorbed in listening to the radio. With one hand, she indicated they should sit on the braided rug and be quiet. Pete was next to his older brother, Hank, on the couch, leaning forward with his hands flat on his thighs, intent as the others. Since graduating from the schoolhouse, Hank had gone to work in Providence, but he came home weekends. Betty, the oldest of the Gibersons' children, worked in a department store on the weekends and couldn't get home as often.

The president was talking about the war, as usual. Alice listened to his familiar, resonant tone. The hands on the clock on the mantelpiece seemed to inch forward to the cadence of his voice. It was too late now;

they wouldn't broadcast "Your Hit Parade." You couldn't count on anything coming on the radio when it was supposed to these days.

As soon as the president finished, Mr. Giberson flipped off the radio and raised his head. For a moment, Alice couldn't think what had given his face such a tired, defeated look. She knew she should feel the same way, but the war was so remote, a vague threat on the other side of the ocean.

Hank jumped to his feet. "Don't you see? England's going to fall, and then he'll head straight for us. There won't be nothing left."

"Anything, Hank," Mrs. Giberson interrupted.

"Anything, nothing, what's the difference? There won't be anything left of Europe or us by the time he's through, and we're just going to sit here and watch it happen."

Hank paced agitatedly over to the window where he stood looking out, his back to them. Mr. Giberson watched him. He opened his mouth as if he were about to say something, then closed it again.

Hank turned and faced them. "If and when we do get into this war, I'm going down to enlist the first day, the minute they'll take me."

"Oh, Hank," Mrs. Giberson said. "We're not getting into this war —"

"Yes, we are, Mother."

Hank skirted Alice and Lydia, and strode from the room. Mrs. Giberson stood up, but without a word Mr. Giberson waved her back into her seat.

"Guess I'll go after him," Pete said as he rose to his feet and shoved his hands in his pants pockets. Seconds later, the sound of the boys' footsteps came from the kitchen, followed by the slam of the screen door.

"Ben," Mrs. Giberson pleaded. "Can't you talk some sense into him?"

"He won't listen to me. It's nothing but talk anyway. He's got this fantasy about being a big war hero. Well, he can fantasize all he wants because we're not getting into this war. I don't care what anybody says, we're not."

Mrs. Giberson glanced anxiously around the room. When her gaze fell on Alice and Lydia, she seemed to realize for the first time that they were present. "You should be getting ready for bed, Lydia."

"But it's not a school night."

"Well, it's time for Alice to go home and for you to wash up. Go on."

Alice said goodnight to the Gibersons and followed Lydia into the hallway.

"What a gyp," Lydia said. "No 'Your Hit Parade.'"

Alice nodded. "You think Hank'll really enlist?"

"Naw. My father won't let him unless we get in the war. And everybody says we won't. Hank's crazy. He wants to be a flier, a bomber pilot. Fat chance. I guess I'll see you in church tomorrow."

Alice waved as she stepped out onto the porch. Behind her, the lighthouse beam tracked over the sand and swung away. She took the main road home, following it along the shore. On the horizon, the lights of the mainland were just visible, flickering hesitantly in that place which was for Alice the edge of the world. Could the Germans make it that far, all the way to Barton? It did not seem possible.

She was well past the inn, with the darkened shapes of the summer cottages on one side and the water on the other, when the rattle of rocks sounded below the road. She stopped, expecting to hear the snort of a deer as it emerged from the brush and bolted past her. Instead, Ethan Cunningham stepped out of the dark and fell in beside her.

"Want a cigarette?" He extended a pack of Lucky Strikes.

Alice shook her head, trying not to appear startled.

"Wasn't that you I saw smoking earlier, by the lighthouse, with that girl from the inn?"

"Lydia."

"Is that her name, Lydia? You two are like the Bobbsey twins. I saw somebody out there tonight. I thought it was the two of you."

"I guess it was," Alice said weakly.

He laughed. "Hey, I'm not going to tell anybody." He took a cigarette from the pack, cupped his hand around the end, and lit it. "Would you get in trouble if I did?"

"I don't know. My mother smokes herself."

"I guess it's hard to find much trouble to get into on Snow. What are you — eighteen?"

Alice hesitated before answering, feeling, for the first time she could remember, that her age was a liability. "Sixteen. I'll be seventeen in November."

"Sixteen? I thought maybe you were about to graduate at the schoolhouse. You could have fooled me, driving that big old truck around. You look like an old man behind the wheel of that thing."

Alice kept her gaze on the wavering lights across the water. "I have another year at the schoolhouse."

Walking beside him, she was aware of how tall he was. He wore chino pants and a white shirt rolled back at the cuffs. His body was long and angular, and he moved in a deliberate way, as though considering each step before he took it.

"Another year of Miss Weeden. Does she still use monkeys and giraffes for the multiplication tables and give out foil stars? I used to have my bedroom wall covered in those foil stars. I'd lie there counting them before I went to sleep at night, figuring how many more I could get before the year was over. Somebody told me I still hold the record for the most stars in a year." He laughed and flicked the half-smoked cigarette to the side of the road. "Isn't Miss Weeden about a hundred by now?"

"Owen Pierce says she's around seventy."

"We thought she had to be pushing eighty when I was at the schoolhouse, and that seems like a very long time ago. I hated going to the schoolhouse. I was bored out of my skull. I learned everything Miss Weeden had to teach by second grade, and then I just had to sit there for six years, staring out the window and praying that she'd drop dead of a heart attack or something. Then I went away to boarding school, and I had to scramble to keep up. I used to sit there in Latin class cursing Miss

Weeden, thinking how she didn't teach me a thing."

"You took Latin?"

"Latin, French. Wasted a couple years of my life memorizing verb forms. You still don't have French at the schoolhouse, do you? No, Miss Weeden's never heard of it. She's never heard of chemistry, either."

"We have biology."

"Biology. Collecting ferns in the woods and mucking around in the tide pools, that's biology, right? I guess it doesn't make a difference if you're all just going to grow up to be quahoggers."

"Or storekeepers?" Alice tried to stop her answer from sounding too sarcastic, but her voice had an edge to it.

"Or lighthouse keepers." He laughed. "I haven't gone all that far, have I? But you're not going to spend the rest of your life minding the store on Snow. You're too smart for that. I could see it in your face the minute I first saw you there behind the counter. That girl will get off the island, I said to myself. She's bigger than Snow."

Alice had never thought much about the time after she graduated from the schoolhouse. She had assumed she would stay because her mother couldn't run the store on her own. His words made her feel strange, as though she had been presented with a picture of herself she didn't recognize.

"If I had a choice, I wouldn't be here," he said. "I'd be in New York or Boston. I like the city. You feel alive there. Here —" He gestured toward the shoreline. "Here you feel stuck. Snow was always just a place to leave for me. For as long as I can remember, I knew I would leave. And now I have to stay. Beautiful, isn't it?"

"Were you going to be a painter?"

He smiled. "Yes, I was going to be a painter, and I'm still going to be a painter. But it's not exactly a profession, not in the money-making sense. It's more like a calling, a fairly stupid one. Does the world need paintings? Does Snow Island need paintings?"

Alice had never considered such a question, but he did not seem to want an answer.

"Art's an indulgence. A wonderful indulgence, but it's still an indulgence. I've got no business painting, but I do it anyway because I can't stop myself."

Alice paused as they reached the turnoff to her house.

"That your place?" he said, gesturing up the hill.

She wished he wouldn't walk her all the way to her house. What if her mother saw and wanted to know what she was doing wandering around at night with Ethan Cunningham?

He kept talking as they climbed the hill. "You shouldn't listen to me. There's nothing wrong with being a quahogger or running the store. I look at people like that, like your mother, and I think, they're happy. If I'd never left Snow, I'd probably be as happy as anyone else."

A light shone through the living room window, but Alice could not see her mother or Will inside. The thin sound of piano music carried down the hill.

"Where's that music coming from?" he asked.

"Phoebe Shattuck, playing the piano. Sometimes she plays half the night." She gestured toward the Shattucks' house, on past her own.

"She's married to Nate, that character who runs the fix-it shop? You wouldn't figure them for having a piano."

"She's from the mainland. She brought it with her."

They reached her front yard, and the music suddenly went silent. "I'm always around if you want to come over and have a tour of the lighthouse or anything," he said. "Just knock on the door."

She thought he was going to extend his hand for her to shake, but instead he took a cigarette from his pocket, lit it while she stood there staring, and went back down the hill.

# — CHAPTER 4 —

The thin, shaky voices of the congregation carried through the open windows of the Union Church. George Tibbits stopped for a moment on the road to listen. He thought he remembered the hymn, though he had not set foot in a church for twenty-two years, since the day of his aunts' funeral. It was difficult to discern the words; they were enveloped and disguised by the uncertain voices that veered toward the high notes and fell back as if rebuked. Then the hymn came to him, and he found himself whispering, "Breathe on me, breath of God, Till I am wholly thine, Till all this earthly part of me glows with thy fire divine."

Fire divine. Did such a thing exist? He thought of his time in the war, of the night sky lit by the red flares of rockets. He was helping load wounded soldiers into an ambulance near the border with Belgium when a shell hit, and he became one of the wounded himself. During the weeks he spent in a Paris hospital, he consoled himself with one thought: when he was healed, he could go home. He could try to forget the things he had seen. It was months before he was able to board a ship for America, and in the confusion of the war's end, his records were mistaken for another soldier's, one who had died at the battle along the River Selle. The telegram was sent announcing George's death. In the letter of apology which arrived later from the Army, they called it "a lamentable bureaucratic error."

The voices carrying through the open window joined in a quavering "amen" and went silent. George remained at the top of the hill, listening for what came next. He could just catch the sound of a single voice leading a prayer. His aunts had never attended services at the white clapboard church on the hill above the dock, though they read the Bible every day and said the Lord's prayer with him before bed. He started going to church by himself when he was older, fifteen or sixteen. He went out of curiosity more than anything else at first. He kept returning because he loved the quiet simplicity of the services and the restrained beauty of the little church with its bare wood walls and rows of unadorned pews, and the cross made of two pieces of driftwood lashed together above the table that served as an altar. Most of all, he loved the hymns. There was so little music in his life then. They did not have a radio or a piano or any other instruments at the twin houses. The only music he knew as a child came from the sound of the surf and the wind, the cheeping of the crickets in the summer, the calls of the winter birds.

In the Army, he found God. He went to the services conducted by the chaplain and carried a slim edition of the New Testament in his breast pocket. He came to believe in miracles when he saw men who were standing on the threshold of death pulled back into life. He came to believe in prayer. His beliefs were dashed the day he returned home to the island and found Sarah and Bertie gone. If there were a God, George did not believe He could play such a cruel trick on the women who had been like mothers to him. The fact of what had happened seemed proof that God did not exist, or if He did and allowed such things to occur, George wanted nothing to do with Him.

George stood a moment longer at the top of the hill, then took the path toward the store and the dock. The store was not open; the islanders were all at church. He sat on the porch bench and stared at the still surface of the water. After a while, the ferry came into view around Gull Island. He thought of all the other years when he had boarded the ferry by himself and gazed wistfully at the island's diminishing form as the boat

44

pulled into the channel. This year would be different.

The islanders came spilling out of the church moments before the ferry's horn sounded. He watched the people stream down the hill. The arrival of the ferry would make no difference to them; there was no mail service on Sundays, and chances were the boat carried no passengers. The people came anyway, because the arrival and departure of the ferry was the only thing that ever happened on Snow, and someone might get off, there was no telling. He remembered how it was. This much, at least, had not changed.

The crowd assembled at the foot of the dock. He knew some of them, old Owen Pierce and of course Miss Weeden, his teacher at the schoolhouse. He glanced at them quickly and looked away. The girl who had passed him on her bicycle the day before came bounding up the porch steps and pushed open the door. "Morning," she said before hurrying inside. He waited a moment and followed her.

She was busy straightening piles of paper on the counter and did not look up immediately. George stood in front of her and finally resorted to clearing his throat. "Do you run the store?"

"No," she said uncertainly. "My mother does. I mean, we run it together. The ferry's here." She gestured toward the door.

He nodded. "I'll be needing some groceries. Do you deliver?"

"Yes."

"Can I leave you a list and have it by this afternoon?"

"Yes."

She stared at him dumbly. George knew he should have expected this reaction, but it annoyed him nonetheless. He wished he could stay on Snow without anyone knowing, but of course this was impossible.

"Could I have a piece of paper?" he asked.

She rummaged through her pile and produced paper and a pencil.

He had already formulated the list in his mind. It did not take long to reproduce it. He was just adding the last item, tea, when the door swung open and a small woman in a straw hat entered.

"Mr. Tibbits," she said in a tremulous voice, "the ferry's waiting for you."

He could not think what to say. He did not want to voice his plans openly. There was something so naked about it.

"He's staying," the girl said.

"Staying?" The woman stared at him. George turned his gaze to the list beneath his hand, seeking reassurance from his own neat lettering and the fact of sugar, and bread, and canned peas.

"Then I'll tell Captain Tony to go on?"

He nodded.

When the shrill woman left the store, he felt relieved. The girl did not intrude so much. He handed her the list. "You can leave the delivery on the porch. I'll pay you at the end of the month." She set the paper by the cash register, and he turned to go.

George made his way down the porch steps and up the hill, avoiding the looks the islanders gave him. Why shouldn't he stay? He owned the houses, didn't he? And he had kept them all these years with this day in mind.

He took the long way around, going down Bay Avenue past the Improvement Center and the dump, as he had the day before, but this time, finally, he was truly coming home to stay. He carried the suitcase. It did not contain much. He could wear the clothes left in the house; he had not gained any weight to speak of, and the shirts and old pants still hung in the closet, as though they had waited for him all these years.

At the fork where one road went to Gooseneck Cove and the other to Snow Park, he turned left, toward the western side of the island. He had not been out to Gooseneck Cove since just before he left for the war, when he spent a day going around the island to say good-bye to the places he loved best. He had saved Gooseneck Cove for last, remembering how he used to bicycle out to the windswept spot by himself on summer days. He was not sure if he could return to the cove now. He was half-afraid he might meet himself there, a teenaged boy running over the

46

rocks and down to the water, plunging in.

The dirt road wound along the marsh and through a stretch of woods, then came to the open water. In the distance, he could see the houses of Snow Park dotting the green hillside. It was different, making the trip today, just as he had imagined it would be. The twin houses seemed like something that could, just possibly, return to life. He climbed the hill and took the path through the trees. When he caught sight of the houses across the field, he doubted himself for a moment. They appeared to lean together, toward each other, like old women shaking their heads. They seemed to say it was too late; they had been dead too long. Perhaps they were right. He had not slept a night in either of the houses since before he left for the war. He wondered if he could do it now, actually put his head down and close his eyes, or if this plan that had been silently present inside him for so long were just another piece of folly.

He had waited for years to take a summer off from his job at the drug store. First, he had to be certain enough of his position that he knew they would not replace him. Then he had to find a suitable person to make deliveries while he was gone. The owners, Mr. and Mrs. Lily, had a son. George had watched him grow, progressing from one grade to the next until at last he was in high school. It was only then, when the son was old enough to take his place for the summer, that George proposed the plan. He had not imagined he could step out of his ordered life so easily, but when the time came, it was simpler than he thought. He pulled the shades on his apartment windows and left enough to cover the rent. He took the bus to the train station, secure in the knowledge that his old life would be waiting when he returned.

George unlocked the padlock over the door to one twin house and then the other. He had known for a long time which house he would live in when he came back to Snow, but he wanted to keep both houses open. It would be too strange to have it otherwise. He took his suitcase into Sarah's house and carried it to the upstairs bedroom, where the quilt she had made for him lay folded across the bottom of the bed, a bright hodgepodge of triangles of fabric. Each pattern held a memory: the flowered print from the dress she wore summer after summer, the ginghams from old tablecloths. Sarah insisted that the quilt she constructed for George consist only of scraps from clothing she had sewn herself. She would not accept any of the scraps in Bertie's fabric bag, though Bertie pestered her about it for weeks.

George went through the house, opening the shutters and the windows. Despite the cleaning he had done the day before, the sunlight falling into the rooms in slanted shafts was full of dust. It swirled in the air. He entered Sarah's room last. Her brush and comb lay on the dresser beside a pile of hair pins. That day when he returned from the war, he had found her in the bed with her hair cascading over her shoulders, her head slumped to one side. She only left her hair down on the bad days, the ones when she didn't get out of bed. On the table beside her sat the books she loved to read and re-read: *Jane Eyre, David Copperfield, Adventures of Huckleberry Finn.* "I like books with names for titles," she told him once. She read the books in a set order he could not remember, and once she had finished them, started over again. She could not tell him how many times she had read them. When he suggested she might like to try new books, she said that these ones were so good, it seemed a shame to spoil them by reading others that might not come up to the mark. It would be like ruining the idea of a book, and she didn't want to do that.

Ernie Brovelli and that coroner from the mainland searched both the twin houses without finding any evidence of how she obtained the poison she used to kill herself. George suspected she had kept the vial hidden for years, just waiting for the time she feared might come eventually, though how she got it into the house and kept it concealed from Bertie's frequent and diligent searches was the greatest mystery. "I'm watching you, Sarah," Bertie used to say. "Remember that. I'm watching you, day and night. Don't forget it." When he was young, George did not know what Bertie meant by saying these things, but as he got older his understanding gradually grew. There was the time Bertie hauled Sarah out of the hip bath in the kitchen, screaming that she was trying to drown herself. George had never known if Sarah had really made such an attempt or if this was just another of Bertie's fabrications, though he believed Sarah when she whispered to him that night, "I didn't mean to do anything but wash my hair, honey."

He had not thought of these memories for a long time. They had remained like cloaked figures at the edges of his mind. Perhaps it was opening the windows that brought back the sound of Bertie's nagging voice and Sarah's soft replies. The fragmented scenes rushed in with the light, filling the empty rooms. A night in winter. They were seated around the stove in Bertie's house. Sarah's knitting needles made a clicking sound. "You'll drive me to distraction," Bertie hissed suddenly, setting the sock she was mending on a table. George looked up from his reading, surprised as he always was by her outbursts. "You're not even making anything."

"Yes, I am," Sarah answered timidly.

"What?"

"It's . . . it's a piece of knitting."

"It's a waste, that's what it is. A waste of good yarn. I won't get you any more from the mainland if you're just going to waste it."

Sarah's mouth puckered, and George thought she was going to cry, as she often did when Bertie "took her to task," as she put it. "I just like the feel of it, knitting."

"Well, you can like the feel of it and make something while you're at it. Like a sweater for George. He could use another sweater, wearing that same old one I made for him every day to school."

Sarah bit her lip and shook her head. George knew as well as she did that the complexity of knitting to a pattern and putting the finished pieces together was too much for her. Quilting was easier; she simply joined one triangle after another in no set pattern. A "crazy quilt," she called it. "Crazy is right," Bertie commented with a snort when the quilt was done.

That winter night Sarah began sniffling. "I take the stitches out and start over," she said.

"Don't cry on me, Sarah. I can't take it. It's bad enough I'm stuck here on this godforsaken island for the rest of my life because of you and your infirmities."

"Leave then." Sarah jumped to her feet. The knitting fell from her lap to the floor. "George and me can stay here by ourselves and do just fine, can't we, George?"

"George and I," Bertie said icily. "Pick up your knitting."

But Sarah was already heading for the stairs. Later that night, Sarah lay beside George in his narrow bed, pressing her wet face to his. "Promise you won't ever leave me, George."

He grasped her hand and answered in a whisper so Bertie couldn't hear from the next room. "I promise."

The first time George could recall having any real sense of Sarah's infirmities, as Bertie called them, he was only seven or eight. "I get muddled in the head," Sarah told him as they were hanging clothes on the line one afternoon. "You got an aunt who gets muddled in the head." She laughed and gazed toward the houses, and he knew that her getting muddled in the head didn't make a difference to him in the least, that it only made him like her better.

During the winters, when the three of them lived in Bertie's house, George and Sarah shared a room on the second floor with two narrow beds. He often woke to find that she had crawled beneath the covers beside him in the night. Muddled mind or no, she was careful to wake before Bertie and return soundlessly across the floor to her own bed. Summers were better times because then Bertie let Sarah live in the other house and allowed George to stay there with her, sometimes for weeks on end. Bertie said it was her only chance to get some peace, when she was free of the two of them. They still ate meals together, but the rest of the time George and Sarah walked in the woods behind the houses or went clamming or searched the tide pools for treasures. "Look," Sarah would exclaim, holding up a perfect oyster shell. "Isn't it the prettiest thing?"

As the land was sold off and the houses in Snow Park started to go up around them, Sarah stayed closer to home, afraid of meeting strangers. One summer she refused to go down to the tide pools at all. "Too many people," she whispered to George. They spent afternoons in a small clearing in the pines behind the houses, leaning against either side of the same tree, reading. George remembered those afternoons as the happiest time of his life.

When he announced he was going off to war, she locked herself inside her house and would not come out. She emerged the day before he left holding a lumpy woolen mound. "You have to serve our country, George," she said as she handed him what looked like an old animal's skin. Then he realized it was the yarn she had raveled and unraveled for years, finally assembled into something useful, the most misshapen of sweaters.

He knew, as he pulled off his jacket and pushed his arms through the narrow sleeves of the sweater, that she had forgiven him, that she saw going off to fight as his duty and not the breaking of that promise he had made years earlier. Through the months in France, he kept the sweater with him, thinking of it as the proof he and Sarah shared that he would be coming home, that he had not left her for good.

George closed the door to Sarah's room now and crossed the hall to the bedroom where he had spent all those summer nights. He opened his suitcase and took out the shirts and extra pair of pants and hung them in the closet.

# — CHAPTER 5 —

The islanders talked about it for the rest of the day. George Tibbits staying? What had possessed him to do such a thing? "Those houses are a sight," Miss Weeden said. "I wonder if they're even fit to live in. Did he say how long he would be here?"

"No," Alice responded. "He didn't say."

"But what did he want, coming into the store?"

He just wanted to set up an account, she explained to one person after another. No, she didn't know if he was planning to live over there all by himself, or which of the two houses he might inhabit. No, she wasn't sure if he planned to stay for a week or a month or a year. No, he didn't say whether he was on vacation or not. He didn't say much of anything at all.

"Isn't that just like him?" Miss Weeden sniffed delicately and held her handkerchief to her nose. "I always said he was peculiar. I've known some mighty peculiar people in my time, but he takes the cake."

Alice nodded and wrapped up the throat drops Miss Weeden had purchased.

She did not tell anyone, even her mother, about the grocery delivery to the twin houses, afraid that the whole island would come along for the pure curiosity of it if they knew. She waited until the ferry crowd had cleared out, and Owen Pierce had ambled up the road — to see about his boat, he said. Then she took an empty carton and began filling it with the order.

"What's that?" her mother asked, peering into the box.

"A grocery order."

"Who for?"

"George Tibbits."

"You didn't tell me he wanted anything delivered."

"Well, he has to eat, doesn't he?"

"I suppose." Evelyn struck a match and lit a cigarette. "Man looks like he lives on air, if you ask me. Did he pay you?"

"No. He said he'd pay at the end of the month."

"You think he's good for it?"

"Yes."

Evelyn shrugged, as if to say it was no concern of hers. "Who's taking this delivery over?"

"I will."

"You gonna go into those houses?"

"No. He just said to leave the groceries on the porch."

"Which one?" Evelyn sucked on her cigarette and laughed.

"I don't think it makes any difference."

"It's just that there's two. Houses. I wondered how you'd know which one."

Alice continued moving through the store's aisles, taking cans and boxes and setting them in the carton.

She drove the truck to the west side, passing the Improvement Center, a long one-story building that served as the island's lending library and the gathering place for events like the chicken supper. Past the Improvement Center, she came to the dump, and beyond the dump, out toward Gooseneck Cove, there was the barn-like structure of the dance hall. Silas Mitchell opened the dance hall on weekends through the summer, bringing bands over from the mainland, though he couldn't always be counted on to open when he said he would. He used what money he could scrape together to buy the beer and had nothing left over to pay the bands. The musicians were always canceling at the last minute.

When she came to the fork heading toward Gooseneck Cove in one direction and Snow Park in the other, she turned toward the Park, taking the long way around to avoid Schoolhouse Hill. If the truck stalled on that hill, she could roll right into the bay in the time it could take to get the thing started again. Besides, she didn't want to go past the lighthouse, afraid she would run into Ethan Cunningham. "Just knock on the door," he had said. She could not imagine doing such a thing.

The truck rattled over the dirt road. She tried to avoid the ruts left by all the rain, but in places this was impossible, and her head banged against the top of the truck's cab. She was moving along the flat stretch by the rocks when the truck sputtered and came to a stop. Alice was fairly certain she knew what was wrong. The carburetor was plugged up again. She hopped to the ground and opened the hood. She was reaching to open the valve when she heard a voice.

"Need some help?"

Alice emerged from beneath the hood to find Pete Giberson leaning against the side of the truck. "No. I think the fuel line's clogged with some rust."

He held a fishing pole in one hand and wore an old pair of sneakers riddled with holes.

"Catch anything?" she asked.

"Naw. Nothing's biting. The tide's turning now anyway."

Alice rolled up the sleeves of her blouse and leaned over the engine. She turned the valve and a trickle of gas and sediment drained out of the carburetor.

"Where are you headed?" Pete said.

"The twin houses. George Tibbits wanted some groceries delivered."

"And you're going all by yourself? Aren't you scared?"

"No." Alice closed the valve cover.

"You should have told Lydia you were coming over."

"I know, but I didn't want a whole crowd with me."

"How long do you think he'll stay?"

"I don't know. Maybe forever." Alice climbed back into the truck. "I think it'll start now."

She turned the key and pressed the starter on the floor with her heel. After a second, the engine caught. "Could you put the hood back?" she yelled through the open window.

Pete set the hood in place. "Mind if I come?" he asked, resting a foot on the running board.

Alice shook her head, and he put his fishing rod in the back of the truck and got in beside her.

When they reached the turnoff for Snow Park, the truck climbed the hill slowly. At the top, Alice took the lane to the twin houses. The doors were closed, but the shutters in both houses had been opened. Alice pulled up at the side of the road and shut off the engine.

Pete came around to the back of the truck and helped her unload the first of the two boxes. "How were you planning to get this up there?" he asked.

"I don't know. I figured I could manage somehow."

"You'll hurt your back doing things like that."

They carried the box together, holding it between them. Pete went first, facing Alice and walking backwards. "I can help you with things like this, you know," he said. "You just have to ask."

They left the box on the porch of the twin house on the left and went back for the second one. There was no sign of life behind the open windows, but at least, Alice thought, the windows were open and free of the black shutters. It was the first time she had ever seen the houses this way. The bare windows gave the places a startled look, as though they had been caught undressing.

Alice took a note from her pocket and stuck it between two cans in the second box, then started back through the grass.

"What was that?" Pete asked, hurrying to keep up with her.

"Just a note."

"What'd you say?"

"That we'd be happy to make deliveries whenever he wants them."

"So you think he's staying?"

"You saw how much we just left. That's more than a week's worth of groceries."

"I guess."

Pete gave her an admiring look, and Alice thought how she knew things, working at the store and selling people their groceries, that no one else knew. "You want a ride back?" she asked.

"Sure. I walked over."

The truck coughed, but the engine started. Alice backed the truck into the road and turned around, watching for George Tibbits to emerge, but the porches and the windows remained empty. As she eased the truck down the hill toward the water, she thought how Pete was the only person she knew, besides George Tibbits, and she didn't exactly know him, who would take the time to walk all the way to the other side of the island. Anyone else would have at least ridden a bicycle.

"You must think of your father over here," Pete said as they rattled along by the water.

He was referring to that March day when her father's boat washed up along this stretch of the west shore, empty. Three days later his body washed up in almost exactly the same spot. Alice did not want to be reminded of these memories, not at that particular moment at least. She kept her gaze on the muddy surface of the road.

"I wish I had met him."

Alice nodded.

"What was he like?"

"He was like anybody else — a quahogger. He went out in his boat every day and came home . . . " Alice trailed off, aware she was lying. Her father was not like anybody else, but she could not find words for the way he was different. With his deep laugh and quiet eyes, he made people feel he knew and understood everything about them, that there was no hurt he could not put right.

"That's what I want to do."

"Be like everyone else?"

Pete laughed. "In a way, I guess. No, I meant be a quahogger. Go out in my boat every day and come back."

"It's hard work."

"I know. I think that's why I want to do it."

"You don't have a boat."

"I'm saving for a down payment."

Alice wondered if his parents knew he had gotten this far with his plans, but she didn't say anything. They passed the dump and the store came into sight. Pete placed his hand on her arm.

"Nobody knows I'm saving for a boat. Don't tell Lydia, okay?"

"Okay," Alice responded blankly. She coasted the truck down the hill to the store and pulled up beside the gas pump.

"Thanks, Alice," Pete said as he climbed out.

She could tell by the steady look he gave her that he was thanking her not for the ride but for agreeing to keep his secret. She wished he hadn't told her.

"Hey, where have you been?" Lydia called. She was sitting on the porch with her feet dangling over the edge.

Pete retrieved his rod from the back of the truck. "Fishing."

Lydia turned her gaze on Alice as she swung the truck's door closed and slipped the key in her pocket.

"I was just making a delivery."

"Who to?"

"George Tibbits."

"George Tibbits?" Lydia put her hands on her hips. "Well."

# — CHAPTER 6 —

On a piling at the end of Owen Pierce's dock a lone cormorant sat glistening in the sun. Alice watched as the bird spread its sleek feathers and probed them with its beak. In the bright light, the wings were like a knife blade slicing the air, a shade of black so deep they appeared blue. With quick, nervous jabs, the cormorant groomed its feathers, stretched out its curved neck, and settled into a brooding squat on the tip of the pole.

School had been out three days now, three luxurious days Alice had spent lying in the sun and bicycling around with Lydia. The store was stocked and the orders had been placed. The summer people would not arrive in substantial numbers for another week. Alice's mother told her to go on and have a good time. She would work hard enough the rest of the summer.

She and Lydia had not planned to stop at Owen Pierce's when they set out for the clam flats that afternoon, but he waved them over and began talking. With his pipe cradled in his puffy hand, he leaned back in a wicker rocking chair and squinted at a pile of old wood and tin cans below the porch railing. From her place at the bottom of the porch steps, Alice had an alarming view of the bristly hair protruding from his nose.

"It was my great-great-grandfather, you know. The one who got speared by a British bayonet in the Revolutionary War. Right here, right on Snow. Took a bayonet straight through the gut."

Lydia rolled her eyes at Alice. Each year at the schoolhouse, Miss Weeden gave a lesson on the fate of Snow during the Revolutionary War, and they knew for a fact that no one was killed or even wounded by the British. The islanders evacuated before the British arrived; by the time the British came and burned everything in sight, no one was left on Snow besides the goats and sheep and a couple of cows.

"There's John Sparr's stone up in the cemetery, the one with the bite taken out of it." Owen Pierce pointed his pipe in the direction of the cemetery. "Top of the thing was taken clean off by a cannon ball all the way from a British ship out in the bay. Took a chunk out of the headstone and kept right on going."

This was one story Alice knew he had not invented or gotten wrong in his confused state. The headstone with its missing top sat up in the cemetery for anyone to see.

"How about George Tibbits?" Lydia broke in. "Did you know him?"

Lydia had become obsessed with George Tibbits in the weeks since he decided to stay on Snow. She was always begging Alice to ride over to the west side just to see if they could get a look at him.

"I've known George Tibbits since he was a baby. Not that he gives me so much as a hello these days. Looks right through me." Owen widened his eyes and took a puff on the pipe.

"Why do you think the one sister killed herself?"

"I guess she thought she couldn't live without her sister and George. That's about all anybody's ever come up with. A terrible shame, her getting the news like that about George when it wasn't even true. I don't know that the Army ever even apologized."

This was all he had to say on the subject, though he was glad to go on about other things, like the fire over in Snow Park in the twenties, when half the fancy houses burned down.

Lydia did not wait to hear about the bucket brigade that stretched close to a quarter-mile by the time the fire was extinguished. She jumped to her feet and grabbed Alice by the sleeve. "We have to go now. We promised we'd bring some clams home for supper."

Owen squinted down at the water. "Tide's about dead low."

They waved good-bye, cutting through the tangled brush to the flats. Climbing over the barnacle-encrusted rocks, they made their way across the mud and waded through the shallow water. The dark sand oozed through Alice's toes, thick and mucky.

"Silas Mitchell postponed the dance, did you hear?" Lydia said. "The band canceled. He said there weren't enough summer people here yet to make it worth it anyway. That gives us more time."

"For what?" Alice sank her rake into the mud and began moving it carefully back and forth.

"I don't know. Practice dancing and smoking. Get your legs shaved."

Alice eyed the thin down of hair on her legs self-consciously. She had not planned on shaving them.

"I'll have to ask my mother."

"If you can shave?"

"She said once she didn't think a girl should do that until she's eighteen."

Lydia raised her eyebrows. "How's she gonna know?"

Alice sank her rake in the mud, pulling it slowly toward her, feeling for lumps. She discarded a series of rocks and hit some clams, stooping over to retrieve them and drop them in her bucket. "She might look at my legs sometime."

"Yeah, and by then it's too late. She can't do anything about it."

Alice could see no point in arguing about whether she should shave her legs, of all things. Lydia gave her one of those looks, as if to say she was hopeless, and dug her rake into the sand.

They worked on in silence, growing gradually farther apart on the flats. The heat of the sun on the back of Alice's neck made her skin damp and itchy. She and Lydia were looking for littlenecks, the small clams. To get quahogs — the big, hard-shelled clams — you had to go farther out. The men rowed out to the quahog skiffs they kept moored off shore and worked over the side of the boats, bringing up the quahogs in the wire baskets at the ends of the tongs. She and Lydia worked more slowly, raking the sand. Alice tried to remember those times of clamming when she was younger, or better yet, going out with her father in the boat. She had loved the sticky feel of the water as it dried on her skin, a salty crust. Now she didn't go clamming for fun but for food. What Alice gathered would be supper for that evening, with the last jar of pickles and some brown bread left over from the day before.

"My bucket's full," Lydia called after a while.

Alice tackled one more square of mud and managed to get another handful. The original settlers on Snow had clammed this way for years, but to clam year-round and get quahogs in quantity enough to sell now required a boat and one of the big tongs that could drag up bucketsful at a time.

Alice made her way back to the rocks and hoisted the bucket over them. In the process of searching the flats, they had moved down the shore toward the lighthouse. Owen Pierce's place was almost out of sight. They crossed the rocky beach to the road.

"Let's go swimming," Lydia said. "I'm burning up."

They reached the sandy beach in front of the lighthouse and set down their buckets and rakes. Alice glanced up at the Cunninghams' house. The car was parked out front, but there was no one in sight. Together they collected seaweed from along the shore, wet it, and used it to cover the clams. Lydia peeled off her blouse and shorts, revealing her bathing suit underneath. Alice stripped down to her bathing suit and followed Lydia down the beach. They waded out to where the bottom dropped away, and they were in to their shoulders. Alice took a deep breath and dove beneath the surface.

The water swept through her hair and ran over her body, clean and cold. When she opened her eyes, she saw the rocky bottom in the green, murky depths below. Farther out, a smooth plain of sand stretched to the dark edges where the water closed in, too deep to penetrate. Alice moved her arms in wide strokes and shot to the surface.

Lydia floated on her back, her face turned toward the sun. "Let's swim out and take our suits off," she said.

Side by side, they swam toward the still water beyond the point by the lighthouse. From off shore, the beach appeared to be no more than a slip of white below the houses. Even the lighthouse looked pitifully small, squatting in the grass as though trying to pull itself up to full height.

Alice moved her arms to stay afloat while Lydia unzipped her suit. The water flowed over Alice's back, warm now that she was used to it and soft as washed hair. When Lydia finished, she rotated so Alice could unzip her suit. It was hard to keep afloat long enough to work the zipper free, but Alice kicked her legs in a quick scissor stroke until finally, her fingers thick and clumsy beneath the water, she wrestled the zipper down. Together they wriggled out of the bathing suits.

Diving beneath the water, they tied the straps of the suits to their ankles. The racing sailboats that had dotted the horizon earlier were gone, back toward Newport, leaving the channel empty except for the bell buoys and markers bobbing on the surface. The water felt like a pair of sleek hands on Alice's skin.

The first time they went swimming out past the lighthouse and took off their suits beneath the water, the idea was Lydia's, one of her suddenly inspired dares. Lydia turned thirteen that summer, the summer before the 1938 hurricane. One hot afternoon while her mother watched them from the lighthouse beach, it came to Lydia. They could slip off their bathing suits and swim around out there, and no one would be able to tell. Alice refused at first, but when at last Lydia shamed her into taking the dare, they discovered she was right. Naked, they dove and came to the surface, and the women on the beach went on knitting with barely a glance in their direction.

When they reached the boundary edge, where they could see the movement of the current out in the channel, Alice brought her legs together and dove. She came up and found herself looking at the windows on the second floor of the Cunninghams'. The small squares of glass gleaming in the sun were blank.

After a while, they turned and started back to land. Fingers of light penetrated the water, wriggling like golden eels in the transparent layer beneath the surface. Alice turned and caught a glimpse of Lydia's chest under the water, round and white and full, covered in a latticed pattern of yellow. Surprised, she pulled her legs together and dove again. It had been a while since she had seen Lydia naked. Even though Lydia had been wearing a bra for a couple of years now, Alice did not quite think of her as having breasts. But what she saw through the water were clearly breasts, big enough to hang down and touch her chest.

Alice struggled to untie the bathing suit straps knotted around her ankle. She held her breath as long as she could, until the last unbearable second, and gave up. Her eyes smarted from the salt.

"You want me to try?" Lydia asked. She was swimming toward her, the round whiteness of her body shimmering in the water.

"No. I can get it."

Alice dove again and picked at the straps with her fingernails until she pried the knot loose. Lydia was still there, close beside her, when she bobbed above the water with the suit clutched in one hand. She had just struggled into the suit when she felt Lydia's fingers against her skin, tugging the zipper up.

"The water's warmed up a lot in the last week. I thought after this winter it'd stay freezing all summer," Lydia said, finishing with the zipper. She dove under the water, the white of her body flashing away.

"Come on," Alice said impatiently when she emerged. "I've got to get back."

She waited while Lydia climbed into the suit, keeping her eyes averted, and zipped her up as quickly as possible. Then she set off for shore doing a fast overhand crawl. She could hear Lydia behind her at first; when the muffled splashing faded, she knew she had pulled away. She swam faster, raising her head for a moment to check the distance to the beach. She and Lydia had never been modest with each other in the past, a word Lydia used in a tone of disgust to describe her sister, Betty, who dressed in the bathroom with the door bolted. Alice slapped the water with her arms, reaching forward as far as she could with each stroke, and thought of all the times she had spent the night at Lydia's when they took hour-long baths together and unabashedly pulled on their nightgowns in full view of each other. Now it was different. She felt she shouldn't see Lydia naked.

By the time Alice reached the shore, Lydia was far behind. She hobbled over the mounds of rocks and dropped to the packed sand. "Beat you," she called as Lydia emerged from the water minutes later and struggled over the rocks.

"It wasn't a race."

"I still beat you."

Lydia plopped to the sand next to her and stretched her legs in front of her. "Want me to go get some towels?"

"No. Let's just dry in the sun."

Lydia pried a rock from the damp sand and tossed it toward the water. The rock landed with a dull plunk, out beyond the breaking waves. They sat side by side without speaking while Lydia gathered a pile of rocks and methodically threw them, one by one, out over the water.

"When did you get so big?" Alice finally asked.

"Big? What do you mean?"

"You know. Your chest."

"It just sort of happened. One day my bra was so tight I could hardly breathe."

"Did you get a new one?"

"Yes."

"Why didn't you tell me?"

"I don't know. I wasn't exactly thrilled about it."

"I would be. Mine never fit to start with, and it still doesn't. It just hangs there."

"You should try those exercises Betty showed us, to make you develop."

"I have. They don't do anything."

"Sure they do. It just takes a while. Keep doing them. Maybe you won't get that big . . ." Lydia paused. "But you'll get bigger."

When their skin had dried and the suits only clung to them damply, they pulled on their clothes and headed for the inn. They had almost reached the road when Ethan Cunningham emerged from the lighthouse and crossed the path to his house, waving in their direction but not stopping to speak. Alice wondered when he had gone into the lighthouse. She had a sudden and acute awareness of her appearance: the wet, stringy hair hanging to her shoulders; the damp spot on her blouse where her bathing suit showed through.

"He sure is strange," Lydia said when Ethan had disappeared through his kitchen door.

"What do you mean?"

"You know, strange, odd. Different."

"I don't think he's that strange."

"No." Lydia arched her eyebrows. "You wouldn't."

It was just as well, Alice thought, that she had not mentioned the chance meeting with Ethan to Lydia.

They came to the porch of the inn, and Lydia hauled her bucket up the steps, taking the rake she had loaned Alice. Pete stood on a ladder nearby, hammering shingles beneath a second-floor window. He and his father had been reshingling the inn ever since school let out.

"You got a good haul." Pete paused in his work and nodded in the direction of Alice's bucket.

"Yes, but I'm sick to death of eating chowder."

Mr. Giberson appeared from around the back of the inn with a hammer in his hand. "There's been a news bulletin on the radio. Hitler's invaded Russia."

"Russia?" Pete said. "I thought they were allies."

"Not anymore, apparently."

Pete came down the ladder slowly.

"This isn't good." Mr. Giberson's tone was grave. "The farther that man goes, the more likely Congress will be persuaded we've got to get in the war."

"I thought that wasn't going to happen," Lydia said.

"That's what I like to think. Maybe your brother Hank is right."

Pete stood there watching his father closely. "I'm going to get some iced tea. Want some?"

Mr. Giberson shook his head.

"How about you two?"

"I should get back to the store," Alice said.

"You want me to help you carry that?" Pete asked.

"No, it's not that far."

Alice said good-bye. The Gibersons crossed the porch and went inside as she made her way to the road, switching the bucket from one hand to the other. She had not gone far when she heard a car behind her. Ethan Cunningham pulled up next to her and called across the front seat, "Get in. I'll give you a ride."

Before Alice could answer, he got out of the car and came around to the passenger side, holding the bucket while she slid into the front seat.

"I saw you out on the flats," he said as he climbed in on the driver's side. "You and your sidekick. Bringing home dinner?"

Alice curled her hands in her lap, concealing the mud caked beneath her fingernails, and nodded.

"I guess you are a quahogger, then. I shouldn't have said all those things I said that night on the road. I'm not really such a snob, I just sound like one sometimes."

"I don't think you're a snob."

"That's charitable of you. School's out, huh?"

"We finished on Wednesday."

"I was going to come over for your little ceremony, but my mother was having a bad day. Anyone graduate this year?"

"No."

"Your friend's in the same grade you are?"

"And her brother, Pete. The twins."

"He must be that gawky kid who's been hammering shingles on the inn all day, driving me nuts. I'm about ready to go over there and help him. He's making about an inch of progress a day. So what was your end-of-year recitation?"

"I read an essay on the causes of the Civil War." Alice was glad Ethan had not been there to witness her performance.

"And what were they, the causes of the Civil War?"

"Cotton and slaves."

"Cotton and slaves. I guess that about sums it up."

He turned the corner by the dock and started up the hill to her house, churning up dust as he pulled in and shut off the engine. Alice saw through the front window that her house was empty.

"That was quite a show you and your friend put on out there in the water," he said, turning to face her across the seat. "You looked like a couple of mermaids."

Alice blushed so deeply, the roots of her hair felt hot. "We didn't think anyone could see."

"Nobody but me. I kind of had an aerial view up in the lighthouse." He smiled. "Don't worry. I won't tell anyone you're a secret nudist. You do that often, just take your clothes off in broad daylight?"

"No." Alice tried to think of something else to say, some way to explain what she and Lydia were doing, but she was genuinely speechless.

"We used to go skinny-dipping sometimes at night, but not in the middle of the day." He let out a whistle of appreciation. "Now that's gutsy. I knew you had guts, Alice. I could tell the way you drive that crazy truck around."

Alice reached for the door handle, uncertain whether she was mortified or flattered.

He put his hand on her shoulder and squeezed it. "It's okay. I didn't see much. Just some white skin."

For one panicky moment, she feared he was going to slide across the seat and wrap his arm around her, but he let go of her shoulder and brought his hand back to the steering wheel.

In her haste to get out of the car, Alice caught the bucket handle with her foot as she opened the door. Ethan reached over and grabbed her ankle. He kept his fingers wrapped around her foot for a moment and met her gaze. "Be careful."

She nodded and swung her leg over the bucket. Somehow she managed to extricate herself from the car, but not before he had come around, lifted the bucket out, and carried it to the front stoop.

"Let me know the next time you're going skinny-dipping," he said.

He made her feel naked all over again, the way he looked at her. Alice ran to the house, grabbed the bucket, and slammed the door behind her, listening as he started up the car and pulled away.

# — CHAPTER 7 —

The summer people were full of questions when they arrived each year. How can you stand the winters? Isn't it terribly dull? What do you do without movies? Alice would remember the incredulous, condescending expressions on their faces when she set off for the schoolhouse on one of those sharp January mornings and found herself blinded by the diamond-studded surface of the bay. The summer people never saw the island in the winter light, when the setting sun turned the brittle fronds of beach grass into golden fields. They never felt the stiff force of the wind on the west side, so steady off the water the icicles hung sideways from the eaves of the houses. They never experienced the profound quiet when only one or two cars drove past on Bay Avenue all day. Now that the summer people were beginning to arrive, thronging the deck of the ferry and littering the dock with their oversized trunks, barking dogs and screeching cats, and boxes full of whiskey and gin and groceries, Alice tried to remember the other Snow Island, that windswept place it seemed only she knew.

She spent her days at the store, waiting on customers and reviewing inventory. The delivery business was an instant success, especially when Alice explained that she was not ordering her produce from Morton's but direct from the farmers around Barton and suppliers in Providence. "Morton's produce wasn't much good last year," Mrs. Lamprey told her.

"He sent us his cast-offs."

Alice set up crates on the flatbed of the truck, filled them with whatever she thought the summer people would want, and drove over to Snow Park each morning. When she tooted the horn, the women came running out on their porches and flagged her down. No one was sending grocery orders to the mainland. Morton's son still came over in the boat with fresh-baked bread and went cruising back and forth by the summer people's docks. Alice and her mother couldn't compete with him in baked goods; she didn't care if they purchased bread from him, as long as they weren't buying anything else.

By the first of July, they had enough to pay the mortgage on the fifteenth. Alice counted the money out on the counter one night when there were no customers in the store.

"See?" she said to her mother, trying not to sound too triumphant.

Evelyn stared at the pile of bills as though she had never seen money before. "That's good, Alice."

"This is the earliest we've ever made enough for the payment. This year we can really get ahead."

Evelyn closed her eyes and nodded wearily. "Fourteen hours a day, fifteen. I didn't think it would be like this when we bought the store."

"This is always the busiest time, Mom, after the summer people first get here. You forget. It'll slow down some."

"They're so demanding, wanting this and that and the next thing. Mrs. Sibley wants us to get canned pineapple. Can you imagine?"

Alice figured they should get Mrs. Sibley anything she requested. Mrs. Sibley had more money to spend than the rest of the summer people put together, but Alice refrained from pointing this out to her mother. She poured a cup of coffee and set it on the counter.

Evelyn raised the cup to her lips, blinking at the light bulb hanging from the ceiling.

"Do you have a headache?" Alice asked.

"No. I'm just tired, dog-tired. I don't know where you get the energy,

Alice."

Alice took the pile of bills and set them beneath the cash drawer. She thought it was a question of desire, not energy. If her mother truly wanted the store to do well, she wouldn't care about the long hours, but there were times when it seemed she did not want the store to succeed. Evelyn still acted as if there were someone else to take care of the three of them, someone wiser and stronger who could pay the bills and worry about making a living, when this person did not exist any longer, not in this world at least.

When the hurricane had hit on that Sunday in September of 1938, the store didn't stand a chance. Alice and her mother and Will rode out the storm at their house. They spent the afternoon and evening huddled against the inside wall in the kitchen, praying that the house would hold, and emerged to find the world strangely altered. Though the water had not reached their house, it had left nothing but piles of wood along the shore, tearing up one summer place after another. A few timbers were strewn about where the store had stood, along with some rusted cans of food. Everything else was swept away. Evelyn stared, speechless, and burst into tears. "We're finished," she said. "We're through. I want to move to Kansas. I want to go as far from the ocean as a person can get."

On the mainland they were giving grants to small businesses to rebuild. Alice helped her mother fill out the papers. The grant covered the cost of the wood and enough money to restock the store. The men of the island donated their time, working nights and Sundays, and by December, they had a store again. Alice thought of this as she shut the cash drawer. She took a pride in the store her mother didn't understand.

The sound of voices and laughter carried through the screen from outside. Evelyn removed her apron and began stacking the ledger books beneath the counter.

"You're closing?" Alice asked.

"It's almost nine."

"But the summer kids just showed up."

"Alice, we have been here since seven this morning."

"I know. You go up to the house with Will. I'll close up after they're gone."

Evelyn shook her head, but said nothing more until she and Will were leaving. "Make sure the padlock's on when you close."

Sometimes Lydia came and worked her way into the group on the dock, or kept Alice company in the store, but tonight she had not appeared. Alice sat behind the counter, flipping through a copy of Movie Mirror while Molly slept on a pile of newspapers beside her.

"How's Your Clothes IQ?" the magazine headline read. "The best way for a girl to get places fast is to wear the right clothes. How is your style sense? If you're in the smart class, you won't have any trouble with our little quiz." Alice studied the pictures on the page. She couldn't imagine she would ever see a woman in a paradise fur hat with a matching muff, even Mrs. Giberson, who cared about such things.

She had gotten the first two questions of the clothes quiz wrong and was working on the third (name three new styles that are a direct loan from the Navy), when Nate Shattuck appeared, whistling in fits and starts.

"Why aren't you out there wi' the other kids?" he asked, leaning on the counter so he was as close to her as he could get.

Grease and dirt covered the legs of his dungarees, and he wore a tattered plaid shirt. A bristle of dark hairs sprouted from his chin.

"My mother's gone up to the house," Alice answered, stepping away, pressing her back against the wall of mailboxes. She could smell the liquor on his breath.

He stared at her for a long moment as if trying to place her. The whites of his eyes were yellow.

"Do you want something, Nate?"

"Nothin'. No, I don't want nothin' but to look at your beaut'ful face. Just out for a lil' stroll. See what's going on." He steadied himself by placing his hands flat on the counter. "Ain't it time for you to close?"

"I will when the summer kids leave."

"Gimme me a pack of Lucky Strikes then."

Alice considered refusing. Nate Shattuck had paid almost nothing on his tab since January. Phoebe had come in and paid five dollars on their bill a few days earlier, but a sizable balance remained. Nate held her look, as though he knew what she was thinking. She reached behind her and set the cigarettes on the counter.

"You're gonna have to put that on my tab. Wife cleaned me out th' other day." He placed his hands in his pockets, swaying away from her, and tugged at them. "See that? Nothin'. Not even a nickel."

"Fine," she answered, keeping her voice low, aware of voices moving closer outside. "I'll put it on your tab." She tried to hand him the pack.

He gazed at it, confused. "I said Lucky Strikes." A wild look came into his eyes. He held the edge of the counter for balance.

"These *are* Lucky Strikes," she said. "Here, Nate. Take them."

"Take them? Course I'm gonna take them. I'll take every damn thing in this store if I want, and there's nothin' you can do to stop me. Writing every last penny down in that book like I'm some kind of criminal, like I don't deserve to eat like everybody else, like I'm some kind of . . . I ain't somebody for you to be pitying, Alice Daggett."

He raised his hand as if to hit her, and she shrank back against the mailboxes.

"You think you're so goddamn high and mighty wi' your own store, think you can tell us all what to do, make us do a little dance for a blasted bag a flour. Bag a flour. Is that too much to ask?"

He brought his hand down on the counter with a loud smack and swept away the stack of newspapers. Molly let out a loud mew and jumped to the floor, barely avoiding the cascade of papers. Alice didn't move. Outside the voices had gone silent.

"Are you gonna give me what I want or not?" he growled.

"I did, Nate. I got you the cigarettes."

"What about the flour?"

He leaned over the counter again and swayed back, then spit on the floor. Molly circled around him and pressed against Alice's leg.

Alice was scared to move from behind the counter and scared to stay. She was still trying to decide what to do when the door opened, and Pete Giberson came quickly toward them.

"Nate, what're you doing?"

Nate turned his head slowly, like a dog waking from sleep, and stared at Pete as though he had never seen him before. "Nothin'. What're you doing?"

"Just came by to say hello to Alice."

"Me, too. Alice. Ain't she a beauty?"

"Yes, she is. You have what you want now, Nate?"

"Cig'rettes. I just wanted some cig'rettes."

The door opened again, and a group of summer kids came inside. Alice recognized David Sibley and his sister, Meg, and Jack Cheaving. They paused inside the door, eyeing Nate as though they were not sure whether to advance or retreat.

Aware that something had happened, Nate turned toward them. "What're starin' at?"

None of them spoke.

"Nate," Alice said through clenched teeth. "Just take the cigarettes." She held them toward him.

Nate slowly turned his head and peered at her.

"I've got other customers. You need to go."

"Need to go? I don' need to go anywhere." She thought he was going to erupt again, but he kept his voice low.

She could feel her heart in her chest, beating fast and loud. After a long moment, he picked up the Lucky Strikes, fumbled for his pocket, and shoved the cigarettes into it. He was about to leave when he turned back. "Got any matches?"

Alice reached beneath the counter and handed him a matchbook.

"You're a princess, Alice. Hard as stone but a princess all th' same."

He did not seem to be aware of the trio by the door, staring at him. Pete hooked his arm through Nate's and said, "Come on. I'll walk you home."

Together they crossed in front of the summer kids, Nate stumbling for a moment. Alice kept her eyes on Pete's back, too embarrassed to look at the others.

No one moved until their steps died out on the porch and Nate's ragged whistling started up again. Then David Sibley spoke. "Are you about to close up?"

"In a few minutes."

"We just wanted some sodas."

"Help yourselves." Alice gestured toward the cooler.

David retrieved the sodas and brought them to the counter. The others stayed by the door, as though they were afraid to get too close.

"Boy, he was stinking drunk," David said.

Alice nodded. "You want to pay for these or put them on your bill?"

"I'll pay you for them. Does he get like that often?"

Alice shrugged, taking the dollar he handed her. "Not to speak of."

"If you have any trouble with him again, come outside and get me."

The offer struck her as insulting. "He wasn't bothering me," she said quickly.

David gave her an appraising look, as if to say he didn't believe her, slipped the change in his pocket, and gathered up the sodas.

"Come on, let's go back to our place, see if we can get some music on the radio," he said to Meg and Jack. He handed them the sodas, and the screen slammed behind them. Moments later, she heard cars starting up outside.

Alice waited until the cars had crested the hill and gone off toward Snow Park. She went to the porch and searched the dark beyond the streetlight up by the road. There was no sign of Nate Shattuck. She could still feel the sense of shame that overtook her when David Sibley stood there staring at her, as though she were the one drunk and making a spectacle. In the eyes of the summer people, she knew it didn't make a difference. She and Nate were one and the same, part of that peculiar breed known as islanders.

Inside, Alice took a rag and cleaned Nate's spit from the floor. She picked up the newspapers and set them on the counter. Molly followed her, rubbing against her legs and mewing. When Alice collected the money from the till, shut the register, and pulled the string on the light bulb, the cat jumped back to her spot on the newspapers. "Sleep tight, Molly," she whispered, leaning down to bury her face in the cat's fur. Molly purred and rolled over, curling against the cash register.

Molly closed the outer door and snapped the padlock together. She did not think she had ever truly feared Nate before, but now she felt for the bills in her pocket and wondered if she should carry them back to the house. She imagined he was there, waiting for her behind one of the old cars parked by the dock.

As she started down the porch steps, she realized someone was there, coming toward her on the path. The person was shorter than Nate and walked more steadily. Pete.

"Sorry about that," he said.

"It wasn't your fault."

"No, but it's terrible to see him like that. Maybe you shouldn't stay alone at the store."

Alice laughed. "I don't think Nate would really do anything. You think it's not safe?"

"Well, what would you have done if I hadn't come along?"

"I don't know."

"David Sibley and Jack Cheaving weren't any help. They just stood there outside."

"I guess if he'd gone any further, they would have come in."

Pete shook his head in a way that made Alice angry.

"I think I can handle the store," she said.

He shrugged. "Okay, then I won't stop in to see how you're doing again."

"That's not what I meant, Pete. I'm glad you came in. You calmed him down."

"Yup. That's what I'm good at. Calming people down. I can practically put someone to sleep if I try. See you, Alice."

He turned away. She realized he was angry now, and that it was somehow her fault. "Good night," she called after him. "Thanks."

He waved his hand but did not look back.

Alice made her way up to the house, fingering the wad of bills, the mortgage money, in her pocket. When she opened the front door, she saw that her mother was already stretched on the couch asleep. She let herself back out, following the path by the chicken coop to the outhouse. Up the hill, the curtains were pulled over the windows at Nate Shattuck's.

Letting herself into the outhouse and sitting on the wooden seat, Alice thought of the times she had heard Nate's shouts carrying down the hill. Phoebe rarely gave any response that she could hear, which made the sound of his yells that much worse. Alice used one of the squares of newspaper stuck through a nail on the wall and stepped out of the outhouse.

A few years earlier, Nate Shattuck had gambled and lost his boat in a poker game on the mainland. He still went out quahogging in the winter when he could walk across the ice and in warmer weather when he could borrow a boat. The rest of the time he ran a fix-it shop in a shack next to his house, repairing cars, toasters, furniture, whatever people brought him. Most of his customers were summer people, and he hadn't caught up yet from the lean winter months. He couldn't find the money to pay his food bills, but he managed to get the liquor somehow, though Alice had never seen him drunk like that before.

Phoebe Shattuck came from one of the "better families" in Barton, as people put it. No one knew why she had left a big house on Front Street and a chance to study piano at the conservatory in Boston to marry Nate, though Alice's mother claimed he was handsome once. Now she tried to make ends meet by giving piano lessons and working as the organist at the Catholic church. She had converted to Catholicism since she came to Snow, a choice that only made her more isolated. Her three children attended the schoolhouse with Alice. Rachel, the oldest, was nine, and the boys, Nate Junior and Phil, were six and eight.

Inside the house, Alice crossed the room quietly and put the money in the cookie jar on the kitchen table. Her mother let out a loud snore and rolled over without waking up. Alice climbed the stairs to the attic and ducked beneath the blanket that hung over the rafters, dividing her side of the room from Will's. He was already asleep, his knees pulled up to his chest in a tight ball beneath the sheets.

Alice sat on her bed and watched as the lighthouse's beam tracked across the window. She thought of Pete, wondering what she had done to make him angry. Maybe she shouldn't have responded to him as she did that night, but she hated it when people suggested that just because she was a girl, she wasn't capable of running the store. She had known for a long time that she couldn't count on other people, that she could take better care of herself than anyone else could, or maybe ever would.

# — CHAPTER 8 —

George Tibbits finished painting the last bare spot on the hull of the boat and stood back to inspect his work. The only paint he had on hand, left over from the last time he painted the houses, was a deep shade of maroon-red, not the color he would have chosen for a boat, but he was sure Sarah would understand. She knew the importance of "making do."

They had planned the trip for years. George remembered the summer day when the idea came to Sarah. He was ten years old, and Bertie was in one of her moods. She yelled at Sarah for leaving the wet laundry sitting in a basket by the clothesline to follow a bird into the woods. Bertie ran after Sarah and dragged her back by the sleeve of her blouse, going on about mildew and forgetfulness and how she couldn't take her eyes off either of them, her or George, for more than a minute, and it was enough to drive any sane person to madness.

"It was a wren," Sarah said in her smallest of voices. "I've been watching for her. I thought I might find where she has her nest."

"You can go bird-watching after you hang up the clothes, Sarah. First things first, remember?"

Sarah nodded stiffly and reached for a wet nightgown.

George went to help her. "Maybe we can find the wren this afternoon." He kept his voice low and handed her two clothespins.

Bertie went back inside her house, where she was busy canning blueberries. Canning always put her in a bad mood.

"The wren will be frightened of me now," Sarah said sadly.

"No, she won't. She knows you're different from Aunt Bertie."

Sarah took the clothespin he extended and stabbed it over a sock.

Later that afternoon, they set off in search of the wren. Bertie was lying down after the long hours of canning. She did not ask where they were going or call them back, for once. They wandered through the brush and the pines, heads tilted toward the high branches, without speaking. They walked for a long time. It was hot and still in the woods. Finally Sarah sat down, slumping against the trunk of a tree.

"I think it's gone."

"It's not gone, Aunt Sarah, not for good."

"I think it's abandoned the nest. She scared it right off."

"No. We'll see it again tomorrow. You know it always comes in the morning."

"But where do they go in the afternoon? Birds have secret lives, don't they? I wish I could be a bird, a little one, like a wren. They're so delicate. Don't they look like they're made of velvet? Brown velvet. I always wanted to hold one. That's what I was thinking, if I could just make friends with that wren, if I knew where she lived, maybe she would trust me enough to come to my hand."

She saw the look on George's face, bit her lip, and laughed. "I'm awfully foolish, George."

"Not awfully. Just a little bit."

"Well, why wouldn't that wren eat out of my hand? Stranger things have happened. What we need is a journey, George. A journey to find out where the wren goes in the afternoon."

"You mean going farther into the woods?"

"No. We need to see the way a bird sees. We need to go all the way around the island."

"That could take all day."

"Not if we do it in a boat."

George was never certain he understood the relationship between the boat ride around the island and the secret life of the wren, but before long neither of them thought much about how the plan got its start. The boat ride became the point in and of itself, the focus of their dreams from the beginning of each day to the end. First, Sarah said, they had to find a boat. You would think such an object would be easy to obtain on an island, but finding a boat proved more difficult than she at first imagined. They didn't want a sailboat that would be complicated to maneuver. Something small they could handle themselves, that's all they needed, Sarah said.

At night they lay side by side in her bed and planned their trip. They would leave just at dawn, before Bertie was up. They would push off from the flat place past the rocks, down near the sandy beach. They would stay close to the shore, where it was most safe. Sarah thought they could make it clear around the island by early afternoon, before Bertie had time to get too worked up. They would have to choose the day carefully, of course. No wind and not too hot. June would be the best time, but it was already the end of July by the time they began making plans. They would have to hope for a June day in August, for a bit of luck, but first there was the matter of the boat.

"I think we will have to row around the island," Sarah said one night, in a solemn voice. "Do you think we can handle rowing, George? We can each take an oar and pull together. We can do that, can't we?"

George nodded. "I can probably row all by myself."

"We just might be the first people ever to row all the way around Snow Island. Maybe we'll get in the paper. Oh dear, now we've got to think about what we'll wear."

Sarah decided that an outing on a boat called for a dress, a flowered one, and a pretty wide-brimmed hat. The next day she set about mending her best summer dress and searching through her sewing basket for a bit of trim for her old hat.

That night when George climbed into her bed for their nightly talk, she said, "I've got it, George, what we should bring to eat on our trip. I'll make a blueberry cobbler and a pitcher of lemonade and some hard-boiled eggs. And we'll take some of those crackers you like so much. And you can wear your new shorts with a long-sleeved shirt. That will look good for the newspapers."

Their talk went on like this all through August and into September. They were no closer to finding a boat, but they had planned the rest of the trip down to the smallest detail. The first week of September passed and then the second. George was back in school, and the three of them were living in Bertie's house again. When Bertie went to get something in the kitchen one night, leaving George doing his homework on one side of the table and Sarah knitting on the other, she whispered, "I don't think we can take our trip this year. It's hurricane season now." She pursed her lips and shook her head, but George knew that neither of them had given up the idea.

That year at Christmas, they made a secret exchange of gifts before Bertie woke on Christmas morning. George presented Sarah with a jar containing eighty-two cents, and she gave him an old pocket handker-chief with a dollar thirty-four tied up inside. It seemed like a sizable beginning toward the purchase of a boat. Sarah held his hands in hers and said, "Next summer, George."

Each year they renewed their promise to each other; by the follow-ing summer, they would have a boat and make the trip. Sarah kept their boat savings in the dresser drawer, beneath her undergarments. Every time they took the money out and counted it, the bills and coins seemed like a small miracle they had created all on their own. A boat did not pre-sent itself, however. George asked around as often as he could, but no one seemed to have a spare rowboat they wanted to part with. There were boats they might have been able to borrow, but this was out of the question, since they could not accomplish such a thing without alerting Bertie. The less likely the trip appeared, the more Sarah clung to the idea. As George grew older, he secretly came to believe they would never row around the island and was no longer even sure why they had wanted to, but he did not let on about his change of heart. He continued to contribute to the boat fund and simply nodded when Sarah said, "I think it will be this summer, George. I've got a feeling about it."

The night before he went to enlist, Sarah crouched by his bed. "Bertie's asleep," she whispered. "I just wanted you to have this." She handed him a handkerchief tied in a knot, heavy with coins. "I don't think we'll be making our trip now. You should take the money. You might need it over there."

George shook his head. "We'll get a boat when I come back. You keep the money. When I come back, we'll take that trip."

She argued with him in whispers. The money was rightfully his. All these years, he had given her whatever he could spare out of his allowance and clothes money and what he made raking lawns. She couldn't keep the money now for an old boat they might never have. George pushed the worn handkerchief back into her hands. "Keep the money for me, till I come back," he said.

When he returned from the war, he hurried into Sarah's house, hoping she had already moved out of Bertie's for the summer, and when he got no answer to his calls, he climbed the stairs to the second floor. It was as if he knew. Afterwards he wondered at this. He seemed to be drawn up the stairs, though there was no evidence of life in the house. Once he discovered Sarah's body, he went to the other house and found Bertie. It wasn't until later, after the men had taken the bodies away, that he spotted the boat under Sarah's house. He followed the men across the lawn, glancing back at the last moment as though he expected to find Sarah coming after them, bringing up the rear of the procession. He saw the boat then, turned on its side, a sturdy rowboat with two oars lying next to it. The boat remained the only piece of those last months that was still a mystery to him. All the rest of the time before Sarah's death he had been able to reconstruct, up to the last night when she climbed the stairs and slid beneath the covers and waited for the end, but he had never learned how she obtained the boat or what she told Bertie, if anything.

The boat had been protected under the house and was in fine condition, except for needing a little paint. George wanted the boat to look the best for its maiden voyage. He felt that Sarah would be watching in some way, taking a distant delight in seeing him make the trip at last. He would even bring hard-boiled eggs, though he would not attempt the blueberry cobbler.

George spent the rest of that afternoon seated on the porch, trying not to stare at the boat. He resisted the impulse to cross the lawn and touch his hand to the hull until nearly sunset. By then the paint was dry. He went inside, made himself some supper and boiled a few eggs, and went to sleep hoping to wake to a fine day.

The wind came up in the night. He stood at the window for a long time in the morning, wondering if he should go. At last he decided against it. He could hear Sarah saying, "We need just the right day, not too hot and no wind." The following morning was better. The air was still, and the water on the west side had a blank, placid look. It was sultry, hot already, but he thought this was preferable to a day that brought choppy waves. He would wear his hat.

# — CHAPTER 9 —

"Alice, every soul on this island is going to that parade. What kind of business do you think we're going to do?" Her mother sat behind the counter at the store, carefully applying polish to her nails.

"I just think it's better if we stay open."

"Nonsense. They'll think we're crazy, staying open on the Fourth of July. It's disrespectful. I for one don't plan to give up that parade. We've been looking forward to it all year."

"You go, Mom. You and Will. I'll stay here."

"Stay here and do what?"

"Catch up on the paperwork, do inventory."

Evelyn inspected her shiny, red nails, and sniffed. "You're getting greedy, Alice. Everything's a dollar sign to you."

Alice flipped open the ledger and stared at the columns of figures, biting the inside of her lip to keep herself from responding. At least, she thought, one member of this family cares whether we starve or not. Her mother had been up since five that morning, ironing her best dress and fussing with her hair in preparation for the trip to Barton. She had not even considered how many customers they could get that day or checked to see if the penny candy was stocked.

"Who's that out on the porch with Owen Pierce?" Evelyn asked.

"Pete."

"He's up early. I bet he's going to the parade."

Alice nodded and went to the back, where the boxes of extra stock were piled. She took a handful of peppermint sticks from one, returned to the counter, and filled the candy jar. Once she finished with the penny candy, Alice went up and down the aisles taking canned goods and boxes of cereal and soap powder from the shelves. Pete had not referred to the night with Nate Shattuck again or shown any further signs of being angry with her, and Alice felt relieved.

Evelyn eyed her as she began loading the groceries into cardboard boxes. "What're you doing now?"

"Getting things ready to drive over to Snow Park."

"Today? When everybody's going to the parade?"

"People still need to eat."

Evelyn rolled her eyes. "Suit yourself."

Pete came through the door and saw what Alice was doing. Without asking if she needed help, he took one of the boxes and carried it out.

"Isn't he a lamb?" Evelyn said, as she finished touching up her nail polish.

Alice gave her mother a withering look and grasped a box in her hands. Pete held the door for her. When the truck was loaded, Pete swung up alongside her on the seat. "Mind if I come?"

She shook her head.

Alice turned the key and pressed the starter with her heal. The engine caught. She moved the lever on the steering wheel to give it gas, hoping the truck would make it up the hill. When the gas was low, it sloshed to the back of the tank, and the truck could suddenly die. This time it made it.

"I'll drive if you want," Pete said over the truck's rattling.

"That's okay. I know this thing better than anyone else."

They went bouncing down Bay Avenue. Alice kept her eye on the road, veering around the ruts.

"There used to be four schoolhouses on Snow. Did you know that?"

Pete said. "Owen was telling me."

"Did he tell you about that snowstorm? He's always talking about that."

"I don't mind listening to his stories. He doesn't have much else to do."

"Except going out quahogging." Alice felt the meanness of her words as soon as she spoke them, but it was too late to take them back.

"So he's a little confused sometimes. If I get my boat, I'm going to take him out with me. He can teach me better than anyone. You didn't mention it to Lydia, did you?"

"No."

"I don't want anyone to know until I have the money for the down payment."

Alice made the turn by the marsh and a few minutes later pulled up the hill to Snow Park and came to a stop, beeping the horn. Mrs. Sibley crossed her porch and called, "Got any sugar today?"

Alice filled a sack and weighed it on the scale she had brought with her. Pete remained in the front seat. She waited on four other customers and was ready to head back when George Tibbits emerged from the path to the twin houses. He came up to the truck and took off his hat. "I was wondering if you could take a boat down to the shore for me. I'll pay you. It's a rowboat, not too big."

Alice nodded.

"It's just in the yard by my houses." He hesitated on the last word, as though not wanting to call attention to the fact that he owned more than one house.

"All right. I'll drive over." Alice climbed into the truck. "He wants us to take a boat down to the water for him," she told Pete.

"I didn't know he had a boat."

"He says it's a little rowboat."

"Wonder what he wants with that."

Alice shrugged.

George Tibbits walked ahead of them on the path with his hat perched awkwardly on his head. Alice inched the truck along behind him. The rowboat sat on sawhorses in the middle of the lawn with two oars inside it. George Tibbits did not speak as he and Pete eased it off the sawhorses and carried it slowly to the back of the truck. When the boat was settled, George reached into his pocket and pulled out a dollar. He handed the bill to Alice. "Could you just leave it down below, by the sandy spot next to the rocks?"

George thanked her and turned toward the twin houses. Alice and Pete jumped into the truck, not waiting to watch him cross the lawn.

"Did he ever say how long he plans to stay?" Pete asked as Alice nosed the truck down the path and onto the road.

"Not to me. Maybe he's moved here permanently."

"I wouldn't want to spend a winter in one of those houses."

At the foot of the hill, Alice pulled over and helped Pete tug the boat from the back of the truck. They left it in the sand, well above the tide line.

"It's a good thing you came with me," she said when they reached the other side of the island and the dock came into view. "I couldn't have handled that boat by myself. Here." She took the dollar from her pocket and handed it to him.

"That's yours."

"No, you did all the work. You take it. For your down payment."

Alice felt his shyness as he slipped the bill into his pocket. Sometimes Pete reminded her of her father, with his quiet ways. She pulled the truck up next to the store and saw that the ferry was chugging toward the dock. A knot of people stood waiting, and the inside of the store was packed.

The crowd was so large that Captain Tony had to make two runs back and forth to Snow to bring everyone over for the parade. Her mother stayed to help between the first and second ferry, selling sodas and penny candy and newspapers, but when the last ferry pulled away with a blast of the horn, Alice found herself alone. She watched from the porch as the ferry inched away from the dock. Her mother leaned against the ferry's railing with Miss Weeden. Even Mrs. Cunningham was going to the parade. The Brovellis had helped her up the gangplank and settled her on the bench. Pete sat between her and Owen Pierce.

Alice was relieved to see Nate Shattuck board the ferry with Phoebe and the children. He had been in the store once since the night when he was so drunk. "I want to pay you for those cigarettes I got the other night," he said sheepishly. She saw that he was embarrassed and took the coins from his hand. She supposed that was his way of making an apology.

Once the ferry was gone, Alice spent the rest of the morning behind the counter, swatting flies and paging through the order forms. No customers stopped in, and no one drove by up on the road. The heat blanketed the dock in an oppressive silence. She made a sandwich up at the house at noon, brought it back down to the store, and ate behind the counter, offering bits of apple butter to Molly, who roused herself for the occasion of a meal. As soon as Alice finished eating, the cat returned to her cool spot against the rear wall of the store and flopped over.

By two o'clock, Alice had finished filling out the order forms, swept the floor, and taken inventory of the canned goods. There was more to be done, of course. She could go through the ledger and total customers' accounts for the last week, but in the heat, the numbers running up and down the page in uneven rows made her dizzy. She shut the ledger and went out to the porch, taking the *Movie Mirror* she had not yet finished with her.

She sat on the bench and leafed through the magazine. Lana Turner had declared "No more divorces," a headline proclaimed. A photo showed the actress in a tight red bathing suit and platform sandals, standing by a swimming pool, holding an air mattress. Alice thought of Lydia and how she wanted a bathing suit like that, one that fit so tightly you could barely breathe. Alice dropped the magazine on the bench beside her. Her mother was right, she realized. She might not do any business at all that day. She hadn't wanted to go to the parade anyway, she told herself. It was the same every year, first the veterans' band, then the farmers and their tractors, and the fire trucks coming last. She didn't relish the idea of standing in the heat that long. She hoped someone would have the sense to take her mother inside somewhere, out of the sun, or she would be laid up with a headache for days.

Alice locked the store and went up to the house for her bathing suit. She pulled on a pair of shorts over the suit and tied a towel around her waist. It would be cool by the water, she thought, and on her bike she might find a breeze. She rode her bicycle down the hill and away from the dock. The summer houses along Bay Avenue were deserted, and shades covered the windows at the Improvement Center.

The sun was hot on the nape of her neck, though the air cooled her face. She had not planned on going all the way to Gooseneck Cove, but when she came to the cutoff, the shaded stretch of road was too inviting to pass up. Alice rode by the dance hall and the trail to the sandy beach and kept going.

There were few houses out this way. Past the last summer place, a path wound through fields and patches of blueberries, with a vast marsh on one side and Gooseneck Cove on the other. Alice rode over the rutted grass, following a red-winged blackbird that flitted ahead of her. When she was almost to the bluff where the land gave out, she left her bike in the tall grass and climbed Pine Hill, the highest point on Snow. There were no boats in the cove. On the other side of the hill, the gold-tipped marsh grass stretched to the end of the island, a skinny finger of land in the distance. At low tide, it was possible to walk from this point to the small mound of Despair Island, whose twin, little Hope Island, lay in the waters off the east side.

Alice scanned the horizon. They said her father must have gone overboard somewhere off the rocks surrounding Despair. He was not a swimmer. Alice could not recall ever having seen him in the water. He wouldn't have lasted long in it that day, the men said. If she had been there, she would not have been able to save him. She knew this. She just wished she could have been there, that she could have made him feel for a moment he was not alone.

Silas Mitchell was the one who found his body, three days after the empty boat washed up on the west side. In the winter, Silas cleaned the schoolhouse and did other odd jobs around the island. He was making his daily walk along the shore, on his way back from the schoolhouse. Alice wasn't supposed to know the details, but she had heard Ernie Brovelli repeating what Silas said, how he saw what at first looked like an old coat draped over a rock. Daggett always was an independent cuss, Mr. Brovelli said to the men assembled on the porch at the store, but that day he just hit bad luck. At first Alice was wounded by his words, but then she felt proud. Her father wasn't like the other men.

She never saw the body herself, except in her dreams, the bad ones, when he walked out of the bay, a skeleton in sodden clothes, and she woke with a start, her back damp with sweat. The casket was closed, and the women of the island prepared him for burial, not even allowing her mother to view him. Alice sometimes wondered if it would have made a difference to see the body, to know for herself the awful truth of what he looked like, but at the time, she did as she was told, going through each day in mute surrender, thinking and feeling almost nothing.

The quahoggers went out at dawn each morning and returned by mid-day with their catch. When Bill Daggett didn't show up that day, the other men knew something was wrong. Then his boat washed up. Mrs. Brovelli appeared in the doorway at the schoolhouse, her lips white, and motioned for Miss Weeden to follow her outside. Miss Weeden returned, walked slowly toward Alice's desk, put her hand on her shoulder, and led her to the vestibule. An awestruck silence hung over the schoolroom. Everyone knew that something out of the ordinary had happened. In whispers, Mrs. Brovelli told Alice and hugged her, enfolding her in her fat arms. Alice remembered with a strange clarity the feel of Mrs.

Brovelli's arms around her, and the looks the children gave her as she went to get Will, and the sensation of the chill air on her face as they crossed the lawn to a waiting car. Later, she wondered where her mother was (out in one of the boats, looking for him), but at the time, it seemed perfectly natural that Mrs. Brovelli was the one to come and stand in the doorway of the schoolhouse like a figure carved out of stone. Everything seemed to happen that day exactly as it should, as if each moment had been rehearsed beforehand, and yet Alice could not remember ever feeling more strange, more distant from herself or her surroundings.

By nightfall, they knew there was little hope, but the men kept searching the following morning and the one after that. Each day was like the first, like being in a play where she was given lines to speak. She spoke her lines without knowing what she said; she moved when she was directed to move. She performed her part perfectly, she thought, until the search was called off. Then another kind of strangeness set in.

For a long time, she was troubled by not knowing exactly how and where the accident occurred. He was a good quahogger, the men said, one of the best. John Brovelli, Ernie's son, told her it could have happened to anybody. The deck was icy, and he slipped as he put the quahog tongs in the water and went overboard. That must have been what happened, a simple accident, but she needed to see the place where he went into the water before she could begin to believe he was gone. There was no place, though, just the endless, flat surface of the bay. The water stretching on all sides of the island met her again each day, revealing nothing.

Alice scrambled down the steep path to the cove. Gulls wheeled over the water, flashing their white wings in the sun, and the tide was high, coming in. She left her shoes and towel by the beach grass, picked her way over the rocks, and waded into the water.

When she dove beneath, the cold gripped her chest, and she came up gasping for air. The sand on the bottom was soft against her feet. She dove again and surfaced to float on her back and hold her face to the sun.

Sometimes she wondered whether things might have ended differently if her father had known how to swim. Could he have made it back into the boat? Or even to the shore of Despair? John Brovelli said no, the water was so cold in March, it was a question of minutes. If he didn't get his boots and oilers off right away, he couldn't have made it. Still, she kept reliving those minutes, unable to let go of the belief that he might have had a chance.

Alice righted herself and turned toward shore. There was someone on the beach, sitting on a rock, watching her. She knew immediately who it was, though she was so startled, she thought she might have created Ethan Cunningham out of the hot air.

He waved as she waded out of the water, retrieved her towel and other things, and crossed the beach. She had not spoken to Ethan at any length since the day he drove her home with the bucket of clams. For a moment she was tempted to run back into the water or turn the other way down the beach, where she could disappear into the marsh grass.

"You knew where to come today," he said when she was within earshot.

"I stayed home from the parade so we could keep the store open, but there haven't been any customers, and it was so hot . . ." She trailed off, realizing she did not have to explain to him why she was swimming at Gooseneck Cove. Against his black hair and pale skin, the blue of his eyes had the shock of something rare, like a butterfly's wing.

Alice wrapped the towel around her shoulders and sat on a rock next to him. Though it was the hottest day of the summer yet, he wore long khaki pants with a button-down shirt and sneakers. Alice wondered if he ever went swimming. The sleeves of his shirt were rolled to the elbow, exposing his white forearms.

"You kept your suit on today, huh? When I realized it was you out there, I thought you'd come prancing across the beach naked."

Alice felt the blush rising into her face and stared at the sand, trying to hide behind the strands of hair that fell over her forehead.

He chuckled. "Don't be embarrassed. I'm paying you a compliment. Really."

"I'm not embarrassed."

"Yes, you are, but you shouldn't be. You're beautiful, Alice. Did anyone ever tell you that before? Probably not, but it's true. I'm old enough and I've been enough places to know. I tried to paint you even."

This was a stunning piece of information. Alice fished through the sand for a broken clam shell and held it in her hand, rubbing the smooth surface. "I thought you didn't paint paintings of people."

"What do you know about my paintings?"

"Just what I've heard."

"And what's that?"

"You only paint rocks."

"Who told you that?"

"Owen Pierce."

"You mean I don't paint pretty scenes?" He sounded scornful.

"I don't know. Owen said they were mostly just rocks, nothing he recognized."

"When did that old geezer see my paintings, anyway?"

"Your mother showed them to him one time. That's what he said at least. It's hard to know if you can believe anything he says these days."

"He's right. I paint a lot of rocks. Rock formations. Rocks and sky. Rocks and grass. You could call them landscapes, but they're not those kind of landscapes, not pretty ones. That's what my sisters always say. 'Why don't you paint something pretty for a change?' They can't understand any painting that's not decorative. They think everything should look like Norman Rockwell. But I do paint people sometimes. Like you. I tried to paint you swimming around by the lighthouse, but it came out all wrong."

Alice gave him a nervous glance.

"Don't worry, it's not that kind of picture. You're just a tiny figure in the water. Nobody would ever know it was you. What else has Owen

Pierce been telling people about me?"

"I don't know."

"Oh come on, Alice, there's nothing to do on this crazy island but sit around and gossip. What do they say about me? Do they say it's strange for a man my age to be living at home with his mother, unmarried?"

"No." Alice had never heard anyone voice such an opinion, though she supposed people thought it.

"Well, they must say something. Come on, tell me."

"They say you sleep late and don't turn off the lighthouse when you should, and you don't believe in God."

Ethan let out a guffaw.

"Well, you don't go to church."

"Looking for God in church is like looking for quahogs in the woods. You could spend your whole life doing it and come up with nothing. God's not in church. God's here." He swept one arm toward the water. "Why would God stay cooped up in a church with a bunch of hypocrites who think they're better than everyone else? He's got better things to do. Going to church is about proving to your neighbors that you're holier than they are, not about spending time with God. If I want to spend time with God, I come to Gooseneck Cove, I don't go to church."

"So you do believe in God?"

"Well, that's a whole different question. I guess I do sort of. When the chips are down, I'll pray. The rest of the time I don't think much about it."

"Do you believe in Jesus?"

"Sure, I believe there was a man who lived two thousand years ago and went around preaching and died on a cross. I don't know if he was the son of God, but I believe he existed. He was probably even a great man."

"I always thought there must be a God, but Jesus feels kind of far away."

Ethan turned to look at her. "You're too damn smart, Alice. Smart and pretty. Snow Island doesn't deserve you."

Alice had never thought of herself as smart. Curious, maybe, and prone to feeling things in ways others didn't seem to, but not smart, the sort of smart that meant you should go to college or be a teacher. She wasn't sure about being pretty, either. She had always thought of her looks as perfectly respectable, but nothing out of the ordinary.

"Aren't you hot?" he asked. "I'm roasting. Come on, I've got the car here. I'll give you a ride." He stood up, brushing the sand from the palms of his hands.

Alice wasn't sure how to get into her shorts with Ethan standing there, looking at her. When she took them from the rock beside her, he seemed to sense her discomfort and started for the path. She pulled on the shorts and followed him.

They reached the top of Pine Hill and descended the path in silence, making their way along the marsh to the place where he had left the car. Alice pushed her bike over the dry ground. The grass crackled beneath the bike's tires, and the humming of the cicadas filled the air. When they reached the car, Ethan lifted the bike and wedged it into the back seat. Alice gripped the hot handle and opened the front door.

He started up the car, and they went jolting over the grass to the road. Alice squinted through the windshield at the hard light, wishing she had brought a blouse to put on over her bathing suit. The car sent dust billowing around them on the dirt road. Ethan rolled up his window. Neither of them spoke as they rattled over the flat stretch past the sandy beach and made the turn onto Bay Avenue. When they came to the dump, Ethan asked, "Who's that?"

Alice glanced toward the piles of trash.

"No, out on the water. In the rowboat."

"It must be George Tibbits. He asked me to take the boat down to the water this morning in the truck."

"Is he really crazy, the way everyone says?"

"No, he's just quiet."

Ethan gave her an appreciative smile and drove on toward the dock.

# — CHAPTER 10 —

It happened quickly. One minute Ethan was asking if she wanted to come up and see his paintings, and she was saying yes; the next they were back in the car and racing to the rowboat tied up at the Gibersons' dock. Alice was the one who spotted George's empty boat out in the channel. Scanning the horizon simply to avoid Ethan's eyes, wondering why she had said she would continue on to his house, she spotted the empty boat drifting away in the swift current of the channel. Ethan ran into the lighthouse and grabbed a pair of binoculars, which he swept over the water. "He's on the island. Hope Island. He's not moving."

They did not talk about what to do. Ethan simply asked, "Where can we get a boat?" He drove right to the dock, cutting across the edge of Mrs. Giberson's pristine lawn. For one idiotic moment, Alice thought how angry she would be.

Alice cast off the painter and Ethan took the oars. He rowed with a strained concentration, pulling as hard as he could. Alice sat there watching his arms go forward and back, forward and back, like a movie short in slow motion. She wished there were something she could do to make them move faster.

The wind had come up, the way it always did in the afternoon. They were rowing into it now. Ethan seemed to be stuck in place, like one of those tin wind-up toys. She kept her eyes on the island over his shoulder, and told him when he started drifting off course. The oars dipped into the water and came back with a methodical stupidity, as though they had nothing to do with the motion of his arms. She felt the sun on her back, but the fact of heat or cold did not matter. The only thing that mattered was getting to the island, now.

As they grew closer, she could see George Tibbits, plastered to a rocky ledge on the island's shore like a wet rag. On any other day, the channel would have been full of boats, but everyone was at the parade.

Ethan rowed without looking at her. His eyes were fixed on nothing in particular, cold, blue, and terribly distant. "When we get to the channel, you better stay still and hold on." His voice had the same quality as his eyes; he did not seem to be speaking to her.

Alice felt the water run more swiftly around the boat. When she glanced down, she could see the furrowed lines in the surface of the water, shooting past. She felt him digging in, holding the boat against the current. They were almost there.

The minutes went on, punctuated by the groan of the oars in the locks and the splash as they went into the water and came back. Alice did not take her eyes from the limp form of George's body. Then they were there, and Ethan was shouting at George Tibbits, "Do you think you can make it into the boat?"

The island was nothing more than a pile of rock. There was nowhere to land and few places where they could even get close to the jagged outcroppings. George Tibbits was draped over a narrow ledge. He did not respond. Alice prayed that he was not dead.

Ethan maneuvered the boat next to the tiny island. "There's nowhere to tie up. Do you think you can hold on?"

Alice leaned over the side and grabbed the pointed end of the nearest rock. It was cold and slimy. She watched Ethan climb from the boat, holding the painter in his hand, and balance precariously on the ledge. He was just able to reach George Tibbits. He took George's legs and pulled. Leaning over, he wrapped his arms around George's chest and dragged him over the side, into the boat. Alice tried to keep the boat steady. Ethan climbed back in, took the oars, and pushed off. "I'm getting out of this channel," he said, almost shouting, although the whole world seemed to have gone quiet.

George Tibbits lay on the bottom of the boat, his gray face turned toward the sky. Alice could only think this must have been what her father looked like, gray and limp, no longer human but not yet something else.

"Raise his arms," Ethan barked, pulling hard on the oars and starting back toward shore. "You've got to pump the water out."

Alice was scared to touch him, but she inched her way toward George Tibbits.

"Loosen his shirt."

Alice tugged at the wet cloth, pulling apart the knotted tie, and undid the top button of his shirt.

"Now raise his arms and lower them."

There was not much room in the boat, but Alice leaned over him, holding each of his wrists, and moved his arms back and forth.

"Keep doing it."

She repeated the action, once, twice, three times.

"Now push on his chest."

Alice placed the flat of her hand on George's chest and pushed down. He sputtered and opened his eyes, then leaned over and coughed up a mixture of vomit and water in the bottom of the boat. Alice moved her leg just in time.

"You all right?" Ethan asked.

George nodded weakly.

Alice moved back to the plank where she was sitting, her body shaking. She watched George Tibbits coughing like a baby, unable to believe he was alive.

"It's okay," Ethan said. "He's going to be okay."

"I know." Alice's voice was shaky.

Ethan nodded. "We're okay now."

Alice could not take her eyes from George's gray face. He was alive. She had to keep looking at him to believe it. She wrapped her arms around her chest to still the shaking.

The boat met less resistance as Ethan rowed closer to shore. They passed the lighthouse and came alongside the dock by the inn. Ethan rowed all the way to shore and jumped out, pulling the boat up onto the sand. He helped George Tibbits out, holding him beneath one arm. George stood unsteadily but found his balance and stepped out of the boat.

"I'm sorry I put you to so much trouble," George said in a thin, raspy voice.

"It's all right," Ethan responded. "We'll take you over to the house and make sure you're okay."

George hesitated. "What happened to my boat?"

Ethan shrugged. "It must have been carried away. Maybe it'll wash up."

"I was just . . ." George gestured vaguely toward the water.

"Just what?"

"Rowing around the island."

"It's a hot day for that."

Ethan led George to the car and helped him into the front seat. Alice sandwiched herself in the back with her bicycle, and they made the short drive over to the Cunninghams' house. When George got out of the car, he stared at the water for another long moment. Then he followed them up the porch steps and into the kitchen.

"You better get out of those wet clothes," Ethan said.

George regarded him warily, without expressing agreement or disagreement. Ethan went upstairs and returned with a worn pair of work pants and a shirt. "These were my father's. I think they'll fit you. You can change in there." Ethan gestured toward a room off the kitchen. "You can use one of the towels to dry off."

George Tibbits took the clothes and shut the door behind him.

"Rowing around the island," Ethan muttered. "That's nuts." He moved around the kitchen, taking glasses from the shelf and filling them with water.

Alice accepted the glass he handed her and drank. Her hand was still shaking.

"You were a trooper out there. Come here." Ethan took the glass from her and set it on the table. He put his arms around her, pressing her against his chest. "I know how scared you were, but you didn't show it."

Alice let her cheek rest on his chest. He smelled sweaty. He rubbed his hands up and down her back. "Okay? You're going to be all right?"

"Yes."

Ethan released her and tapped lightly on the door of the room off the kitchen. There was no response. "Mr. Tibbits?" he called.

He turned the handle and opened the door slowly. It squeaked on its hinges. He motioned for Alice to come closer. George Tibbits was stretched on the bed in the clean clothes, asleep. He lay curled on his side, his shoulders rising and falling with each breath. Ethan laughed and closed the door. "I guess he's moved in."

He went to the stove, struck a match, and lit the burner. The Cunninghams had a propane stove, one of the few on the island. Ethan took a soup pot from the back burner and moved it to the front. "Why the hell do you think he was rowing around the island? And today of all days, when nobody's around? Did he say anything this morning, when you took the boat down?"

"No."

"He must have drifted out in the channel. He's damn lucky you saw the boat out there. Old eagle eyes. That's what I'll call you from now on — eagle eye Alice. How the hell he fell out of the boat is anybody's guess. Did he ever go quahogging or anything?"

"Not that I ever heard of."

"So where'd he get the boat?"

"I don't know."

"George Tibbits isn't a sailor or a fisherman or — what does he do?"

"People say he works in a drugstore in New Jersey."

"So what would make him try to row around the island on the hottest day of the year? I guess he is nuts."

Ethan took plates from a shelf above the sink and set them on the table with the silverware. He sliced some bread and filled a glass dish with his mother's pickles. When the fish chowder was heated, he spooned it into two bowls.

"Should we wake him up?" Alice asked.

"No, let him sleep. Long as we get some water into him when he wakes, he'll be okay. Shoot, I could use a nap myself. Eat, Alice. You must be hungry." He set the bowl in front of her.

When they finished the chowder and bread, he brought a custard pie from the pantry and served two slices. Alice listened for signs of life through the closed door off the kitchen, but there were none. Ethan cleared the plates when they were done with the pie and motioned for her to follow him up the stairs. "Come on. I'll show you some paintings."

At the head of the stairs, he opened a door. A standing lamp without a shade sat in the middle of the bare floor. There was no furniture in the room, save for an old sofa with torn upholstery, and an easel with a straight chair in front of it. Unframed canvases circled the room, leaning against the walls behind them. Tubes of paint were scattered on the floor. Most of the paintings were small in size and depicted groups of rocks in shades of gray and black and brown. In some of the paintings, there was a view of water. Others showed massive rocks in the center of fields. There were no houses or people in the paintings, only the looming shapes of the rocks. The images were made with thick layers of paint that revealed the brushstrokes. They had a rough, unfinished look.

"You really do paint rocks," Alice said.

"Rocks and a few other things."

"I like them."

"What exactly do you like about them?"

"They're not quite real. They look like something you might have dreamed."

He pulled a pack of cigarettes from his pants pocket, extracted one, and lit it, dropping the spent match on a plate covered with cigarette butts in the middle of the floor. "Sit down," he said, gesturing toward the sofa.

Alice positioned herself on the edge of a lumpy cushion. He went to the straight chair and reached for a nearby pad of paper. Without saying anything, he began moving a pencil over the paper, raising his head to look at her from time to time. Alice watched the movement of his hand. At first, she felt acutely self-conscious, but after a few minutes, she grew used to having his eyes on her. He studied her dispassionately.

"Are you comfortable?" he asked, putting the cigarette out against the edge of the plate.

She shrugged.

"You look terribly uncomfortable. Here." He ripped the sheet from the pad and tossed it to the floor. "This one's no good. I'll try another." He crossed to the sofa and stood over her. "Stretch out." He took her feet and pulled them up, extending her legs the length of the sofa.

Alice did as he said, leaning back against the sofa's arm, feeling like she was out in the boat again, following his instructions without thought or sensation. She could not look at him in this position unless she turned her head, which she sensed he did not want. She stared at the gold light beyond the window. The sun would be setting in another hour or so, and then the ferry would return. This did not seem possible. She imagined that she and Ethan would live in the strange silence of this time forever, with George Tibbits sleeping downstairs like a lost child they had found.

The scratch of Ethan's pencil was a tiny voice on the other side of the room. She followed its whisperings as long as she could and let her eyes close. Her skin still held the sun's heat, flushed yet prickly with cold at the same time. She tried to resist the closing of her eyelids, but she couldn't. She seemed to be wandering through the paintings ranged around the room, looking for something.

When she opened her eyes, Ethan was seated beside her. "People are dropping like flies around here," he said, smiling. "I think you got sunburned." He touched his finger to the tip of her nose and leaned down to kiss her.

She thought of struggling to get away, but it seemed too late for that already. His lips were moist and hard at the same time. He laced his fingers through her hair, cupping the back of her head in his hand. Nothing, she thought, had ever felt so good.

"Did you think we might not reach him?" he whispered. "Out in the boat?"

"Yes," she answered, surprised to find she could make her voice work.

"I had my moments, too. If you hadn't held the boat the way you did, I couldn't have gotten him into it."

He wrapped his arms around her and held her tight. "How'd you get so tough, Alice Daggett?"

"I'm not tough."

He leaned back and looked at her, then kissed her again, a long kiss that went clear through her body. "You're tough enough."

The click of a door opening sounded downstairs, and footsteps.

"I guess Prince Charming's up." He took her hand and helped her off the couch.

She searched the floor for the drawing he had done, but the sketch pad was closed. He kept hold of her hand, leading her across the room and down the stairs. At the foot of the steps, he let go.

"Been up long?" Ethan asked.

George shook his head. "I must have fallen asleep," he said. "I'll change back into my clothes." He held his damp shirt and pants and tie pressed to his chest.

"You can keep what I gave you."

"But I'll get them back to you." George glanced at the faded clothes he wore.

"You don't have to. They're my father's. I think you probably got a touch of sunstroke out there. You should have some water." Ethan filled a glass and handed it to George, who gulped it down. "There's some fish chowder here."

George shook his head. "I'd best be going back."

He started toward the door. Ethan motioned for Alice to follow. George glanced uneasily back at them. "I'll walk," he said. "You've gone to enough trouble."

"No, I don't think that's a good idea, Mr. Tibbits. We'll drive you."

George said nothing more. He stood beside the car as Ethan took Alice's bicycle out, then climbed into the front seat next to him while she got into the back. Later, she remembered that drive around the island as though it had happened in another time and place, suspended in the warm air. None of them spoke. The car jerked over the uneven road, and when they crested Schoolhouse Hill, the moon hung above the bay.

Ethan drove down the narrow path, all the way to the edge of the lawn in front of the twin houses. George Tibbits stepped from the car, holding his clothes loosely in his arms. "I'm sorry," he said, "to have caused you so much trouble. You — you saved my life."

"It's all right," Ethan said. "It's really Alice you have to thank. She spotted you."

George glanced toward the twin houses and back. "Thank you."

Ethan nodded. "Don't try that again, huh, rowing around the island. Not alone, at least."

"No. I won't." George Tibbits addressed the words to the ground. He turned and walked toward the twin houses.

Ethan waited until George had climbed the porch steps and opened the door of the house on the right. He turned the car around, and drove slowly toward the road. He took the other way back, going along the western shore, past the marsh and the dump. Alice thought of how they had driven past the dump earlier that day. It seemed like a terribly long time ago. The lights of the ferry shone out on the water, inching toward the island. He pulled to a stop when they reached the store. "The ferry's almost here."

Alice nodded.

"I'm glad you saw him out there."

"So am I."

He reached across the seat and pulled her toward him. He kissed her, moving his tongue between her lips. They had been holding each other only a few moments when the ferry's horn sounded. She broke away and stepped from the car, worried that the returning passengers would see her, though in the dark it was not likely.

# — CHAPTER 11 —

"There were more people at that parade than ever." Evelyn set her pocketbook on the table and wagged a finger at Alice.

"You shoulda seen the fireworks," Will said. "Bang! Bang! Bang! I watched them set 'em off. They light that fuse and run like crazy and then KAPOW! You can get your head blown off if you ain't careful. Owen Pierce said it was the biggest crowd he ever saw."

"Will, stop that chatter and go wash up. Your hands look like something the cat dragged in."

Will held his hands in the air and smiled ghoulishly. The palms were gray with dirt and the ends of his fingers crusted pink with the remains of cotton candy.

"You heard me." Evelyn pointed at the sink and sat down at the table. When her cigarette was rolled and lit, she gave Alice a long look. "So how did you happen to see George Tibbits out there?"

Alice shrugged. "I was just sitting on the porch at the store. I saw him go by in the boat, and then I looked up, and the boat was empty."

"And how'd Ethan Cunningham get involved?"

"I couldn't think who else was around. I went to get him on my bike. It's still there, at the Cunninghams'."

"What in the world did George Tibbits think he was doing?"

"He said he was rowing around the island."

"Of all the foolish things. Well, I guess it's good you didn't go to the parade, otherwise that man would be dead. But I don't like him putting other people in danger like that. The current's terrible out in that channel."

"The boat drifted right away. We didn't even see where it went."

"Good. Maybe that lunatic will stay on land now. Who even knew he had a boat?"

Alice closed her eyes as she sat down at the table, seeing again George's gray face as Ethan pulled him off the rocks.

"Did you finish with the order forms?" Evelyn asked.

"Yes. I did that this morning."

"And you've got enough stock for the delivery truck tomorrow?"

"I think so."

"Look." Will came away from the sink, waving his hands in the air.

"That's better," Evelyn said. "Now brush your teeth and go get ready for bed."

"Aww, Ma."

"Don't 'aww, Ma' me. It's been a long day, and you were out in that sun for hours. Scoot."

Will reluctantly returned to the sink, worked the pump, and brushed his teeth noisily.

"It sure was hot over there. Must have been ten degrees hotter than on the island. Those sidewalks just bake." Evelyn flicked the ash from her cigarette and inspected her nails. "Will you look at that? Chipped already." She held one finger in front of Alice's face. "On the way over on the ferry the ladies were all saying how much they liked the delivery truck. They all said what a good job you do. If we carried more in the line of bread and so forth, they wouldn't buy anything from Morton's, they said. I was thinking —"

"Do I haveta go to bed?" Will interrupted.

"Will, it's way past your bedtime. Now give me a hug and run along."

Will grimaced, but complied, wrapping his arms around his mother's neck and pressing his face to hers before dashing for the stairs.

"Don't ask me why, but I let him have that cotton candy, even though I know it'll rot his teeth. It's only once a year, I told myself. What can it hurt? What'd you have for supper?" Evelyn eyed the empty sink.

"I just made myself a sandwich."

"The problem is, I don't get out enough, Alice. I realized that, being in town today. It did me good just to look in the store windows. I was thinking, we should go to the mainland once a month, make it a regular thing, and not just for business. Take in a movie, see what they have in the shops. We couldn't even get into the picture show this afternoon. The crowds were terrible. But we had a fine picnic in the park. We ate with the Brovellis and Mrs. Cunningham. I'm going to have to start going over to Mrs. Cunningham's for our quilting nights again. I bet she misses it. I know I do." Evelyn paused. "How'd you get so red? Going out in that boat to rescue that dimwit George Tibbits? You're so fair, Alice. You should watch that. Wear a hat if you're going out in the sun. With what the ladies were saying on the ferry, I was thinking maybe we should get Phoebe Shattuck to do some baking for us. Breads, pies, that sort of thing. We could have a pretty little table right down front in the store, and you could put some of her goods on the truck, too."

"We already tried that, remember?" Two years earlier, Phoebe had agreed to supply them with bread and other baked goods, but after a week, she gave it up. She was not much of a baker. Her bread dough wouldn't rise, or it would rise too much, so the bread was either dense as a rock or so airy it fell apart when sliced. The store was doing fine now; they were having the best summer since they bought the place. Alice didn't think they needed to add to the merchandise.

"You don't like my idea," Evelyn said.

"It's not that. I just think it's a lot to start up now, in the middle of the summer. Phoebe's got her work at the church, and she's giving some piano lessons. Maybe she doesn't want anything more."

"Nate still hasn't paid off that tab."

"No, but he's getting there."

Evelyn pursed her lips. "The one idea I have, and you don't like it."

"I didn't say that, Mom. Maybe next year we could try. It's not a bad idea."

Evelyn sniffed. "Of course it isn't. Better than yours of keeping the store open on the Fourth of —"

"I'm going to bed," Alice said, cutting her off.

"All right. I'm beat myself. 'Night, dear." Evelyn leaned over and brushed Alice's cheek with her lips. "You want some salve for that burn?"

"No. It's not that bad."

Alice climbed the stairs, trying to hold on to the memory of Ethan bending over the couch and touching his finger to her nose. Will was still up, reading a comic book. "Did you get that today?" Alice asked, crossing to his side of the attic and sitting on the edge of the bed.

He nodded. "I wish I was here to help you rescue George Tibbits. Was Ethan really brave?"

"Very brave."

"And he just dragged him into the boat? Was George Tibbits still breathing?"

"I don't know. I raised his arms and pumped his chest, and then he was okay." Alice smoothed the tousled hair on top of his head. "'Night."

She undressed slowly. She still found it hard to believe that George Tibbits was alive. She had to stop herself from slipping out of the house and taking the long walk to the twin houses to make sure.

By the time the last ferry had pulled in to the dock that night, the clouds were thick overhead. The crowd came spilling down the gangplank, many of them headed for the store. They wanted cold drinks and cigarettes and milk and eggs for breakfast. Lydia had pushed through the people thronged around the counter. "You missed the best parade ever," she said. "And we're going over to Snow Park for a bonfire."

"Who's we?"

"Me and Pete, and Sally Farnwell and her sister, and Jack Cheaving.

Jack's got his car here. I heard you're a big hero, saving George Tibbits. You rowed all the way out there with Ethan Cunningham?" Lydia raised her eyebrows.

"Ethan did the rowing."

"And then you came back with both of them? Sheesh, I leave for one day, and you're in a boat with the two weirdest people on the island. I guess that was pretty exciting."

"He could have drowned if we didn't get there."

"Would have served him right, rowing around the island all by himself. Well, I've gotta catch my ride to the bonfire." She turned with a flounce of her navy skirt. "See you." A flash of bare knee showed beneath the pleated skirt as Lydia moved off.

While Alice packed up some groceries for Mrs. Lamprey, she watched through the window as Lydia and Pete climbed into Jack's car. Jack tooted the horn a few times and took off up the hill. Down the beach, someone was setting off firecrackers.

Alice peered around the edge of the blanket hanging in the attic. Will was asleep with the comic book open on his chest. She went to him, closed the comic book, and set it on the floor. He did not stir as she pulled the sheet up over his shoulders. She wouldn't have gone with Lydia and the others even if they had asked her, Alice told herself.

She had considered not telling anyone about the rescue, for she couldn't recall George Tibbits lying in the bottom of the boat without remembering Ethan beside her on the sofa in the upstairs room. She feared the truth of the day would be written all over her face when she told the story, but she couldn't stop herself. It came spilling out as soon as her mother stepped from the ferry with the Brovellis and Mrs. Cunningham behind her, and they went and told everyone. She had imagined herself standing on the porch of the store, surrounded by all those swaggering summer kids, Jack Cheaving and David Sibley and Meg. They would look at her with awe and admiration, following her every word and gesture, and know there was a reason why she stayed behind and didn't go to the parade, because she was meant to save a life that day. They would see how fearless she and Ethan had been, jumping into the boat without a moment's hesitation. They would know her finally for who she was, not a thin, quiet-voiced girl eternally stuck behind the counter at the store but someone of importance, ready to act and capable of bravery.

Naturally, it did not happen this way. She was too busy in the store to tell the story properly, so others told it for her. The news slowly filtered through the crowd and was quickly absorbed. The effect did not seem to last long. Alice wondered whether the event might have had greater impact if someone else had rescued George Tibbits, like Jack Cheaving and David Sibley. Maybe her actions only reinforced their sense of her strangeness, hers and Ethan's, staying behind instead of going to the parade.

Alice went downstairs to use the outhouse. She made her way across the bare floor and eased open the screen. Evelyn let out a jerky snore from the sofa where she slept. Alice followed the worn path to the outhouse and lifted the latch. It was close and hot inside, the thick air so oppressive it seemed to cling to her skin. Alice let the wood seat fall shut when she was done and hurried out the door.

She had not entered the front bedroom in a long time. She almost walked past the closed door when she returned to the house, shrugging off the impulse, but at the last moment, she found herself reaching for the handle and slipping inside. A flash of lightning flooded the room for a brief second, followed by a bolt of thunder that sounded in the distance. She saw the high mahogany bed with its lace cover, the thin curtains at the window, and her father's shirts hanging in the closet.

The thunder sounded again, closer. Lowering herself into the chair by the dresser, Alice folded her legs on the seat and rocked slowly back and forth. For a moment everything outside remained unnaturally still. The gnarled apple tree by the window seemed to draw itself up and hold its breath. Then the rain came in a rush of sound and a wave of coolness.

Alice watched the rain slide down the black windowpane. She had
not asked for Ethan Cunningham to notice her. She had avoided him,
waiting on other people when he came into the store, glancing away so
she wouldn't meet those unsettling eyes. She had not gone looking for
this, but it had found her, had found both of them that day under the flat
light of the sun. Never had she thought of kissing Ethan. She was certain
of this, but when he leaned over and pressed his lips to hers, she realized
that she was not surprised, that in some hidden part of herself, she had
been waiting for him to touch her. Was this wrong? She thought it should
be wrong, but it didn't feel wrong.

Pushing herself from the chair, Alice went to the bed and climbed
into it. The old lace cover was scratchy against her skin. She pulled her
knees in to her chest and listened to the patter of the rain. The
*Providence Journal* her father had read the night before he died lay neatly folded on the nightstand, though the pages were yellow now.

Since the day of the accident, Alice's mother had slept on the sofa in
the living room. There were too many memories in that bedroom, she
said; they'd keep her up all night. Once a year, Evelyn asked Alice to dust
the furniture and sweep the floor, but the rest of the time, the room was
off limits. Alice found her mother's reluctance to enter the room hard to
understand. She had always taken comfort in sneaking inside and closing
the door behind her. Here, more than anywhere else, she felt her father's
presence and heard his voice. When she pressed her face into the old
clothes hanging in the closet, she imagined she could smell his skin, that
unmistakable scent of the flats at low tide mingled with Castile soap.

Alice did not mean to go to sleep. She just wanted to lie there for a
moment, to see if she could piece together what she felt after a day that
had turned out to be so unexpectedly full, but before she knew it, she was
asleep with her head on the old pillow.

She dreamed she was in the field by the twin houses. It was hot and
still, a day in the middle of summer. A person came toward her, walking
through the high grass. She was confused. Hadn't George Tibbits mowed

the lawn? Then she understood, this was a different time, and the grass was long again. The man reached her. He stopped and smiled. The expression seemed to move over his face in slow motion, as though he wanted to take as long about it as he could to make her understand. This was no ordinary meeting. No, of course it wasn't, he did not need to convince her of that.

"I didn't know you were here," he said.

Neither did I, she thought fleetingly, but no words came out of her mouth.

He stepped forward and leaned over her, again with a deliberate slowness. It was then Alice realized the man wasn't her father but Ethan Cunningham. He kissed her, a light, soft touch of a kiss, holding his face to hers for what felt like minutes. He moved away, turned, and walked across the field. She watched as his back slowly turned to grass.

"Alice?" Her mother was outside the door. "Are you in there?"

Alice woke with a start. "Yes."

"Well, come on out here. You nearly gave me a heart attack. What are you doing in there?"

Alice realized that it was morning, and she was stiff and cold.

\* \* \*

She was busy until noon, driving the truck over to Snow Park, coming back and counting the money she had made, and helping unload supplies when the ferry arrived. As she slid boxes of canned goods onto the wagon and pulled it across the gravel to the store, she kept watch for Ethan and his mother. They did not appear in the crowd gathered for boat time, but Alice could not shake the sense that he was there anyway, giving her that knowing smile over the heads of all the people by the dock.

"What were you thinking, sleeping in there?" her mother hissed as Alice carried a box inside and set it in the first aisle.

Alice had to stop for a moment to figure out what her mother was talking about. "I told you — I didn't mean to sleep in there."

"Well, what were you doing in that room?"

"Nothing. Just watching the rain."

Alice continued stacking boxes and ignoring her mother's hurt looks, but Evelyn kept coming back to the topic whenever the store cleared out. "Do you go in there often?" she asked.

"No. Just to clean . . . and last night."

Evelyn pursed her lips. For the rest of the day, she gave Alice wounded looks. Alice had to resist the urge to grab her by the shoulders and shake her, to say, "It's only a room. Maybe if you went in there just once you'd get over it finally."

Alice unpacked the boxes between waiting on customers. Her mother sat behind the counter, listlessly paging through the newspaper. Alice could tell she had a headache coming on. She supposed her mother believed the headache was her fault; she even supposed her mother was right.

Alice was halfway through shelving a box of cleanser and other cleaning supplies when a car horn sounded. "I'll take care of it," she said.

Evelyn nodded without raising her eyes from the paper.

Outside, she found Jack Cheaving pulled up to the gas pump in his family's Chevy. Sally Farnwell sat next to him on the front seat. "Fill it," he said, hanging one arm over the open window.

Alice hated pumping gas. She never knew what to do while she stood there with the pump in her hand, what to say to the summer people staring expectantly at her, as if just waiting for her to display some eccentric island behavior.

She inserted the nozzle and saw that Lydia was in the back seat of the car. Lydia rolled down the window and leaned out. "Hi," she said.

"Rescued anybody today?" Jack asked.

Alice shook her head.

"I guess you're a regular her-o-ine," Jack said. "Did you get old

George Tibbits to talk to you?" .

"A little."

"Shoot, you save a man's life, and he still won't talk to you."

"He talked, just not a lot."

"What'd he say?"

"Thanked us, said he was sorry to put us to so much trouble, I don't know." Alice squirmed under Jack's stare.

"Thank you for saving my life." He spoke in a sneering falsetto, imitating George Tibbits. "We practically live next door to that nut, and we can't get him to say boo to us. He's like a scared rabbit, scooting in and out of the house, sneaking around his own yard."

"Are you working all day?" Lydia said.

"Probably."

"That's too bad. Jack was going to take us out in his boat."

Alice did not say anything.

"You should have come over for the bonfire. When it started raining, we all went over to the Sibleys' and danced. Maybe we'll be there again tonight. What do you think, Jack?"

"I don't know. Have to see who's around, what's going on. Maybe."

"Why don't you come?" Lydia said to Alice.

"I can't close the store until ten."

"You can't work all the time, Alice. It's ridiculous."

Alice stared at Lydia. She could feel the others' eyes on her, but she didn't look at them. She hung the hose back on the gas pump and replaced the Chevy's gas cap.

"You can put it on our tab," Jack said. He started up the car and tooted the horn. They pulled out in a cloud of dust.

Alice watched as the car climbed the hill, with Jack's tanned arm hanging out the open window.

# — CHAPTER 12 —

George Tibbits began this day as he had begun every day for a week now. He rose early, with the sunrise. He pumped water at the sink in the kitchen and splashed it over his face. He dressed quickly and ate a hasty breakfast. He made his way down to the shore, walking furtively past the houses in Snow Park. Today, as on most days, he found the houses quiet, the front doors closed and the curtains drawn over the bedroom windows.

He carried binoculars on a strap around his neck and wore an old wide-brimmed hat he had found in Bertie's house. He moved slowly, scanning the horizon as he came to the foot of the hill. Quahoggers were out on the water already, sinking their tongs into the muddy bottom. The sun, just climbing into the sky behind him, left a golden trail from the rocks to the open water. The fishermen looked like bronze statues, frozen in the early light. He wondered if one of them had found his boat and taken it already. It was nothing more than a small rowboat, but he supposed even so it would be valuable.

He made the hardest part of the journey first, when he was fresh, walking around the wooded north end of the island. He followed the shoreline, but in many places this was a challenge, requiring him to climb over rocks and grab onto the branches of the scrubby brush that came right down to the water. The beach roses were in bloom, filling the air with a pungent fragrance that made him think of Sarah. She loved the beach roses more than anything she could cultivate in the garden behind the twin houses, and every year they had spent at least one afternoon gathering the fruit for beach plum jelly. "Take a deep breath, George," she would say, throwing her head back and beaming. "Isn't that the most divine smell?"

George paused frequently as he made his way over the rocks, searching the ragged shoreline and the flat, still water with the binoculars. He could not say what had happened the day he tried to row around the island. The sun must have overpowered him. One minute he was rowing, straining to keep the lighthouse in sight, and the next he was sitting in a pool of water, wondering where it had come from. He had nothing to bail the water with. The boat he had felt so certain of had begun to leak, water seeping in through a break in the hull. There was enough water pooled in the hull that the boat began to sink. The oars were out of his hands and he was leaning forward, trying to get the boat to right itself. Then the boat went from under him, and he was in the water, thrashing, beating his arms against the surface. He watched as the boat went bobbing away, carried off on the current. He struggled to reach the small island of rock. Suddenly it was there, and he was clinging to the rock, and then the girl and the lighthouse keeper were bringing him in. He supposed the events of that day should make him believe in God. He supposed he should offer a prayer of thanks, but it had been so long that he didn't know how to pray anymore.

Seven days had passed now, and he had not found the boat, though each of these days he had walked the entire perimeter of the island, searching. He told himself he would spend the rest of the summer searching for the boat if necessary. It could still wash up somewhere. He did not think it had sunk because he had watched it go floating off. The boat was Sarah's last gift to him. He remembered the moment when he had spotted the boat beneath the house as they took her body and Bertie's away. The sight of the overturned rowboat was like her voice, speaking to him again, urging him to go on without her. For all these years, he thought of the boat lying there under the house, and it was the same as hearing her laughter, and seeing her knitting, and feeling her breath on his neck when she whispered goodnight.

George paused at the northern point of the island and lifted the binoculars to his eyes. The sun covered the water now, playing tricks on him in the hollows, making the dark places between swells look like the bow of a small boat. He stared and stared at the moving surface. Could the boat still be drifting on the open water? He did not think so, but he had never paid much attention to the tides, beyond taking note of the times of high tide and low. He had never studied the currents around the island the way the quahoggers did. The boat had been swept into the strong current of the channel on the island's east side, of that much he was sure, but what this current did once it met the end of the land and merged with the bay, he could not imagine. He only knew that the boat had to exist somewhere still, and that he had to find it.

Lowering the binoculars, he moved on. He could not shake the sense of shame that kept overpowering him, the knowledge of his own stupidity. To have lost Sarah's boat was unthinkable. At night, lying in the narrow bed on the second floor of her house, he whispered to her, "I'm sorry, Sarah."

He had been in the store once since the accident. The girl who came to rescue him was not there, and he was relieved. Her mother gave him the same suspicious look she always did, pursing her lips and wrapping up his purchases with a little shake of the head. He wondered if the girl and the lighthouse keeper had told anyone about rowing out to save him.

The strangeness of their coming to rescue him was enough to make him believe in fate. He had encountered death, a wet hand, closing his eyes and pulling him under. He fought it, but not too hard. He felt himself giving in to the grip of that hand in a matter of moments, felt himself bowing to death. He was ashamed to remember this, how he gave in so quickly, but it was as though a part of him had been waiting for the arrival of death for a long time, expecting it like an overdue train. Then something hovered over his face, and he was resting against a hard surface, and his eyes jerked open, back in this world. He had come so close to leaving. In those last moments before he found himself lying in the boat with the girl bending over him, he was walking down a path lined with trees on either side, the path to the twin houses. The trees were terribly tall, rising so high above him he could not see the sky. Sarah stood at the end of the path in a pool of sunlight. He thought he saw her wave; certainly she was smiling. He was just about to run toward her when his eyes opened and he began to cough up a thin, salty vomit.

If it was fate that the girl at the store had seen him out on the water, the rest of life was fated, too. It was fate that Bertie died suddenly, leaving Sarah alone and frightened. It was fate that the telegram came from the Army, falsely informing her of George's death. It was fate that he did not arrive home three days earlier, in time to stop her. George could not believe the same fate that allowed Sarah to take her life, based on such a hideously stupid mistake, saved his. What kind of fate was this, that damned and saved in equal measure, that did not care? People who believed in fate, or God, did so when things went their way, when these unseen forces operated for their own good. This was meant to be, they said, but as soon as fate turned on them, they saw it differently. George had a problem with selective belief. Either things did exist or they did not. Either his entire life was fated, from start to finish, in which case God was malicious and cruel, or everything was random, with no particular meaning or order. George did not think you could have it both ways, believing in the benign guidance of God when it was convenient and rejecting God when it was not. So he believed in nothing but the random occurrence of events. He could have died that day by the buoy just as easily as he had lived. Perhaps it would have been better if he had died.

George labored along the rocky shore, finally reaching the southern end of the island, a stretch of wilderness where he and Sarah used to come to pick blueberries. The berries would fall into their buckets with a dull plunk until there were enough to cover the bottom. Sometimes this seemed to take forever, the wild berries were so small. George always felt an overwhelming relief when he could no longer hear that plunk, because it meant that their work might actually end before sunset. One year the mosquitoes were especially fierce. They tied handkerchiefs around their necks and paused every few minutes to swat the bugs away. George finally dropped his bucket and said, "I can't stand it anymore."

Sarah set her bucket down and threaded her way to him. She put one hand to the side of his face. "They won't leave you alone, will they? Come on, we'll go now."

The buckets were only half full, and George knew that he and Sarah would meet Bertie's wrath back home. He didn't care. He just wanted to get away as fast as he could. He walked so quickly that he left Sarah behind, struggling with her bucket. He knew he should go back, but he couldn't. The thought of the road and of a breeze blowing off the water drew him on, until he stopped glancing back to make sure Sarah was following. When he reached the road, he sat on a shaded patch of grass and waited. It seemed to take a long time, but finally she appeared, gripping the bucket in front of her with two white-knuckled hands. He felt disloyal, and too embarrassed about leaving her behind to look her in the face, but she simply smiled and said, "It's cooler here, isn't it?" As they started the climb up Schoolhouse Hill, she said, "The mosquito is one of God's creatures, too, George."

George rounded the southern tip of the island now, and the lighthouse came into view. He stayed to the shoreline until the thick brush gave way to houses and bits of lawn; then he made his way up to the road. He had always remembered her saying that about the mosquito. It struck him as remarkable now that Sarah was able to convey so much in a few words, the single sentence serving as a gentle reprimand to him and at the same time a statement of her simple and expansive faith. He missed her faith most of all, not a faith in God necessarily, though she did believe in the kind, old gentleman she prayed to each night, but a faith in the rightness of things. She even made room for Bertie in her view of the world. "She doesn't mean to say those things," she would whisper to George across the space between their beds when the lights were extinguished at the end of the day. "She can't help herself. She was just made that way. Imagine being saddled with that sort of disposition. It must be a terrible cross for her to bear, don't you think?"

Even as a child, George puzzled over what she said, for it seemed clear to him that Bertie was *their* cross to bear, that she was the last person who deserved their sympathy. Now he realized how much he had learned from Sarah. Yet once she was gone, he could not put the lessons she taught him to use. She took that sense of the rightness of things with her and left nothing in its place.

George kept his gaze on the shoreline below, still looking for his boat, as he made his way down the road. He was almost to the lighthouse when he heard a shuffling step behind him and turned his head.

"What you looking for?" the old man asked. A pipe was clenched in his teeth, and his face was rough and red.

George stared at him for a moment and resumed walking.

"Must be looking for something. I been seeing you out here every day with those binoculars. You one of those bird watchers?"

George realized that the man was Owen Pierce, the old quahogger. He had not recognized him at first; he seemed to have shrunk somehow.

"I have a boat that I lost," George said.

"A boat that you lost? How'd you do that?"

"Floated away."

"Floated away. Ain't that the damnedest thing? I never had a boat just float away, except in the hurricane. Smashed to bits, it was. Those waves took everything they could find and smashed it into the rocks. Made a terrible racket, the wind and the waves and everything breaking up. You weren't here then, were you? Hell of a storm."

George expected Owen Pierce to turn back after a few minutes or stop at one of the houses along the way, but he kept plodding along beside him. George slowed to accommodate him.

"I've still got my quahogger's skiff if you want to borrow it," he continued.

George shook his head.

"Eighty-two, and I can still handle a boat and quahog tongs. That ain't an easy trick, you know."

George wondered when Owen Pierce went quahogging, since he seemed to be always sitting on the porch at the store whenever George came over to the east side.

"Young men don't have the toughness today. They complain about going out in the winter. When I started out, we didn't have nothing more than a little rowboat. Fill 'er up with quahogs and bring 'er in, then head back out and do it again, or work the flats with a flour sack hanging off your shoulder. They don't know the meaning of work today. You planning on staying on Snow now?"

George gave him a quick glance. "Just for the summer."

"Oh, just for the summer, eh? People like it here in the summer. Cooler than on the mainland with the breezes we get. Course it was never a vacation for me, living on Snow, but I don't begrudge it for anyone else, summer people and all. They got a right, I suppose. Lot of those summer people like that bird-watching. I never paid a whole lot of attention myself. There's the gulls and then the ones you can recognize right off, like a red-winged blackbird, but all the rest is the same to me. Can't tell one bird from another, really. There ain't no vacation for a quahogger, that's for sure. I never would have made it if I took a vacation, never would have got where I am today." He removed the pipe from his mouth and regarded it for a moment, as if it symbolized his accomplishments. "I ain't sorry. I'm proud to be a quahogger. It's honest work. Ain't a lot of work that is, you know, just plain, honest work. I wouldn't have wanted anything else."

They seemed to be inching toward the dock. George longed to move on and leave the old man behind. A car passed them, stirring up a cloud of dust. Owen raised one hand in a wave. "Summer people," Owen said.

"Ain't got nothing better to do than drive around wasting gas."

When they reached the path to the store Owen did not turn off. He kept shuffling at George's side, taking his pipe in and out of his mouth. George pointed to the path. "We've come to the store."

"You need something? I'll go down with you."

George went reluctantly with him on the path, unable to think of any other way to get rid of the old man. He held the screen door for Owen and entered the store. The girl sat behind the counter with a pencil in her hand.

"'Bout out of tobacco," Owen said.

The girl reached beneath the counter and gave him a pouch of tobacco.

"Don't have any cash on me today. You think you could put that on my tab?"

The girl opened a ledger book and made a mark with the pencil.

"He's lost a boat." Owen jerked his thumb in George's direction. "Been out looking for it."

"Did you find it?" the girl asked George.

"No."

"Can I get you something?"

"Pack of tea."

She went and retrieved the tea from a shelf in the back, and told him she would put it on his bill.

George thanked her and slipped the tea in his pocket. He ducked his head and made his way quickly out of the store, before Owen could follow him.

Up on the road, he resumed scanning the water and the shoreline. He felt less certain, this day, that he would ever find the boat, but he couldn't return to the twin houses without trying, without having something to report to Sarah.

# — CHAPTER 13 —

On the Sunday when the chicken supper was scheduled to be held, a heavy rain fell. The foghorn sliced through the damp, chill air, and like almost everything else, it made Alice think of Ethan Cunningham, of how he had climbed the spiral staircase in the lighthouse and set the foghorn going in the fog signal building. She had waited for him all week, her glance darting toward each newcomer entering the store. She closed as late as she could at night, ignoring Lydia's entreaties to come over to Snow Park, but he didn't come. She began to wonder if that hot, strange day had happened at all.

In the crowded main room of the Improvement Center, the windows were steamed over and the close smell of baked chicken and rhubarb pie filled what air there was to be had. The rain continued to fall, a silent presence, inaudible beyond the din of conversation and clinking silverware. Alice spotted Ethan the moment she stepped inside, seated at a long table in the back beside his mother. She had imagined how she would thread her way through the crowd and take a place next to him, not caring who saw or what they thought, but his table was nearly full, with Miss Weeden and Owen Pierce and Ernie Brovelli and his family.

Alice took her place in the line of people waiting to pick up plates of food and handed her ticket to Mrs. Brovelli. The supper was a fundraiser for the volunteer fire department. "Don't miss Mrs. Cunningham's biscuits," Mrs. Brovelli said, pinching her on the cheek.

"Alice," Pete called when she turned with a plate of chicken and peas and potato salad. He beckoned her toward the table where he sat with Lydia and Jack Cheaving and Sally Farnwell.

She tried to catch Ethan's eye as she made her way to the empty chair beside Pete, but his head was turned toward Owen Pierce.

"Here she is, the one-woman rescue squad," Jack said as she set down her plate. "Saved any lives lately?"

Alice shook her head.

"Shoot, I wish I'd been there to see that, you rowing all the way out there and hauling old George Tibbits into that boat. You must have muscles like a prizefighter. Here, lemme see." He reached across the table, wrapped his hand around Alice's upper arm, and let out a low whistle. "Not bad."

Alice gave him an exasperated look and pulled her arm away.

"She didn't row out there all by herself. Ethan Cunningham was there," Lydia said.

"What, were you two the only people left on the island besides old George Tibbits?"

Alice shrugged, trying not to blush.

"Who knows if they really rescued him? There weren't any witnesses, were there? Maybe they made it up just to impress everyone." Jack looked around questioningly.

"We didn't make it up," Alice responded woodenly.

"It's just a funny thing, the three of you left on the island, everybody else goes to the parade, and while we're all gone, something happens. But what? Nobody knows for sure."

"They rowed out and saved George Tibbits. That's all that happened," Pete said.

"That's what you think. Hey, anybody hear 'Amos 'n' Andy' last night?" Jack went on, giving a synopsis of the show, pausing for emphasis before delivering the punch line in a perfect imitation of Amos's drawl. "'Shucks, Andy, I ain't a brick.'"

Lydia threw her head back and laughed convulsively. Alice exchanged a quick glance with Pete.

"Just ignore him," he said softly.

Jack recounted another "Amos 'n' Andy" episode. Lydia reacted with exaggerated enthusiasm to everything he said. Alice caught a glimpse of Ethan across the room, but again he was looking the other way. She wondered if he was turning away deliberately.

"Alice?"

She realized Pete was trying to get her attention. He laughed when she looked at him and quickly said, "What?"

"Would you dance the reel with me?"

For a moment she could not respond. She had been thinking about it for days, and in the scenes she played over in her mind while she lay in bed at night, it was Ethan who crossed the floor of the Improvement Center, took her by the hand, and led her into the dance.

"Sure," she said, trying to hide her confusion. "I'll dance the reel with you."

When everyone was finished eating, the men cleared the tables and chairs from the room, and Silas Mitchell struck up a tune on the fiddle. Alice moved toward the lemonade table, thinking if she stayed there to help serve the drinks, Ethan would come and ask her to dance, but Pete came behind and caught her by the elbow.

"Where are you going?"

"I was just going to see if they needed any help with the lemonade."

"Come on and dance, Alice. We only need one more to make a square." He gestured toward a group in the middle of the floor.

Alice followed him, winding through the clusters of dancers. Lydia was paired with Jack; Sally Farnwell and David Sibley, and Meg Sibley and Charlie Henderson, made up the other couples in the square.

The high whine of the fiddle filled the room, and Nate Shattuck joined in on the guitar and called for the dancers to take their places. He talked them through the first dance slowly, tapping his foot in time. "Okay, you should be oiled up by now," he said when they had walked through the moves. "Let's see what you can do."

Alice do-si-doed around Pete, casting her gaze over the people along the wall. Mrs. Cunningham sat in a chair next to the dessert table, and Ethan stood behind her with his arms folded over his chest. She caught his eye and he nodded. Pete took her hand and swung her round.

Nate shouted commands to "swing your partner" and "bow to your corner." Pete pressed his fingers into the small of her back and twirled her hard. Her hand was the anchor. The rest of her body was like a piece of string, going taut, then slack. The room spun, and her feet skimmed the floor. Alice could feel that they were better than the others in the square. Pete landed her just where she was supposed to be, and when another of the boys handed her off, he was there, arm extended, waiting to catch her. He spun her longer and harder than anyone else, until her hair stood out from the back of her head, and she was panting for breath. She was moving too fast to pick out Ethan in the crowd, though when the music stopped, she found him again behind his mother.

Pete dipped his head and said, "Thanks, partner. Another?"

Alice pushed the hair from her face and said yes.

While they waited for the music to start up again, Lydia leaned across the square and whispered in Alice's ear, "Isn't he too perfect?"

For a confused moment, Alice wondered if Lydia somehow knew about Ethan Cunningham, though she could not imagine she would ever describe him as perfect. Then she realized Lydia was referring to her own partner, Jack. She nodded, and Lydia reached down and squeezed her hand.

She stayed for the next dance and the next, loving the rush of warm air against her face and the feel of her feet skipping over the floor and the way Pete would catch her when she thought she was about to go flying off in a dizzy spin. She knew Ethan's eyes were on her. She could feel him out there, following the twirl of her skirt and the lift of her hair. It made her dance faster and smile harder.

When the music stopped, Pete caught her by the shoulder. "You're so light. It's like dancing with a feather."

"Thanks." Alice ducked her head and slipped away, across the room to the lemonade table. She gulped down the pulpy drink Mrs. Giberson poured for her. Ethan was talking to Ernie Brovelli, standing so his back was toward the dance floor. Over in the corner, she spotted Will, crouched beneath a table with Ernie's grandson, Eddie. She skirted the dancers and squatted beneath the table.

"What are you doing?" she asked.

Will gave her a disgusted look. "Playing marbles."

"Isn't the floor kind of sloped?"

"So?" Will pursed his lips in concentration and took aim with his thumb. The marble he hit went ricocheting off the wall. "It's not a real game."

The music started up again. Lydia and Jack remained on the dance floor, but the others in the square dropped out. Pete stood by the lemonade table with David Sibley.

"Boy, it's hot in here," Alice said to Will and Eddie, who continued to ignore her. "I'm going to get some air."

She went around the edge of the room, hoping no one would notice that she was stepping outside. The rain had slackened and a fine mist was falling. She held her face to its cool touch.

She started when the door opened, ready to move off before she was seen, but it was Ethan emerging from the yellow light, holding a cigarette between his fingers.

"Kind of stuffy in there, isn't it?" he said. "You're quite a dancer."

"You should join us."

"No, that's not for me. I can't keep up with you kids."

"You act like you're an old man or something."

"I am an old man, Alice."

"How old?"

He gave her one of his faint, distant smiles. "Twenty-six."

"That's not old."

"Old enough. Have you seen George Tibbits again?"

"Just once, when he came into the store. He didn't say anything. You know he's been spending every day walking around the island, looking for his boat."

"Yeah, I've seen him. I don't think he's going to find it, not now. I guess he's not one to make a big show of saying thank you. But that's not why we rowed out to save him, is it?"

"No."

"So are we famous on the island now?"

"I guess."

"I thought you'd come by to see me again."

Alice gave him a startled look. "I have to work at the store, you know, and . . ."

"Meet me at the lighthouse. I go to check on it after ten usually. I'll watch for you." He stubbed out his cigarette and tossed it into the grass. "You're getting wet." He touched her face, running his fingers down her cheek. "Come on. You'll get sick standing out here in the rain when you're all sweaty." He put his hand on her shoulder and opened the door. As soon as the light fell on them, he took his hand away.

Alice stepped inside quickly, moving past a group of summer people by the door. When she turned around, she saw that he had circled the room in the other direction, going back to his mother.

"There you are," Pete said. "They're about to start the reel."

Pete grabbed her by the hand and pulled her across the dance floor. Alice took her place in the center of a long line of women, facing him. When the music started he stepped forward, grasped both her hands in his, and made a quick bow. As the first couple sashayed down the line and everyone clapped, Alice looked for Ethan, who was bending over his mother's chair. She could still feel the touch of his hand on her face. She circled Pete, thinking she did not care about anything else but that moment out in the thin rain. The rest of this night could fall into oblivion and all the people jammed into the Improvement Center with it. She had what she had come for, in the lingering way Ethan looked at her and the softness of his voice and the feel of his hand on her face.

When it was their turn to sashay down the line of dancers, arm in arm, Pete held her elbow tight and set a fast pace. The other dancers clapped and hooted. She felt her hair flying again and her face radiating heat. She caught Ethan's gaze for a second as they reached the couple making an arch at the end of the line and ducked beneath. She could wipe that quiet, wistful expression off his face if he gave her the chance.

The crowd applauded as the music died out. Pete stepped forward and hugged her awkwardly. "You're the best dancer in the room," he whispered, bending close. "Better than Meg Sibley."

Alice arched her eyebrows. "That's a big claim. I can't compete with her."

"I think it's the other way around."

Alice didn't want to slip into this sort of banter with Pete. "I've got to help clean up," she said. "Thanks, Pete."

He held onto her wrist as she turned away. "Don't go. We're all going over to the Sibleys' tonight."

Alice shook her head. "I better help my mother clean up and get home."

He gave her a disappointed look but let go. By the time Alice made her way to the lemonade table, Ethan and his mother were gone. She just caught sight of them as he took his mother's arm and helped her out the door.

# — CHAPTER 14 —

Alice lay on her back, staring at the patterns in the wood ceiling, old water stains from the winter when the roof had needed repairing and they had not been able to afford it until summer. If she squinted at them long enough, forms began to emerge. An oblong patch above her bed became the body of a woman, a woman with what Lydia would call a full figure. She wore a small dress cinched in at the waist, with a low neckline and no sleeves, and a watery blob sitting on her shoulder looked like her head. Two thin cracks made eyes and another a close-mouthed smile. Alice had stared at the discolored wood for years now, bringing the shape of the woman in and out of focus, making her appear and disappear through the blurred fringe of her eyelashes. Tonight she felt a new kinship with the woman, as though at last she understood why she stood with her hands on her hips and smiled like that.

Bunching the pillow beneath her head, Alice shifted her gaze to the window. A light mist continued to fall. The muffled beam of the lighthouse came round, the only break in the thickening fog. She had always taken the light's sweep beyond her window for granted, rarely stopping to consider that someone climbed the stairs each evening and set the light in motion. Now the beam connected her to that person as surely as if he were entering her room and leaving it hundreds of times a night.

Alice fell asleep and woke later to the faint sound of something striking the window. A branch, she thought, tapping. The wind had come up in the night. She opened her eyes, trying to catch hold of a fleeing dream. There was sunlight in the dream and crystal water stretching before her. She knew the place was Gooseneck Cove, yet in the dream, the cove opened not on the bay and the island's shoreline but on the vast expanse of the ocean. Out in the open water, the waves rolled in, one after another, but in the cove the water remained still. She stood on the sand, watching a man swim toward her. She saw the white of his arms and thought how long they were. He raised his head from the water. At first she thought it was her father, but then she wasn't sure. When did you learn to swim? she wanted to ask. He lifted one hand and tossed a pebble at the shore. Pete, she realized. The face was his, boyish and frank. He threw another pebble, nearer her feet. Each pebble he threw made a pinging sound as it landed.

Alice opened her eyes. Gray light filled the attic. The rain had ended, but clouds covered the patch of sky through the window, and she could not guess the time. Five o'clock? Six? A pinging sound came from the window, and she realized it was not a branch tapping on the pane or Pete tossing rocks at the shore. She made her way to the foot of the bed, holding the sheet to her chest, and peered out. Lydia stood off to the side of the front porch.

"What are you doing here?" Alice hissed through the open window.

"Couldn't sleep. Can I come up?"

"All right. But don't let *her* see you." Alice pointed to the downstairs window.

Lydia propped a ladder that was lying by the side of the house against the front wall, climbed up, and waited while Alice pulled out the screen. She heaved herself through the window and sat cross-legged at the foot of the bed. Clasping her hands together, she gazed at Alice without speaking.

"Well?" Alice said.

"Well . . . " Lydia paused for effect. "He kissed me."

"Who kissed you?"

"Jack. Who else?"

"Keep your voice down," Alice said, glancing toward the blanket.

"I thought Will could sleep through anything."

"He can, but you never know."

Lydia leaned forward and told her in hushed tones how they had driven over to Snow Park, Jack and Charlie and the Farnwell girls and Pete. They played truth or dare in the barn behind Jack's house, sitting around a candle. She dared Charlie to kiss one of the Farnwell girls, and then he dared Jack to kiss her. When the game was over, she and Jack went off by themselves.

"He put his hands on my chest," Lydia whispered.

"Under your blouse?"

"No. On the outside."

"Do you like him?"

"Of course I like him. He's a great kisser. I wish you'd come, Alice. Those Farnwell girls are a couple of drips. They didn't even want to play truth or dare. Neither did Pete."

"Did he play?"

"Sort of, but he wouldn't kiss anyone. I bet if you were there, Charlie would have kissed you. Can't you get off from the store just for once? We might go back tonight."

"I'll see."

"Isn't he gorgeous?"

"Jack?"

"Yes, Jack. Who do you think I'm talking about? He's gorgeous, and he's got a boat."

Downstairs the couch creaked. "You better go before she gets up," Alice whispered.

Lydia squeezed her hand, backed out the window, and climbed down the ladder.

\* \* \*

By mid-morning, the sun broke through the clouds, though the haze was so thick you could not see the mainland. Sailboats appeared and disappeared off the end of the dock in the oppressive heat.

The sweat ran down the back of Alice's neck as she loaded cartons of groceries into the truck. Mrs. Lamprey wanted her to bring over some molasses, and Mrs. Sibley had asked for clothespins the day before. She drove over to Snow Park alone, leaving Will to help with the customers. Evelyn woke up with a headache that morning. "It must be the heat," she said, gazing tiredly into her coffee cup. "When it gets like this, I feel like my head is stuffed with cotton."

Alice had helped her mother into her clothes, pulling the dress over her head while she stood by the table and whimpered.

"Does it hurt that much?" Alice asked.

"Yes. I'm sorry. I think the headaches are getting worse. It's like knives stabbing."

Alice considered not making deliveries that day, but she had promised the ladies. She walked her mother down the hill to the store, holding her arm beneath the elbow.

"This air is terrible," Evelyn said. "There's not even a hint of a breeze."

Alice left her behind the counter in the easy chair with a cold cloth over her eyes and instructed Will to wait on the customers. He had been insisting all summer that he was capable of making change and running the cash register by himself. Now was his chance, Alice said, to prove it.

She drove as fast as possible and tried to hurry through her transactions with the women, but at nearly every house in Snow Park someone came out and flagged her down.

"I guess you all had fun last night," Mrs. Cheaving said. "Jack's not even out of bed yet. What have you got for thread there?"

Alice went through three boxes before she found the thread.

Mrs. Cheaving took her time surveying the colors and fingering the spools of thread. "I'm not much of a seamstress," she said finally, "but I don't see why I can't hem up those curtains myself. Do you mind if I just go inside and match the color?"

Alice said no, she didn't mind. She waited in the sun for what felt like a very long time. When the door opened again, she saw that it was not Mrs. Cheaving but Jack, in a wrinkled shirt, his hair uncombed. He lowered himself into a wicker chair and stared off at the water.

"I hate square dancing," he said after a pause.

"What?" Alice responded.

"Square dancing. I hate it. Don't you?"

"Oh. I don't know."

"When is Silas Mitchell going to get a real band over here?"

"Maybe next weekend, I heard."

He shook his head. "This is the last summer I spend on this island. There's nothing to do."

"Alice, would you come in here and look at this?" Mrs. Cheaving called. "I just can't decide what I need."

The last thing Alice wanted to do was to go inside the house, but she climbed the steps and followed Mrs. Cheaving into a living room with a huge couch and stuffed chairs and shelves lined with books.

Mrs. Cheaving stood by the window with three rolls of thread in her hand. "It's the pattern, you see. I don't know what color I should match, there are so many."

"I'd just go with the background." Alice pointed to a pale green that matched the dominant shade in the floral print.

Mrs. Cheaving studied it for a moment. "I guess you're right. Okay, I'll take two of these. You don't do piece work, do you?"

"No, but Mrs. Cunningham might do it for you."

"Oh, the cripple? Maybe I'll ask her. They're a strange pair, aren't they, she and that son of hers? He wouldn't even dance last night. I was glad to see you out there."

Alice nodded as she backed out the door and went to the truck. Mrs. Cheaving remained on the porch. When Alice returned with the thread, she took it and said, "I'll pay up on my bill next week, is that okay? Mr. Cheaving will be over then."

Alice started up the truck and flinched when it backfired. As she pulled away, she caught a last glimpse of Jack on the porch, laughing. She did not think she had ever heard Mrs. Cunningham referred to as a cripple. All the way back to the store, she could hear the arch tone of Mrs. Cheaving's voice.

The ferry was just pulling in when Alice coasted down the hill. Pete waited by the porch. He came around as she shut off the engine and held out his hand to help her from the truck. "You should have come over to Snow Park," he said.

"Did you have a good time?"

"Not especially. They all just wanted to play stupid games and smoke cigarettes. But the old barn is nice. I'll show you sometime."

Alice nodded. He stood in front of her, blocking the way up the porch steps. "I better get the orders for Captain Tony," she said.

She brushed past him and went inside to find her mother still languishing behind the counter with the cloth on her head. Perched proudly on the stool, Will opened and closed the cash drawer, though there were no customers in sight.

Alice gave Captain Tony her order forms to deliver to the suppliers in Barton, and by the time the crowd thinned after the ferry pulled out, Pete was gone. Lydia remained, though, waiting for Jack to show up. She sat out on the porch until noon, but there was no sign of Jack or of the others from Snow Park. She gave up and went home for dinner.

Alice left her mother on the sofa after their dinner and went back to tend the store by herself. The hot sun covered the parking lot, the dying grass, and the gas pump. Alice stared at the empty scene out the window and waved some sluggish flies away from the penny candy until she could stand it no longer. Getting the fly swatter from a nail on the wall, she went after them, killing eight in a matter of minutes. She scooped them off the counter one by one and dropped them in the wastebasket.

Every time she heard footsteps on the porch or a car up on the road, she expected it to be Ethan, but the hours of the afternoon drifted by, and he did not appear. Miss Weeden came in for cream of tartar and a group of summer children stopped by for licorice and cinnamon sticks. John Brovelli came in later for a pound of coffee, done with his quahogging for the day.

"Have you seen Jack?" Lydia asked when she arrived after supper.

"No," Alice told her.

"I thought we were going back over to the barn tonight. Can you come?"

Alice explained that her mother was up at the house with a headache, and she had to cover the store.

Lydia looked dejected. "Mind if I stay here, just until they show up?"

There were few customers that night. Lydia pulled a stool up next to the counter, and they played casino with an old pack of cards Alice found on the shelf. The couple of times a car went past, Lydia glanced nervously at the door, ready to scoop up the cards and run outside if the car turned down the hill, but by nine-thirty, they were tied at three games each, and no one had showed up from Snow Park.

"Did they say they would meet you here?" Alice asked.

"Not exactly. He just said, 'See you,' when he dropped me and Pete off. Or, 'See you tomorrow.' I think he said tomorrow. I can't remember."

Alice thought she would refrain from pointing out there was a difference. "What's Pete doing?"

"I don't know. Reading or something. He said he didn't want to go out to the barn again. I don't know what's wrong with him. I think Sally Farnwell is sweet on him, but he doesn't pay any attention to her."

Alice watched the hands on the clock behind the counter inch toward ten as they played one more round of casino, wondering how she could get rid of Lydia before the time came to close up.

141

Just before ten, Phoebe Shattuck came in. The previous week she had paid off the remainder of the Shattucks' bill, stopping by first thing one morning before anyone else was in the store. She had come shopping twice since then, either very early or very late, as if she wanted to encounter as few people as possible. She lingered in the back of the store now, going up and down the aisles without picking out anything.

Lydia leaned over the counter. "What's wrong with her?" she whispered.

"I don't know."

"I guess I'll head home. If Jack shows up, tell him to come get me."

Alice watched through the window as Lydia climbed the path, flinging her braids over her shoulders.

"Can I help you with something?" Alice asked Phoebe.

"No. I'm just trying to get some ideas for what to bake for tomorrow. It's hard to cook in this heat. Maybe I'll make some cornbread."

Alice measured out some corn meal for her and weighed it.

"That's enough," Phoebe said, peering at the scale.

She took a dollar bill from her pocket and handed it to Alice, but even after Alice had wrapped the corn meal and made change, she did not leave. She wandered around the notions table, looking at the cloth. "I should make Rachel some new dresses, shouldn't I?" Phoebe paused and studied a bolt of cotton in a solid yellow. "I'll come back tomorrow."

As soon as Phoebe was out of the store, Alice emptied the cash drawer and turned out the light. Setting out along the beach toward the lighthouse, she kept an eye up on the road. Her one fear was that Lydia or someone else at the inn might see her, but she planned to stay in the shadows below the garden and then move quickly along the path above the lighthouse.

When she reached the inn, she saw that most of the windows in the back rooms were dark, save for one on the first floor. This window was not covered by a curtain or shade, and as she passed, she caught a glimpse of Pete sitting on his bed, fully dressed, reading. She hurried behind the cover of the lilacs.

Alice glanced over her shoulder as she started across the open space below the lighthouse. The back porch of the inn was empty and the door closed. She did not think she had been observed. At the Cunninghams', a light shone in the upstairs corner room. She slipped in front of the lighthouse and sat in the cool sand against its wall. The lighthouse's beam swung round above her head while down below, the waves broke with a soft hush. She sat there for a while, fishing rocks from the sand and placing them in a small pile, before she heard the Cunninghams' door open and close.

"Is that the square dancer?" Ethan said when she emerged from behind the lighthouse. "I thought you'd be off at a bonfire party somewhere."

Alice shook her head.

"Why not?"

"I don't like the summer kids."

"What about Pete, the boy at the inn?"

"He's not a summer kid."

Ethan rubbed his hand over the top of her head. "Wait here. I'll be right back."

She leaned against the side of the lighthouse, listening to his footsteps echo on the metal staircase inside. "This way," he said when he returned. She followed him down the path to a patch of lawn bordered by hedges in front of his house. They sat on a bench next to his mother's flower bed.

"He's in love with you," Ethan said.

"Who?"

"The boy at the inn, Pete."

Alice shook her head.

He laughed. "You didn't see the way he looked at you when you were dancing."

She felt the truth of what he said, but she didn't want to acknowledge it. She and Pete had known each other so long. They had grown up together. She couldn't think of him in that way.

"I wanted to dance with you," Alice said quietly.

"In front of everyone? I don't think so. But I'll dance with you now." He stood up, extending his hand. "May I?"

She took his hand, and he waltzed her around the wet grass, humming a tune she didn't know. He held her hand lightly and pressed her body close to his, until she almost believed they were moving across a dance floor at one of those fancy places in New York. She could feel the swish of a long skirt, silky against her skin. He dipped her toward the wet grass and laughed, kissing the part in her hair.

She closed her eyes and let her cheek rest against his soft shirt, smelling the thick scent of his sweat. He wrapped both his arms around her and picked her up off the ground, spinning her in a fast circle. His arms were tight and strong, leaving her breathless. She felt herself giving in to his strength, not caring anymore about the right or wrong of it. He stopped and lowered her to the ground. He put his hand beneath her chin and raised her face to his, probing her mouth with his tongue. The meeting of their lips was like another form of conversation, outside time.

He guided her to the bench, and they sat pressed together. He ran his hands over her body, touching her through the fabric of her blouse, running his fingers down her bare legs. So that's what it feels like, she thought, but there weren't words for the sensation, like a terrible warmth that came from outside and inside at the same time. She didn't think she could ever go home or do anything else but remain where she was, holding her lips to his. He raised his head. "You'd better go now," he whispered.

He stood up without waiting for a response and patted her on the shoulder. "Come on. Before somebody comes looking for you."

He gave her another long kiss, and she whispered good-bye. She glanced back as she reached the road. He was hidden behind the hedge, but cigarette smoke rose above the thick foliage, showing her that he was still there.

# — CHAPTER 15 —

The heat lasted through July and into August. For three weeks, the island had no rain. "My tomatoes," Mrs. Brovelli said one day when she came by the store. "I water them every day, but they still don't look good."

Evelyn Daggett kept the shades pulled over the windows up at the house and lay on the sofa in the afternoons, sipping cold coffee and fanning herself with a folded newspaper. She didn't even feel like smoking, she said. The idea of striking a match made her cringe.

Alice left Will in charge of the store when she had to deliver groceries to the summer people's houses. Most of the customers waited on themselves when he was there and charged their purchases, or helped him make change if he got confused. Alice would drive off with the truck loaded with groceries first thing in the morning, before the heat got bad. As she coaxed the truck up the hill to Snow Park, it seemed she led two separate and simultaneous existences: one making deliveries and tending the store and putting food on the table, the other sitting with Ethan in the dark with her arms around him, smelling the vague scent of oil paint that clung to him.

She went to meet him whenever she could, when her mother did not stay at the store until closing, and there was no one to watch her head off down the beach. He would bring a blanket out, and they would lie hidden behind the hedges. When they talked, he told her about his paintings, and what he had to do to care for his mother, and how he wished sometimes that he'd never left the island and gone away to school, that he had stayed like everyone else. Most of the time, they didn't need to talk; they found each other in the fit of their bodies as they lay side by side. The silence of this meeting was stunning to Alice, how she could know him so completely in the touch of his skin.

One night when her mother was up at the house, she sneaked off down the beach after closing the store. The lighthouse door was open, and when she called, he told her to come in if she wanted to.

Ethan stood halfway up the spiral staircase with a paintbrush in his hand. A kerosense lantern sat on the step below him. "The Coast Guard radioed," he said. "The inspector's coming tomorrow." He dipped the brush in the paint can and moved it over the metal step.

"Do you have to do the painting tonight?" Alice asked.

"When the hell else am I going to do it? It'll take two coats to cover. If I'm lucky the fucking paint will be dry by the morning."

Alice remembered what he had told her about the last visit by the inspector. If he didn't get the lighthouse painted, inside and out, by the next inspection, he would be out of a job.

He kept his eye on the paintbrush, swabbing it back and forth.

"You're not going to stay up all night painting, are you?"

"Why not? They want to play games with me, I'll play games with them. They weren't supposed to be back for another inspection until September." He dipped the brush in the can, contained fury in his face.

"Can you see what you're doing?"

"No, Alice, I can't."

"Should I get someone to help you?"

"Like who? Owen Pierce?"

"Maybe Pete Giberson would come."

He shook his head. "I can take care of this."

"But —"

"Alice, you've got to leave me alone." He raised his voice, loud enough so that she feared someone passing on the road might hear. "You've got to stop showing up like this whenever you take it into your head. It's wrong."

"Wrong?" she echoed.

"Yes, wrong. You're sixteen years old. You shouldn't be out all night, chasing me all over the place."

Chasing him all over the place? Is that what she was doing?

"You're blocking my light," he said, moving down to the next step.

"I'm sorry." She backed out the door and said she would see him later. He did not respond.

The Coast Guard came the next day. Ethan must have finished the painting because he was still the lighthouse keeper, but Alice did not care to know how he had solved the problem. She stayed away, and he did not come into the store when she was there. She drove the truck over to the west side on those dry, white August days and tried to push Ethan and his hurtful words out of her mind, but he seemed to be everywhere, even out on the choppy water, where she kept seeing the two of them rushing to save George Tibbits.

\* \* \*

Alice sat behind the counter playing solitaire while her mother made supper up at the house. She had not seen Ethan Cunningham for two weeks. Perhaps she would never see him again, except to make change across the counter.

Lydia came banging through the screen. She reached in her pocket and fished out a dollar bill. "Give me a pack of Old Golds, okay?"

"Lydia. Since when do you smoke?"

"Since this summer. Come on, before anybody else gets here. I'm tired of mooching off Jack and the other kids."

"You know I'm not supposed to sell you cigarettes."

"Who's gonna know? I can pay for them."

"I know. But —"

"Alice." Lydia glared at her. "Come on. I'm not an infant."

"What if your mother finds them?"

"I'll say Hank brought them over from the mainland. She can't trace a pack of cigarettes to you."

Alice set the cigarettes on the counter reluctantly and made change.

"Why don't you come with us tonight?" Lydia said as she slid the pack into her shorts pocket.

"Where are you going?"

"I don't know. Jack will come by, we'll drive around, maybe go over to the sandy beach or something. It's one of the last nights everybody will be here."

"All right." Alice was not sure why she agreed to go, but she couldn't bear the thought of climbing the hill later, watching for Ethan in the distance.

Over supper, Alice asked her mother if she could go with Lydia. Evelyn gave her a quick look. "What are you doing?"

"Just going over to the sandy beach for a bonfire."

"You can go, but I don't want you smoking cigarettes, you hear me? I'm not going to have you taking up smoking."

Alice nodded.

She closed the store early that night, when Jack pulled up by the dock and honked the horn. He waited with the motor running while Alice set the padlock in place and hurried down the porch steps. Lydia sat next to Jack on the front seat. When Alice climbed in back, she found Pete there.

Jack took off fast down Bay Avenue. The car jolted and rattled over the uneven road. Lydia was telling Jack about the school she attended in Connecticut before they moved to the island. It was nothing like the Snow schoolhouse; they had a football team and cheerleaders and everything. Alice looked at Pete. He shook his head and smiled.

The Farnwell girls and Charlie Henderson and Meg Sibley were already out at the sandy beach, seated in a circle up by the beach grass, all of them with cigarettes. Sally Farnwell called out as they approached, "Where have you all been? We've been waiting forever."

"We went to get Alice at the store," Jack said.

Sally turned and gave Alice a long look, as though appraising whether the wait was worth it.

"Why didn't you start a fire?" Jack asked.

"Too windy," Charlie responded.

"It's dark as hell," Jack said.

Clouds scudded across the sky, obscuring the stars.

"Just the sort of night for a swim," Meg said. She stubbed out her cigarette in the sand and scanned the circle.

Alice was about to explain that she had not brought her suit when she realized no one else had, either.

"Well?" Meg asked.

"It's too cold," Jack responded. "You're such an exhibitionist, Meg."

"I just like to swim. Come on, who's going? Lydia?"

Lydia got to her feet. "Sure. I'm not afraid."

"Who said anything about being afraid?" Jack looked at Charlie for confirmation. "I said it was cold."

"It's not cold. The water was seventy degrees today," Lydia said. "Come on, Meg."

The two of them moved off, up into the beach grass. Jack watched them go and stood up. "Okay, anybody who's not going in gets thrown in, clothes and all."

He went off in the opposite direction, followed by Charlie.

"Guess we're going swimming," Sally said, extinguishing her cigarette and pulling her sister to her feet.

Alice turned to Pete, who sat next to her. "I'm not going in, Alice."

"Me neither."

Jack yelled to the others from up in the grass. On the count of three they would all run into the water together, he said. Moments later, he called out, "One, two, three," and their white bodies went dashing across the sand. The Farnwell girls screamed as they ran into the water and dove beneath the rolling waves. Alice looked away. "Do they do this every night?"

"I don't know. I don't usually come over."

"Lydia always did like to skinny-dip."

"She's got an extra incentive now." Pete inclined his head toward the water, where the others were diving and splashing each other. They stayed far enough out that their naked bodies remained hidden beneath the water. "I don't like him. Lydia's making a fool of herself."

"I thought he liked her."

"Likes her? What does that mean? Charlie told me Jack has a girl-friend back home."

"Does Lydia know?"

"I don't know. He just wants someone for the summer. After that he won't care."

Pete picked up some pebbles and began to toss them across the sand. Alice remembered him tossing the pebbles in her dream.

"I saw you over at the Cunninghams' one night, I don't know, a few weeks ago," Pete said. "It was kind of late."

Alice turned to look at him, trying to get a sense of how much he might have observed, but he kept his gaze on the water. "Oh, Mrs. Cunningham needed something from the store. I was just bringing it over." She knew as soon as she spoke that it was an odd explanation. She couldn't think of anything else.

Pete would not look at her. "What's Ethan like?"

"I don't know. Kind of quiet. He's very smart. He knows a lot, about books and art and music." Alice felt proud as she spoke these words, as though she had something to do with Ethan's gifts.

"I see him up in his room painting. Sometimes I stay up late reading, and his light is still on. What are his paintings like?"

"Kind of strange, lots of rocks and water. They're not real places, they're like places he imagines and then paints. Ethan wouldn't be living on Snow if it weren't for his mother, you know. He'd be an artist in New York or Boston."

Pete nodded.

"None of his sisters could move back to the island, and he says his mother couldn't leave, not after all these years. So he's the one to take care of her. He has to help her in and out of bed every day." Alice knew she should stop talking about Ethan, but she felt intoxicated with speaking his name and telling his story.

The others came running up the beach, the boys to the spot where they had left their clothes and the girls to theirs. It was too dark to see much besides the white flashes of their bodies disappearing into the grass.

"Hey," Jack yelled after a few minutes from down the beach. "Somebody didn't go in."

Pete looked at Alice. "Want to run for it?"

She got to her feet, but they were surrounded before they reached the car. The others had dressed, though their wet hair glistened. Charlie and Jack grabbed Pete. Charlie hoisted him under the arms, and Jack took his ankles. He yelled in protest and tried to squirm out of their grasp, but they held on, starting down to the water with his body swinging between them. Alice backed away as Lydia and Meg came toward her. "Come on," she said. "I don't want to go in."

"You heard the deal," Meg said. "Everybody or nobody. You can take your clothes off."

Alice regarded them warily. She thought of the bra that still did not quite fit, though the band around the cups was gray with wear. She was not about to expose her underwear to the scrutiny of Meg Sibley.

"Hurry up," Jack shouted.

Meg and Lydia stepped forward. "Okay, go in with your clothes on if that's what you want," Meg said.

Before Alice knew what had happened, Meg kicked her legs from under her and caught her by the shoulders. Lydia took her ankles, and they carried her over the sand. She pleaded with them to put her down and cursed herself for not weighing more.

Jack let out a series of whoops as they approached. Alice couldn't see in her inverted posture, but she heard Pete asking to be put down. The next thing she knew she was engulfed by water. A wave washed over her. She closed her mouth just in time. Meg and Lydia dropped her to the sand, but she was drenched by another wave before she could get to her feet. Pete stood beside her, shaking the water from his head.

Alice waded farther out and dove into the deeper water. Her clothes clung to her, heavy and cold, but the water was warm. When she came up, she found Pete beside her.

"What a bunch of rats," he said.

Alice laughed. "The water feels great."

"How can we get back at them?"

"We won't come out."

Alice dove again, wishing she could free herself of the sodden clothes. When she opened her eyes, the salt made them smart. Surfacing, she floated on her back. Pete was treading water beside her. On the shore, the others yelled at them to come out. Finally their voices faded, and they retreated up the beach.

"Why didn't you come to the dance hall last week?" Pete asked.

Alice gazed up at the cloud-covered sky. "We were too busy at the store."

"I was hoping you would be there."

Alice felt Pete's eyes on her. She did not turn to meet his look. "How was the band?"

"Okay. Lydia complained they didn't play enough of the latest tunes, but I don't keep up with that the way you two do."

Alice rolled over and dove beneath the surface. "Ready to go in?" she said when she came up.

They swam in to shore and crossed the damp sand. Everyone was smoking cigarettes up by the grass. Alice did not want to sit down and get sand all over her shorts, so she stood next to Pete, wringing the water from her hair.

"Very funny," Pete said. "You all are very funny."

Jack took a long drag on his cigarette and glanced up at them. The prank was over, his look seemed to say, and the group had moved on.

They all sat there smoking a while longer. Finally they rose to go. Alice climbed into the back seat of Jack's car with Pete. In the front, Lydia slid over next to Jack. He drove with one hand on the wheel and his arm around Lydia. Alice watched the headlights cut a path along the dirt road, afraid Jack would drive them off into the brush. Lydia giggled as he took the turn by the dump fast, just making the corner. She leaned closer and whispered something in his ear. Alice kept her eyes on the windshield, aware of the distance across the back seat between her and Pete. When Jack pulled to a stop at the foot of her road, she got out quickly, saying, "Thanks for the swim."

"Think nothing of it," Jack answered.

The car pulled away. Alice started up the road, then waited by the bushes until they were out of sight. There were no lights in the windows up at her house. She hurried down to the dock and climbed over the rocks to the beach. Her clothes were still damp, and goosebumps covered her arms and legs, but she didn't mind. The swim had given her a new sense of freedom. She ran her fingers through her wet hair.

She crept past the inn. Jack's car had already headed back to Snow Park, and the back door of the inn was closed. The curtains were pulled over Pete's window. Alice circled the lighthouse and lowered herself to the sand on the far side. There were no lights in the windows of the Cunninghams' house. She held her arms around her knees, wishing she could take off her clothes and let them dry in the breeze. She could smell the salt on her skin, the scent of summer and life and everything good.

She had concluded that Ethan was asleep when she heard rustling nearby and turned to see him walking toward the lighthouse from the direction of the beach. "Alice?"

She scrambled to her feet.

He placed one hand on her shoulder. "What have you been doing? You're all wet."

"I was over at the beach with Lydia. They threw me in."

"Come here."

She followed him down the path to his car, parked in the shadow of the hedges in front of the house. He opened the door to the back seat and handed her a towel. She took it and rubbed her wet hair.

"You'll get sick running around like that, all wet." He looked her up and down, as though he disapproved of her damp, rumpled clothes.

"It's warm."

"Not that warm. It's also late."

"My mother's already asleep."

"She won't wake up when you come in?"

"No." She handed him the towel and forced herself to speak the words she suddenly knew she had come to say. "I know you think I'm too young, but I'm not."

He put his head in his hands. "Oh, Alice." He laughed softly and looked up. "Of course you're old enough. I'm the one who's not old enough. Here, sit down." He gestured toward the car, and she slid across the back seat. He climbed in beside her, shut the door, and lowered the window.

"I suppose I don't make a lot of sense to you. I don't make sense to myself sometimes." He stared into the front seat, wrapping his fingers around hers and slowly moving his thumb back and forth over her skin. "I wish I could be who you want me to be."

But you are, Alice thought.

"I missed you," he said, holding her hand more tightly. He pulled her toward him and kissed her, sending a slow tingling from the top of her head to the backs of her knees.

"You're all sandy." He smiled, placing his fingers on her throat and drawing them gently down, over her collarbone. One by one, he unfastened the buttons on her blouse. "Here," he whispered, lowering her to the seat and lying on top of her.

He unzipped her shorts and reached inside, tugging at the band of her underwear. For a moment she was afraid of what would come next, but as he slid the shorts and underpants down her legs, she told herself it didn't matter, that this is what she had been waiting for, longing for. He reached down and pulled off his shoes and dropped them on the floor, keeping his lips on hers. He pushed off his pants and tossed them beside the shoes. "I'll go slow," he whispered.

At first there was only a sharp stab of pain, opening and going away. Then she could feel him inside her, beyond the pain, a strange sensation that was neither good nor bad. He thrust himself against her. She felt his fury and knew this was how it was supposed to happen, though the meeting of their bodies struck her as having to do not with desire or feeling but with something else, need and longing and a vast hurt. She gripped his back with her fingers until he went still.

"It didn't hurt, did it?" he said.

"No," Alice lied.

Leaning down, he kissed her forehead and touched his fingers to her lips.

\* \* \*

Alice saw a stream of smoke through the window as she approached the house, rising above the sofa.

"Where have you been?" her mother asked as she stepped inside. "It's after midnight."

"I told you. I went over to the sandy beach with Lydia and Pete. Why are you up?"

"I couldn't sleep."

"Does your head ache?"

"No. I just couldn't sleep." Evelyn eyed her suspiciously. "What were you doing at the sandy beach?"

"Nothing. Just sitting there and talking."

"How'd you get there?"

"Jack Cheaving drove us over, me and Lydia and Pete."

"Were you smoking?"

Alice shook her head.

"I smell smoke."

"It's your own cigarette."

"No, it's not. I smelled smoke on you when you came in."

"Some of the others were smoking, but I didn't."

Her mother continued to regard Alice closely. "Did you have a good time?"

"Yes."

"Yes, you had a good time?"

"Yes, I had a good time. That's what I said."

"Alice, is it necessary to answer me in words of one syllable? Honestly, I can't remember the last time you talked to me, talked to me like you used to. I remember when you used to come home from school and chatter like a magpie. Now you don't tell me anything."

"Mom, I talk to you. What do you want me to say? I talk to you all the time." Alice felt her face growing warm. "Don't you think you can sleep now?"

"I don't know. Don't you worry about me. Go on upstairs." Evelyn stubbed out her cigarette and waved Alice off.

Alice climbed the stairs to the attic slowly, thinking how everything seemed different: the cramped features of her mother's face, smaller than she remembered; the narrow staircase; the wide darkness beyond the window, a place that could be filled with anything now. She was surprised when her mother said it was after midnight, for it struck Alice as being some other time entirely, hours or even days later. She could still feel the rough, unshaven skin of his face and the length of his body against hers, and an ache between her legs, reaching up to a place she didn't think she had ever felt before, a room within her body that remained wide open and a tiny bit sore. Alice dropped her clothes beside the bed and slid beneath the covers.

\* \* \*

The days were hot, but at night a stiffening of the breeze hinted at the coming of fall. The sun set earlier, casting long shadows over the store before slipping, in an instant, behind the tops of the trees. In another week it would be Labor Day. The summer people were already starting to pack up and go.

Alice sat out on the dock, watching a seagull coast over the exposed rocks down below. Lydia came walking up and sat beside her.

"The Cheavings are going today," Lydia said. "Probably gone already."

"Didn't you go over to say good-bye?"

"No. I found out Jack has a girlfriend back home."

"How?"

"He told me."

"Just like that?"

"Just like that. He said he didn't think he would be writing to me."

"Oh." Alice tried to think of something comforting or encouraging to say. "You'll see him again next year."

"I don't care if I never see him again, the idiot."

Alice stared at the hazy outline of the mainland, thinking how school would start in less than a week. She could not imagine returning to the long hours of lessons and Miss Weeden's creaky voice at the front of the room. She was a different person now, though Lydia, to her surprise, gave no indication she noticed the change.

"Alice," Evelyn called from the porch. "Could you help me move a box in here?"

Neither of them responded for a moment. Then Alice got to her feet. "Race you," she said.

Lydia followed her half-heartedly down the dock.

# PART II
*Home Front*

# — 1942 —

The train was crowded. George Tibbits had to walk through several cars before he found an empty seat next to a young woman surrounded by piles of luggage. He barely found room to squeeze his feet between a small trunk and a wicker basket tied with string. He couldn't think where they were all going, the men in uniform, the girls with painted lips, the mothers with squawking babies.

He spent most of the ride studying the brim of his hat while avoiding the eyes of the soldier across the aisle. He did not want to hear the soldier's story, any of their stories. The air in the car was thick with the smell of roasted peanuts, and human sweat and cigarette smoke, the rank scent train cars gave off in wartime. He knew about war, if anyone cared to hear his story, but they didn't. This was their war.

The uniforms these soldiers wore had a different look, with their wide lapels and squared shoulders. The men wearing them had a different way about them, too. They were young, as young as he had been, but they carried themselves with a cockiness George did not recognize. They appeared to be convinced that nothing as small and contemptible as the Nazis or the Japs could touch them. He did not remember feeling as certain of himself and his fate.

In Barton, he found the platform thronged with people. George had to shoulder his way through the crowd. Once out of the station, he made his way down Front Street, skirting the knots of sailors along the sidewalk. He had read in the newspapers about the Navy base on Snow Island. The entire coast had "mobilized," as they said. Still, he wondered why they had chosen Snow.

A new sign hung over the entrance to the Priscilla Alden. He spotted it when he was still a block away. As he drew nearer, he noticed the windows on the upper floors were open. Inside, he had to wait at the counter for two people to be served before him. The radio blared, but the armchair where he usually found Mrs. Santos was empty. She was on her feet and looking through a stack of papers while furiously hitting a call bell with the flat of her hand. The tinny sound echoed in the lobby.

Mrs. Santos went on ringing the bell without raising her eyes from the papers spread before her. Finally a teenaged boy appeared in a bellhop's uniform and awkwardly gathered up some luggage. "And get right back here," Mrs. Santos called as he started up the stairs.

George glanced down at his lone suitcase. It was then he noticed the new carpet, thick and blue. The feel of it beneath his feet alarmed him.

Mrs. Santos ruffled the edges of more pages as she rang the bell with the same tired fury and sent the next customer on his way. When George was finally alone at the desk, she reached into her stack of papers without looking at him.

"Name?" she asked.

He cleared his throat. "Tibbits," he answered. "I stay in —"

"Oh, Mr. Tibbits, of course. Room twenty." She gave him a quick glance. "Nice to see you again. Been a whole year, yes?"

He nodded.

"Well, let's see here." She pulled a large register toward her. "I don't know that I got room twenty for you this time. Let's see." She ran one finger down the page and stopped at the bottom. "Hm, looks like they left this morning. You got lucky. Now I just need to know how long you be staying, Mr. Tibbits."

George looked down at the tangle of papers on the counter in confusion. She had never asked this question before. "I'm not certain."

She picked up a pen and shook it at him. "No, no, no, Mr. Tibbits. I got a business here, see? Lots of people now. I can't be just keeping a room there for you."

George regarded her blankly for a moment. "One night," he said finally.

"Okay then, one night." She smiled and began hitting the bell. The pimple-faced boy appeared moments later.

"Oh, Mr. Tibbits," she called as he followed the boy to the stairs. "Mrs. Worthington says to tell you she close up the house and go to Providence with her daughter. She got some work in a factory there. We got the dining room open now." She gestured toward the double glass doors across the lobby.

George waited outside room twenty while the boy unlocked the door and set his suitcase on a luggage rack by the dresser. A quick glance reassured him. The worn bedstead was still in its place against the wall, and up in the corner, the patch of torn wallpaper seemed to wink at him conspiratorially. George surveyed the room slowly a second time, as if to make certain it was really the place he remembered. He realized the boy was still there, standing inside the door and pulling on the ends of his coat sleeves. George fumbled in his pocket for some change and placed it in the boy's hand.

He could not hear the sound of retreating steps on the carpet. He waited until he was sure the boy was gone to draw the small rocking chair over to the window and lower himself into it. The years were erased then. He might have been going home, like all the other men in uniform.

A piercing whistle blew down below by the docks, and within minutes a stream of coveralled figures poured out of the opened gates of the pin factory. The women could only be distinguished from the men by the brightly colored kerchiefs tied round their heads. He knew that this factory, like others up and down the coast, had been converted. They were making anti-aircraft gun parts now. The crowd of workers inched through the gates while a long line of men and women waited to go in on the next shift.

Some time later, after the new workers were swallowed up by the factory gates, the sun set behind the rooftops in a haze of thin yellow light. He watched until the last rounded slice of the sun disappeared and rose to go. He had always eaten at Mrs. Worthington's, even that first time, when he came home from his war. He did not know where he would go now.

In the hallway, George met a couple emerging from the room next door. The man was in uniform. The woman glanced at George and let out a high-pitched giggle. Pretending to lock his already locked door, George stared at the keyhole until they cleared the top of the stairs. Down below, he heard the clink of silverware and the murmur of voices. The entire world had taken leave of its senses. The war was like a drug people craved. You could see it in the glassy-eyed stares of the people on the trains, in the streets, in the hallways of the hotel. They were drunk with the war. One glimpse at the dining room as he went quickly past confirmed his sense of it all. The tables were full. Laughter shot back and forth across the crowded room, and he saw, as he glanced in, champagne glasses raised over one table in a toast. George made his way across the lobby without meeting Mrs. Santos's gaze and let himself out into the street. From the corner of Church and Front, he had a view of the water. The sun was sinking into the horizon across the bay. Prim and white, the ferry waited at the dock for the next day's run. He did not believe it would rain this year. The transparent sky arched over the steeple of the church.

At Wilson's Diner, he stopped and peered through the window. There were only a few people seated at the counter. George took a stool at the far end, away from the others, and ordered the hot turkey plate with coffee and pie. The mashed potatoes were dry and sticky, even with the covering of gravy. You couldn't get decent mashed potatoes since the war started; they skimped on the butter and used powdered milk.

Swirling the last of the coffee in his cup, he gulped it down, paid his bill, and made his way out into the street. It was too early to return to the hotel. George turned down Front Street, away from the center of town.

He looked for signs of life as he passed Mrs. Worthington's, but shades covered the windows, and the porch was bare. Yet all the houses appeared deserted as night came on with their blackout curtains pulled tight. George went by one darkened shell of a house after another until the sidewalk gave out, and he walked in the gravel at the edge of the road with fields on either side. Somewhere in the distance, a rooster let out a raspy, half-hearted crow and went silent. He walked with no fixed sense of where he was going. The cars that passed him kept their lights dimmed and surprised him, coming suddenly out of the gray light.

A stone wall ran along the road beside him in a ragged line. When he could barely make out its rising and falling shape, he turned back toward town. The air was warm and still, just the way he remembered it. There was that at least, he thought. George knew the center of town lay ahead, but he could see nothing but the line painted down the middle of the street, a ribbon of white against the black.

When he reached the sidewalk again, people were aimlessly strolling up and down, but like the houses, the streets felt deserted without the warmth of streetlights, or the lit marquee of the movie theater, or the yellow squares of apartment windows over the shops. George let himself into the Priscilla Alden, relieved to find the dining room empty and silent.

The door to room twenty opened with a groaning creak. He closed it quickly and crossed to the window without turning on the light. The sky was a carpet of tiny lights. The stars were so bright without the interfering lights of the town. He remembered nights when he was a child, and he would step onto the porch of one of the twin houses to gaze overhead in wonder. He thought then that everyone in the world saw the stars the way he did. It was only when he left Snow and discovered the oppressive life of towns and cities that he knew many never saw them at all.

The factory kept up a distant hum all night. Beyond, the still water stretched away toward Snow. He imagined the island out there, surrounded by the placid water. It could not have changed that much, he thought. The ferry sat waiting for him like any other year. He waited with it for the first light.

# — CHAPTER 16 —

Alice and Lydia sat with their backs pressed against the sides of the lookout tower, knees pulled in to their chests and eyes fixed on the sky. The entire afternoon had passed with nothing but seagulls coasting overhead. Alice felt her eyes going dry, tense with the constant effort of searching for planes. They rarely spotted one, as most of the planes flew in to the base across the bay at Davisville or Newport, but Lydia said she wouldn't put it past the Japs to bomb Snow.

Alice would always remember where she was on that cold Sunday when the war began. Seated at the store's counter, she was playing solitaire with an old, grease-stained pack of cards. Rain pelted the window behind her like darts thrown by an icy hand. She was alone, the only unusual aspect of the day as far as she was concerned, for in the winter the store seldom remained empty. Someone always hovered by the stove, trying to get warm and hunting for gossip, but that December day her mother was up at the house, preparing supper, and the store was deserted.

When Pete came running excitedly through the door, Alice imagined that the inn had caught on fire. The men were already lined up in a bucket brigade from the lighthouse to the road, she guessed, and Pete had come to get more help. For a moment after he told her (a base in Hawaii called Pearl Harbor was bombed by the Japanese), she felt ashamed for wishing disaster on the Gibersons. Pete said this had to mean war. What a dastardly act. Even his father favored war now. Such a cowardly, disgusting, unprovoked attack, and on a Sunday. It was inhuman.

Alice agreed what the Japanese had done was inhuman, but she could not get her mind around it. Pete's thin, rangy body appeared suddenly taller, broader; he leaned forward, balancing on the balls of his feet. If only he were already eighteen, he could sign up with Hank right away, he said. Roosevelt had to declare war now, the sooner the better, but Pete would have to wait seven whole months to enlist. "By then — who knows?" He flung his arms over the counter. "It could be over."

They gathered at the church that night to pray for the dead. Mr. Giberson read the Twenty-third Psalm, and they sang "America." Silence hung over the island as they left the church. People were mute, grasping each other's hands and shaking their heads. Remote as it was, even Alice could imagine the hundreds dead, the men and ships lined up in the harbor, defenseless. They had woken just as she did that day, thinking of what they would have for breakfast. They had no warning they were about to die.

The reality of the war broke over the islanders in waves, as each revelation of how life would change became apparent. The orders came to darken the lighthouse the next day, with the news that they were officially at war. A complete blackout followed. Hank Giberson enlisted in the Air Force and went into flight training. Nate Shattuck and John Brovelli enlisted in the Army. In the confusion of those first days, Alice watched for Ethan constantly. It was Mrs. Cunningham who finally told her what she wanted to hear, that he had a deferment because of his commission at the lighthouse. Even though all the lighthouses up and down the coast were dark, they still needed to be manned.

Alice had become an expert on ration points and the geography of the Pacific in the months since then. Spending hours on duty with Lydia at the lookout tower, she had become an expert in the study of clouds, too. A new wooden structure on the island's highest hill, the lookout stood in the trees behind the schoolhouse. Ernie Brovelli, the air raid warden, had all of them taking turns watching for planes — Pete and Will, Owen Pierce and Silas Mitchell, even Rachel Shattuck and his grandson, Eddie.

Lydia rubbed her eyes. "Shoot, I think I'm going blind. Everything looks like a big white blob."

"I know — I see the sky in my sleep. I dream about looking for planes."

"I dream that I've got a gun, and I'm shooting every Jap I can find."

Alice was tired of Lydia's bravado, her repeated insistence that she was going to leave and volunteer with the Red Cross the minute she graduated from the schoolhouse, but she understood. Months later, the sense of injury remained palpable. What they had done to those unsuspecting men in Pearl Harbor they had done to every American.

When the ferry's horn sounded, Alice pushed herself to her knees and leaned over the edge of the lookout. The entire island was visible: the meandering shoreline, the thin ribbon of the road above the dock, the ferry coming in.

"You're not watching," Lydia said.

"You watch for a minute. The ferry's here."

Among the tiny figures gathered by the dock, Alice thought she could pick out her mother and Will in conversation with Captain Tony. The ferry was still on the reduced schedule of winter. This summer no more than one ferry a day, if that, would come to the island because of the fuel rationing. Alice watched people moving over the deck. Then she noticed a solitary figure climbing the hill. She reached for the binoculars.

"George Tibbits," she said.

"Where?"

"Getting off the ferry. At least I think it's him."

Lydia took her eyes from the sky long enough to scan the distance.

"He's just at the top of the hill." She handed Lydia the binoculars.

"Must be him," Lydia said. "Who else carries a suitcase?"

Alice followed his slow progress along the shore. He was almost to the dump before the ferry's horn sounded as it pulled away from the dock. He was early this year, though as always on the day of his arrival, the sky was clear and the air warm. Alice wore only a light sweater over her blouse and ankle socks with the new saddle shoes she had ordered from Sears, Roebuck that winter.

Lydia put down the binoculars and returned to scanning the sky. "See anything at the base?" she asked.

Alice turned toward the southern end of the island, which, until a few months earlier, had been nothing but woods and thickets of blueberry bushes. Within weeks of Pearl Harbor, Owen Pierce sold the land to the government, and not long after that, the area was transformed into a maze of bunkers and barracks. The paved stretch of road that cut through the base resembled a long gray snake lying in the sun. Little white specks she took to be sailors moved up and down the dock. "Can't see much," she said.

"My father says they're stockpiling weapons. In the bunkers. See how you can hardly notice the bunkers from here? They just look like a bunch of little hills. Once they finish with the bunkers and everything, he says they'll leave a skeleton crew on Snow."

Alice sank back into place beside Lydia and fixed her eyes on the elongated shape of a cloud that moved imperceptibly, like a ghostly blimp. "What time is it?"

Lydia glanced at her watch. "Almost four."

"My foot's gone to sleep."

"My brain's gone to sleep."

Alice banged her foot against the lookout floor. The tingling spread to her toes, then slowly faded.

"I can't believe Ethan Cunningham hasn't enlisted," Lydia said. "He doesn't even take a turn at the lookout."

"He has to take care of the lighthouse."

"What's there to take care of? He doesn't have anything to do. He just stays holed up in that house all day painting."

Alice tried to keep her voice neutral, noncommittal, as though Ethan and his actions were of no particular interest to her. "He has to clean the lenses and keep the lighthouse painted and everything in order. He has to make sure the lighthouse could be turned back on at a moment's notice."

"That doesn't sound like much to me."

"There's his mother. He takes care of her, too."

"If I were him, I'd enlist, that's all I know."

"Hey, anybody home up there?" Pete called from down below.

Alice was relieved to hear Pete's voice, saving her from any further response. The lookout tower began to shake as he climbed the stairs.

"You can't read when you're up here, you know," Lydia said when he appeared at the top with a book in his hand.

"I know. Seen any planes?"

"What do you think?"

Lydia showed him the blank page in the logbook.

Pete squinted in the direction of the base. "They're busy down there, huh? George Tibbits came on the ferry. Guess he's staying. He went over to the twin houses."

Alice and Lydia got to their feet, swapping places with Pete. Alice's entire leg was numb. She shook it and stamped her foot.

"What have you got, the palsy?" Pete said.

"My leg's asleep."

"Occupational hazard. I've been waking up with cramps in my legs every night."

Lydia started down the steps. Pete gave Alice a questioning look, as if to suggest she stay.

"I've got to get back to the store."

He nodded and turned his gaze to the sky.

Retrieving their bicycles, Alice and Lydia rode side by side down the empty road. Once on Bay Avenue, the girls went flying down the hill past the lighthouse. Alice looked for Ethan in the second-floor window, but there was only the movement of a white curtain in the breeze. She had not seen him for a week now, since the previous Sunday night when she climbed out her window to meet him.

Alice slowed her bike as they approached the inn and said she would see Lydia later. She rode on alone, past the boarded-up summer cottages, hoping that Ethan might come to the window and notice her. But when she glanced over her shoulder, making the bicycle weave, she found no sign of life at the Cunningham house.

Ethan had made a habit of driving around the island at night since the fall, going off to the west side, where he sat and stared at the water. The islanders accepted this as another of his odd habits. Even when she knew he wouldn't be out there waiting for her, in the middle of the day or over supper, Alice found herself listening for the Plymouth's engine and tensing at any stray sound, like the tooting of the ferry's horn or the chords of Phoebe Shattuck's piano. Ethan could be, and was, anywhere, surprising her suddenly as he entered the store or appeared by her side in the car when she bicycled to the inn. The time they spent together, stolen and secret as it was, ran beneath everything else, the truest part of her life. She passed the interminable days at the schoolhouse meeting him over and over in her mind.

Coasting down the hill by the store, Alice found Will at the end of the dock with the binoculars Owen Pierce had given him pressed to his face. "How many U-boats have you seen?" she said.

He gave a start and lowered the binoculars. "None. How many airplanes did you see?"

"None."

He raised the binoculars to his eyes, grunted, and ran his tongue over his lips. Watching for U-boats took a lot of concentration. Will had paid attention to nothing but his war projects since the war started, or rather, since the United States got into the war, as Alice had to keep reminding herself. It seemed like the war had not existed before Pearl Harbor. Will was twelve now, and over the winter he had grown four inches. When he wasn't rooted to his lookout at the end of the dock, he was dragging an old wagon all over the place, collecting tin cans and newspapers and anything else that could be reused in some fashion. He had long ago collected every last old tire and rubber boot on the island; his daily tours did not yield much now, but he kept at it. Captain Tony was goodnatured about hauling Will's treasure over to the mainland. He told him the people at the collection center were very impressed with the island's contributions.

Alice wheeled her bike back to the store and left it leaning against the porch railing. Inside, the few boxes that had arrived on the ferry lay scattered on the floor.

"George Tibbits came over on the ferry," Evelyn said from her chair behind the counter, a cup of tea in her hands. "I thought he might not show up this year, what with the war and all, but there he was, just the same as ever. I don't think you could find a stranger person if you tried. And to think how you saved his life, and now he doesn't say how do you do to you or anybody."

Alice went to the back and began unpacking one of the boxes, methodically lining cans of beans on the shelves. "Did you finish sorting the mail?"

"Yes. There wasn't much. Phoebe Shattuck had a letter from the Cheavings." Evelyn held the teacup to her lips and took a small sip. "They said not to open up their place this spring. They might not come till August, or might not come at all. Jack's joining up. You don't think you ordered too much?"

"There will still be some summer people, and the sailors coming down. You never know what they're going to want."

"Not cigarettes. They can get them cheaper on the base."

"I didn't order any extra cigarettes."

Evelyn sipped her tea and flipped through the pages of the newspaper that had arrived on the ferry. Kicking the empty box down the aisle, Alice glanced out the window. The sun flashed on the water and the bare rocks. Low tide again. Sometimes she found it hard to believe that the tide went on coming in and going out, just as it always had. It seemed that the ocean should have been transformed along with everything else.

# — CHAPTER 17 —

Mrs. Cunningham waited for them at the kitchen table with the quilt spread before her, crutches lying on the floor at her feet.

Evelyn set down her sewing basket and took the chair across from her. "You know, I was thinking maybe we should make up some braided rugs, too. Your rugs are so pretty. We could sell them at the store."

"We'd need more scraps than I have on hand right now."

"We'll take a trip to the mainland, see what they've got for remnants. When was the last time you went to the mainland?"

Mrs. Cunningham squinted at the needle she was threading. "I guess it was the Fourth of July last year."

"That's a long time."

"I haven't wanted to go anywhere."

"I know, but it would do you good to take a little trip. We'll see a movie."

Alice joined them at the table and took the threaded needle her mother handed her. The piecework was done; now they were finishing the quilting, slowly bringing the layers of cloth together with small stitches.

"I don't think Captain Tony will be running two ferries a day this summer," Alice said. "Guido's enlisted."

Evelyn placed a thimble on her finger and frowned. She had not considered that in order to make a trip to the mainland, they would have to stay overnight. "Well, if you can't go to the mainland, I will," she said to Mrs. Cunningham. "You just tell me what you need for the rugs, and I'll get it."

Mrs. Cunningham kept a fire going in the stove in all but the hottest weather, to take the chill out of the air, she said. The cookstove radiated heat now, and a kettle sat at the back, ready for tea. The Sunday night quilting sessions had become a regular occurrence over the winter. On Saturdays, when Silas Mitchell brought girls from the mainland and packed the dance hall, the store was so busy they stayed open until ten. Sundays the dance hall was closed, and the sailors didn't come down. Alice and her mother locked up the store at seven and went over to Mrs. Cunningham's, leaving Will to patrol the beach with Eddie Brovelli.

Footsteps sounded overhead and descended the stairs. Alice kept her gaze on the needle in her hand. She forced herself not to raise her eyes right away, to wait until Ethan crossed the kitchen and said hello. He was wearing his painting clothes, a shirt with holes in the sleeve and chinos splattered with dots of blue and black and red. His hair had the wild, unkempt look it acquired when he spent hours up in his room. She felt a sense of ownership as she watched him spoon tea from a tin and pour boiled water into the teapot. No one knew it, but that uncombed hair belonged to her.

Ethan met her look as he set the teapot and cups on the table. His eyes did not register anything; they simply held hers a moment longer than necessary. This is the way he behaved when they were in the presence of other people, keenly aware of her yet determined not to show it.

"At least we still have Ethan," Mrs. Cunningham was saying. She patted his hand before he moved away from the table. "Pretty soon you'll be about the only man left on the island, besides the base."

Ethan poured milk in the pitcher and set it next to the teapot, ignoring her words. When Mrs. Cunningham asked if he would have some tea, he shook his head. He went to the stairs without glancing in Alice's direction.

Mrs. Cunningham put down her needle. "Painting," she said, as if no further explanation were needed. "He didn't even eat supper. How did I produce such a child? He lives in another world."

Alice brought the needle up and down, working her way through the folds of fabric, but after nearly an hour of the mind-numbing repetition of stitching, Ethan had not reappeared. They heard footsteps overhead from time to time, but that was all. He might have been a prisoner pacing his cell.

Her fingers were sore, curled in what felt like a permanent cramp, by the time they put down their needles. She made the good-byes last as long as possible, hoping Ethan would hear them and come down, but there was no stirring overhead. Alice and her mother walked home under the cover of clouds. Without the lighthouse, the island was cloaked in black silence.

"Mrs. Brovelli came in with her ration stamps this morning," Evelyn said as they made their way over the pebbled surface of the road. "She said she didn't have any sugar on hand, but I didn't believe her. She's been buying sugar all winter. Then I had to figure out how many stamps to take for what she wanted today."

"The instructions are right in the front of the book."

"I know, but she gets me all confused, and then she tries to get more sugar than she's supposed to for the stamps she has."

Alice had gone over the sugar rationing system with her mother repeatedly, until it seemed there was no use in explaining any more. She said nothing now, listening to her mother go on about how if she'd known, she would have stockpiled sugar herself, just like Mrs. Brovelli. When they reached the house, Alice retreated to her room. Peering around the edge of the blackout curtain, she searched the thick night for something she could recognize. Without the lights of the mainland on the horizon, there were no markers to separate water from sky.

Will lay in his bed paging through the comic books he read over and over. She thought he would never turn out his light, but at last the room went dark. Alice sat at the end of her bed, gazing through the window, listening so intently her own heartbeat tricked her for a moment into believing the hum of a car engine approached. She was almost asleep, her head pressed to the cool glass of the window, when she heard the unmistakable sound of his car. Quickly she pulled on her shoes and jacket, and eased up the window. The ladder wobbled but held as she went slowly from rung to rung, descending backwards. The war was a cover for everything: she had told her mother they needed to leave the ladder there, in case the island was bombed, and she and Will had to get out of the attic in a hurry.

Following the car down the road, Alice felt the cool air on her face. She caught up with him by the stretch of summer houses past the Improvement Center. Ethan slowed to a stop and reached across the seat to open the door. Alice slid next to him. Neither of them spoke until they were past the dump, when Alice said, "George Tibbits came today."

"I guess we won't be parking in front of his houses then."

Instead of climbing the hill in Snow Park, Ethan pulled to the side of the road and shut off the engine. The rocks loomed before them, rough shapes bordering the flat surface of the water. "It's strange to have no lights on the mainland," he said.

Alice wrapped her arms around her chest, feeling the cold air coming up from the floor. "It's like there's nothing out there."

"There isn't anything out there, except the rest of the world."

She placed her hand on his, but he did not respond. He fished a cigarette from the pack in his shirt pocket and said, "I'm leaving next week. I'm enlisting."

Alice went still. "But you have your deferment."

"I know. I don't have any illusions about being a hero, believe me, but I couldn't see staying here staring at a dark lighthouse while the whole world's going up in flames. I wrote away for information about the Signal Corps. I thought I could put my vast knowledge of lighthouse keeping to use. It looks like they'll have me."

"But your mother," she said. "You can't leave her."

"Martha will come stay with her. She doesn't have any kids and her husband's in the Navy, so it's just the same to her whether she's home or here on the island. And Martha can take care of the lighthouse. There's not much to it these days."

Alice stared out at the water, feeling that he was gone already. She wondered how long he had been making these plans.

"You don't think I'm being stupid?" he said.

"No," she responded blankly. Cruel maybe, unfeeling, but not stupid, though Alice told herself these were selfish thoughts. He didn't have to go, and he was anyway, because it was the right thing to do. They needed every man they could get. She should feel proud, but she couldn't find it in her.

"You'll come back," she said, making the words into a statement and a tentative question. "I mean, of course you'll come back. But to the island. You'll come back to Snow, won't you?"

Ethan studied the cigarette between his fingers before striking a match and lighting it. He brought the cigarette to his lips. "Sure, I'll come back."

They sat in silence while he smoked the cigarette. Alice tried to pull herself out of her stricken state. Everything was blotted out by the fact of his leaving.

He pinched the end of the cigarette and tossed it out the window, then reached over to rub his hand across the top of her head. "Come on, Alice, don't make it worse than it is. You think I like this?"

She felt ashamed. She was thinking only of herself, when she should be thinking of him. He pulled her toward him and wrapped his arms around her, covering her face in small kisses. Releasing her, he started up the engine and drove back across the island. He came to a stop a ways from the dock.

"Come here, silly." He gave her a long, probing kiss.

She felt paralyzed, unable to respond.

"No tears, okay?" he said.

She nodded in agreement and climbed out of the car.

* * *

Alice was staring out the window the next afternoon, still trying to take in the fact of Ethan's leaving, when George Tibbits entered the store, a brown hat in his hand. He approached the counter slowly, glancing from side to side as though looking for something he had lost among the bins of flour and corn meal, and handed Alice a wrinkled piece of paper. In small, penciled letters, there was a list of items almost identical to the list he had left the year before: bread and eggs, milk and sugar, canned beans and soup.

"I have these," he said, reaching in his pocket and producing a ration book for sugar.

Alice paged through the book and removed enough stamps for one pound.

"Can you deliver this?" he asked. "I'm walking, you see."

Alice suppressed a smile and told him yes, she could deliver the groceries, adding, "We weren't sure you would be coming this year."

"I come every year."

"So many things have changed with the war."

He stood there expectantly, and she realized he was waiting for her to return the ration book. He stuffed it quickly in his pocket when she gave it to him. "I can pay the bill at the first of the month."

That would be fine, she told him. She would bring the order over in about an hour.

George turned the hat in his hands and thanked her. Watching him walk carefully toward the door, Alice wondered if he came to the store on purpose in the late afternoon, when he knew she would be back from school. It seemed he did not want to speak with anyone else.

Evelyn was out on the porch, going over the newspaper headlines with Miss Weeden. She came inside as soon as George Tibbits left. "What did he want?"

"Groceries."

"He's staying for the summer?"

"He said he'd pay at the start of the month, so I guess he's staying that long."

"It's like he's stuck in a rut or something. He has to come over and walk to the twin houses, and then walk all the way back to place a grocery order. Does that make any kind of sense?"

Alice did not think her mother had grounds for criticizing other people when it came to being stuck in ruts, but she agreed that no, it didn't make any kind of sense, though in fact she thought she understood George Tibbits and his speechless ways. There were some things a person had to do, over and over, for no reason but the doing of them. She had to go down to the dock and watch for her father sometimes, just to remind herself what her years with him had been like, to make them feel not so far away.

While her mother continued unpacking the supplies that had arrived the day before, Alice went from shelf to shelf, assembling the things George Tibbits wanted. She was filling a bag with sugar when Ethan appeared in the doorway, holding the screen open for his mother. Alice set down the sack of sugar and tugged at the hem of her blouse. Ethan gave her a quick glance and helped his mother to the chair by the stove.

"I've come to see what you've got for yarn," Mrs. Cunningham said.

Evelyn retrieved a box behind the counter and placed it in Mrs. Cunningham's lap.

"Ethan's just told me he's enlisting," Mrs. Cunningham said quietly. "He's leaving next Tuesday. I thought I might get a sweater made by then."

Evelyn pursed her lips in surprise, but to Alice's relief, she said nothing. Mrs. Cunningham fingered the skeins of yarn, reaching for one in dark blue. Ethan took it from his mother. He liked the color, he said. Alice studied the hand with which he held the yarn. His skin was not callused, like the skin of a quahogger, and yet he was strong enough to survive whatever lay ahead.

Ethan paid for the yarn and a bottle of milk, and helped his mother back to her feet, fitting the crutches beneath her arms. He took the sack Alice held out to him and thanked her. Alice heard other words in the brief exchange, the ones he couldn't say.

# — CHAPTER 18 —

The truck started fitfully. Alice gunned it up the hill and turned toward the dump. The familiar contours of the shoreline met her, yet she barely saw the view of water and rock. All day she had tried to convince herself that Ethan would change his mind. Now, with the day of his departure fixed, there was no question. He was leaving.

She took the long way around to Snow Park, avoiding the lighthouse, and coaxed the truck up the hill to the twin houses. The supplies George Tibbits had requested sat in two boxes beside her. He was waiting on the porch of the house on the left, seated on the top step with his hat in his hand. She pulled over and lifted the first box out of the truck. She had divided the cans to make the boxes easier to carry. Still, she strained to keep her grip as she crossed the lawn. George Tibbits stood up, shifting from one foot to the other awkwardly.

"Should I take this inside?" Alice asked.

George started, as though she had made a shocking suggestion, then opened the door and held it for her. "You can go through to the kitchen," he said.

Alice glanced at the living room as she went past, taking in a wicker couch and end tables covered by lace doilies. She set the box on the kitchen table. A few dishes sat on open shelves, but the rest of the room was bare, save for a calendar hanging over the sink, decorated with a faded drawing of Barton's main street. The month was May, the year 1919.

The house smelled of mouse droppings and dust. The wood floors were dark with age. George followed Alice back down the hall and stood by the door while she retrieved the second box. As she passed inside again, Alice tried to fix what she saw in her mind: an old copy of *National Geographic* on a table by the sofa, a glass bowl full of shells. She placed the box on the kitchen table and took the quarter George fished from his pocket and handed her. Alice wanted to stay and climb the stairs to the second floor, but she retraced her steps, down the hallway past the living room, and let herself out, glancing back to see George on the other side of the screen, peering after her like a child.

Driving to the other side of the island, Alice felt strangely honored to have been inside one of the twin houses. The place was just as she had always imagined, frozen in time. Lydia would be jealous.

Owen Pierce sat on the porch of the store, puffing on his pipe. "Did you hear Ethan Cunningham's enlisting?" he called as Alice jumped out of the truck.

Yes, she said, she had heard the news.

"He doesn't have to go, you know. A true American, that's what he is. If I was a young man, I'd be right there with him. You couldn't hold me back. We're going to show them what Americans are made of, men like Hank Giberson and Ethan Cunningham." Owen waved his pipe in the air.

Alice nodded vaguely as she watched Lydia come flying down the hill on her bike.

Lydia brought the bike to a stop, spewing gravel, and climbed off. "What are you doing driving the truck around?"

"Making a delivery. To George Tibbits."

"I didn't know he ate food."

Alice went inside the store, letting the screen slam behind her. Lydia's comment, and the superior look on her face, did not deserve a response. She wouldn't even tell her she had been inside one of the twin houses.

* * *

That night, and the ones that followed, Alice sat by the window, waiting. She stayed up until one or two, though this was long past when Ethan would appear, and dragged herself out of bed in the morning to go off to school. On Sunday night, she went over to the Cunninghams with her mother and sat at the kitchen table, her stomach tight with dread. Ethan was quite busy getting his things in order, Mrs. Cunningham said. This was the only explanation she offered for the repeated crossing of footsteps overhead and the fact that he did not appear. Alice walked home beside her mother after the quilting session, barely able to speak. He could not leave without saying good-bye. She knew this, and yet with each minute that passed, the time they might have together was slipping away.

Later that night, when she heard the Plymouth going past, she scrambled down the ladder, so anxious to reach him she forgot to stay in the shadows at the side of the road and ran in the open, covered in moonlight. The warm air made it feel like summer. She found this hard to accept. Ethan should have been leaving on one of those raw nights when she wrapped her coat close against the wind.

He drove over to the west side, one hand on the wheel, the other around her shoulder. Alice rested her head on his chest and watched the shapes of the trees move past. At the open stretch of rocky shoreline, the moon shone on the water, making a path toward the mainland. Alice thought of many things to say as they rattled over the dirt road, how she would wait for him to come back, and when he returned, she would be old enough, but in the presence of his silence, such explanations seemed unnecessary, even stupid.

He eased the car into a pull-off past the turn to Snow Park, where they were hidden behind the bushes. Instead of climbing over the back of the seat, he got out of the car and came around, as though the game they had played all winter were over. Alice did the same.

"You won't run off and marry Pete Giberson, will you?" he asked.

"Ethan."

"Just wanted to make sure."

Alice shook her head, afraid to attempt saying more. He moved toward her, putting his hands on her shoulders and squeezing hard. She could just make out his eyes as he lowered his face to hers, small and precise and the slightest bit sad.

He undressed her slowly, as though taking off her skirt and blouse were actions they had rehearsed in preparation for this night. She slid beneath the blanket he had brought and waited while he removed his clothes, dropping them beside hers on the car's floor. He ran his hands over her skin, and she thought of rippling water and her body moving through it, unbearably alive, responsive to the slightest touch. This night would cover them and stay with them, would carry them forward into whatever came next. She returned his kisses, holding her fingers to his face, smiling at the noisiness of their lips meeting. She gripped his back as he slid inside her and held on. He moved in and out, his eyes clenched shut, his breath coming faster. When he was about to pull away, she whispered, "Don't. Stay inside."

He shook his head, raising himself on both arms, but she pulled him back down, wrapping her arms around his chest. He was overcome then, the release hitting him in waves. The other times they had made love that winter, he had pulled out before coming, spilling the cold semen on her stomach. This time she wanted to feel more. She felt the force of his release inside her, and then he rolled away. She ran her fingers through his hair. He kissed her on the mouth and rested his head on her shoulder. After a moment, his breathing evened out. She lay there, holding her hand to the back of his head, listening to his breath come and go. The moon shone down through the car's rear window, bathing Ethan's sleeping face in cold light.

When he woke at last, he lifted his head and kissed her. "It's time to take you home."

They sat side by side in the back seat, dressing, and went around to the front. The road stretched before them, etched in moonlight. Ethan started up the car. Alice tried to remember all the things she meant to say to him before he left. She couldn't think of a single one now. When they reached a shaded spot past the dump, he slowed to a stop and said, "You'll be at the ferry when I go?"

"Yes."

"Then this won't be good-bye."

He held her for a long moment and pressed his lips to hers. Alice did not trust herself to speak. She watched him drive off, until the Plymouth disappeared around the bend past the dock.

\* \* \*

Ethan and his mother did not arrive on Tuesday until the ferry was already within sight. Alice followed the progress of their car through the store's window. The entire island was gathered outside, a quiet knot of people holding small American flags.

Alice joined the group at the foot of the dock and watched as Martha Cunningham made her way down the gangplank. The islanders waited silently while Martha went to the Plymouth and kissed Mrs. Cunningham through the open window, then hugged her brother. When Ethan had said his good-byes, he took a suitcase from the back seat and walked toward the ferry. He went through the crowd, shaking hands, until he came to Alice. He shook her hand like all the others, but as he did so, he pressed a piece of paper into her palm.

The islanders waved their flags when the ferry pulled away. Alice stood there with her fist closed around the scrap of paper as Ethan grew smaller, his figure receding on the ferry's deck.

\* \* \*

There was moonlight again that night. Alice went through the woods instead of walking on the road. The trees were silver, bending over the path. How full they had become in the last week, suddenly leafing out. The lilacs, just opening, made the air unbearably sweet. She held the note Ethan had given her between her fingers and felt certain that by next spring, when the lilacs bloomed again, he would be back.

She had almost reached the cemetery when she sensed there was someone in the trees and stopped. Ahead on the path, a deer emerged. She could not tell if it was a doe or a buck. The deer turned its head, and their eyes met. Sniffing the air, the deer flared its nostrils, remaining for a moment, frozen. Then it bounded off, showing the white of its tail. There were more deer around the island than ever, driven out of the south end by the construction of the base. At dusk, they were like statues among the trees, with their long necks and quiet eyes.

Alice looked for her father's grave as she passed the cemetery. Beyond the stone wall, the marker stood in the moonlight, crisply defined. Her father must know everything, she thought — the war, Ethan, the base on the island. She silently asked him to understand where she was going now and why. An entire hour had passed before Alice was able to read the note Ethan slipped her that afternoon. Finally the store emptied, and her mother went up to the house, and she eased the piece of paper from her pocket. She had never seen Ethan's handwriting before and was surprised by how precisely and neatly he wrote. In blue ink, on a single line, were the words, "Look for an envelope under the lighthouse stair."

When Alice reached the end of the path, she emerged from the woods and walked in the shadow of the chapel wall. Making her way quickly down the hill, she crossed the road, keeping her eye on the windows of the inn. It was past eleven, and there was no sign that any of the Gibersons were still awake. Alice slipped around the corner of the inn, staying close to the lilacs, and took the path to the lighthouse. The door eased open, creaking uneasily. Inside the base of the lighthouse, the dark was cavernous, and the air was damp. She waited a moment for her eyes to adjust before feeling her way to the metal staircase. The concrete floor was covered with sand and had a moist, clammy feel. She ran her hands along its surface until she found the envelope wedged beneath the first step.

Her lungs could not take in the air fast enough as she ran back through the woods, jumping over rocks and tree roots, the envelope pressed to her chest. In the attic, Alice lit a candle by her bed and unsealed the large, square envelope, which was strangely weightless in her hand. She had imagined a long letter, page after page, outlining the life they would have when he returned, but when she reached inside, she found only a single sheet of paper. She tugged at it gently. There were no words on the sheet, save for Ethan's cramped signature in the bottom right corner, beneath a drawing of a girl. The penciled figure lay on a small sofa, eyes fixed on some far off point and hair falling over her shoulder. Alice recognized herself in the drawing Ethan had made the day they rescued George Tibbits, though the girl on the page was prettier than she imagined herself to be. She shook the envelope over the bed, but there was nothing else inside.

# — CHAPTER 19 —

George set out early in the morning, climbing over the rocks and threading his way through the brush. Over the winter, Snow shrank to a distant, gray memory. The return was always startling, as though the island had been dipped in vibrant colors, polished and shined for the occasion. The Snow he discovered when he came back was so much brighter than the place he held in his mind the rest of the year. Cities with their crowded jumble of sensation could not match the pervasive sense of life he felt on the island. The world of trains and restaurants and sidewalks seemed like mere noise compared to the flight of birds and the breaking waves.

Once again, he made his way methodically around the island, searching the inlets and tide pools for any sign. Maybe all he would find now was a piece of wood, the broken remains of what had once been a boat. It made no difference. He had to find something. First, he had returned to the island to make the journey he and Sarah planned all those years; now he came back to finish what he had started, to find the boat or what was left of it, and bring it home.

He had feared that the base would intrude on the island's quiet life, but since returning, he discovered his apprehensions were mostly unfounded. A low hum carried from the southern end of the island during the day, but the sailors seldom ventured off the base. The rest of Snow remained untouched. The shoreline he walked now looked the same as it did when Bertie and Sarah came to Snow, or when the Narragansetts lived on the island. The Indians had called the island Chibachuwesett, which meant "place of the passage of the waters."

The base was separated from the rest of Snow by a long chain-link fence. He could not search the sandy beaches on the island's southern end or wander through the wild terrain where he and Sarah had once picked blueberries. He supposed the government had cleared most of the land to make way for roads and barracks. He hoped they had not found the boat and used it for scrap wood. He had no intention of ever sailing the thing again; he simply wanted it back, so he could place it under the house. For years he had planned his return to Snow with one thought in mind: the boat. He felt it waiting for him when the leaves fell in the fall and snow covered the streets in winter, watching from beneath the house, calling him back.

George reached the fence and turned toward the east, running his fingers along the warm metal of the chain link. The Navy had left a cover of brush on the other side of the fence, so he could not see into the base. Whatever they were building remained well to the interior. He still could not accept the idea of Snow becoming a fortification, a place marked on government maps. He was peering into the thick brush, listening for any indication of activity inside, when a wren flitted over the fence and landed on one of the posts. He stopped walking. She turned her small head, fixing one black eye on him. He tried not to move or even to breathe. They remained locked in a long gaze while the ring of a hammer sounded far off, until she flew on, a flash of brown against the sun. George hurried after her, wanting to keep the bird in sight, but she disappeared over the fence, back onto the base.

Sarah had always believed in signs and premonitions. She could predict the arrival of a letter or the announcement of some national calamity, like the San Francisco earthquake. George was too young to remember that day with any clarity, but Sarah used to relate the story to him. "And then I said, 'I feel bad news coming,' and Bertie laughed. 'What, is the sun going to fall out of the sky?' 'No,' I told her, 'the sun is not going to fall out of the sky, but it will be just as bad as if it had.' 'Oh stop, Sarah, you're scaring the child,' Bertie said. But I knew you weren't scared, because you looked right at me and said, 'Whose bad news is it, Aunt Sarah?' And I told you it wasn't our bad news, it was other people's bad news, people far away. Of course the newspapers telling about the earthquake didn't come for a few days, but when they did, Bertie looked at me all funny. After that when I had one of my premonitions, she didn't say much."

He imagined she had sent the little wren to him now, to let him know he was not alone, to show she made the trips around the island with him. He moved on down the fence, alert for the bird, but she did not reappear. Sarah's suicide was all the more inexplicable because she seemed to have this foresight, this secret knowledge, despite her muddled ways. Couldn't you tell the telegram was wrong? he wanted to shout when he found her there in the bed. Couldn't you feel me getting closer with every day? But her second sight had abandoned her at the most important moment. Perhaps she had become so accustomed to anticipating the bad news of others, she could not recognize the truth or falsehood of her own when it arrived, or maybe without Bertie, she lost the will to trust herself and became uncertain and confused. He tried to imagine those days after Bertie's death, when Sarah lived without her. It was not easy to picture. As much as he had longed to free Sarah from Bertie's grasp throughout his childhood, he understood that the women could not have existed without each other, that they were tied in strange and twisted ways, with a strength amounting to need.

Perhaps Sarah was more present in death than she would have been in life, though the truth of this seemed cruel. George had spent more hours than he could count imagining how he would have lived if Sarah had not gone. He knew she would have lived to an old age, unlike Bertie. She did not have Bertie's restless anger; her simplicity would have sustained her. He imagined marrying and raising a family on Snow, with Sarah there to be grandmother and aunt rolled into one. She would have loved to care for babies. But where would he have met a woman to marry? And what would he have done to support them? George couldn't answer these questions and knew, in the quiet of his private thoughts, that the idea of his marrying was pure fantasy, even if everything had been different. He couldn't extend himself to other people in that way; he couldn't make that leap. Sarah was the only person he had ever been close to, truly. Perhaps they had formed an understanding so perfect, there could be no one else for either of them.

George made his way down Bay Avenue, past the lighthouse and the inn, meeting no one in the bright stillness. The island was oddly deserted. It seemed strange, to have the base on Snow, and yet the place remained blanketed in quiet, as though nothing had changed, or everything had changed. Even the store was closed. Then he heard the thin sound of voices, singing, and realized it was Sunday. He climbed the hill, opened the church door, and slipped inside, into the last pew.

Miss Weeden, wearing a hat adorned with fake flowers, played the wheezing organ. Her bent fingers curled over the keys, rising and falling unsteadily. The voices of the congregation were as quavering as her shaking hands. George felt like he was a boy again, watching the teacher's pursed lips and narrowed eyes, just waiting to be reprimanded. She held the last, long chord of the amen, bringing her hands up with a dramatic flourish. George ducked his head as she scanned the congregation.

There were not many people present: the girl from the store and her mother and brother, Owen Pierce, Mrs. Cunningham from the lighthouse, and a collection of others he didn't know, probably summer people. He supposed the congregation was no larger when he had attended the Union Church, but the meagerness of the gathering struck him. The visiting minister read the story of Isaac and Abraham. George had always loved the part when the angel of the Lord called to him from heaven, and Abraham said, "Here am I." The rest of the story was alarming, to think that God would let Abraham believe he was about to kill his own son. George wondered how he could have listened passively to the Bible stories when he was younger, barely giving them a thought. Now they struck him as wild and frightening, having nothing to do with the paintings that decorated the church walls, airy depictions of Jesus and the Holy Land in shades of pink and yellow and blue, like Easter eggs.

"Doesn't God have a kindly face?" Sarah asked him one winter night.

"I never imagined his face."

"You should, George. You should see him in your mind. He's just a big, sweet old man, really. I see him looking down on me all day. All night, too. That's the thing about God, he never rests, but he doesn't need to, not like us. He's much stronger than we are. It's good to know that there's someone so much stronger watching over us, isn't it? He gives me an awful lot of peace. You have to listen, George, listen real carefully, and you'll hear him. He talks to us. Most people never hear him because they're too busy to listen, but if you just stop and be quiet for a long time, he comes to you."

"What does he say?"

"Oh, private things."

"What kind of private things?"

"He tells me where I left my darning needle when I can't find it, things like that."

George listened after that, long and hard. Once Sarah had fallen asleep, he would force his eyes to stay open, staring at the ceiling, listening so hard his ears rang, but God did not speak to him. He began to wonder if Sarah imagined the voice that came to her. He found it unlikely that if God were going to speak, he would waste his words on lost darning needles.

When the congregation rose for the next hymn, George let himself out, avoiding the startled looks of those who turned to stare. He wished he felt differently; he wished he could return to the church, but he simply experienced the same sense of betrayal that had stayed with him all these years. Sarah's kindly old man had deserted her when she needed him most, and left George with nowhere to turn.

197

# — CHAPTER 20 —

One week passed, and then another, and another. Alice went through the days with a heightened awareness of everything around her, conscious that at any moment news might come. The weather turned hot and muggy at the beginning of June, but the island did not seem to know that summer was approaching. Along the midway, the cottages were still empty, their windows boarded over. The summer people didn't qualify for enough rationed gas to make the drive to Barton, or they had sons and husbands off at war and wanted to stay close to home, or they were busy working in one of the factories.

Alice waited for each run of the ferry and carried the mailbag up the dock to the store, making sure she was the first to open it and peruse the contents before her mother arrived to sort it. She was afraid that Ethan's letter would come when she was at the schoolhouse, and her mother would start asking questions. She hurried down to the store as soon as school let out, but most days the ferry did not come until late in the afternoon, if it came at all. Though she watched for a thin envelope with her name on it, nothing arrived, day after day. Perhaps he thought it was too great a risk to take.

Graduation was less than a week away. Alice and Lydia were tending the store after supper one night, sitting behind the counter sucking on jawbreakers. "Look," Lydia said, fishing the round ball from her mouth.

"Stripes."

"Looks like a sunset." Alice peered down her nose at the jawbreaker on her own outstretched tongue.

The high whine of a jeep sounded up on the road, going fast. Alice expected it to speed past the dock, but with a screech of tires, the vehicle slowed down and turned toward the store. The jeep spun to a stop; two sailors in whites jumped out and bounded up the porch steps. With a quick glance at each other, Alice and Lydia took the jawbreakers from their mouths and dropped them in the trash.

The sailors entered and stood inside the door, appraising the place. This was the first time Alice had been alone in the store when sailors came by. Most nights her mother stayed at the store now, but she was up at the house with a headache.

The taller sailor stepped toward the counter. He had blond hair and an angular face pink with sunburn. The other man, shorter and thinner, showed a fringe of dark hair beneath his cap. They looked like new arrivals, with their shirts so starched the sleeves could barely bend.

"Cute place you got here," the blond one said.

It took Alice a minute to figure out what he was saying. She thought at first the word was *cut*, the way he drew it out in a flat, broad tone. She wondered where people talked like that.

"We're here on official business." He jerked his thumb toward the door, as if to explain why they were driving a jeep. "Got to pick up a newspaper for the Chief. You get the paper daily?"

"It depends whether the ferry comes or not," Alice said.

Lydia hastened to explain that sometimes it did and sometimes it didn't, depending on the fuel situation over in Barton.

Both the sailors had removed their caps when they entered the store. The blond one stuffed his in his back pocket now. Their short, bristly hair shone under the bare light bulb.

"The ferry came today," Alice said, gesturing over the counter at a small pile of papers.

"They don't tell us much down at the base." The blond one picked up the paper and scanned the headlines. "Big difference it makes. We couldn't do anything with the news if we knew it anyways. Stuck on this crazy island without even a telephone." He grinned as he set the paper on the counter. "Guess I have to pay you for this, huh? This your store?"

"Yes. Well, my mother's," Alice said.

"You here all the time then, you girls?"

"Except when —" Alice was about to say "we're in school," but Lydia gave her a swift kick on the ankle bone. She tried not to wince.

"Except when we're being airplane spotters over at the lookout," Lydia finished.

"Airplane spotters? Now that's important work," the blond one said. Alice couldn't tell if he was making fun of them or not. "You think the Chief will pay me back?" He turned to the other sailor as he slid a nickel across the counter.

The dark-haired one shrugged. "Probably. He doesn't seem like a bad guy. So far."

"So far. Okay, take my money."

Alice dropped the nickel in the cash drawer.

"Well, nice to meet you gals," the blond one said. "I'm Ricky, and my buddy here's Brock."

Lydia introduced herself and Alice while the shorter one, Brock, fingered his cap.

"You girls ever go to the dance hall?" Ricky asked.

"Sure. Whenever there's a band or —"

The screen door swung open as Lydia was speaking. "Or anything," she finished, meeting Pete's look.

No one spoke for a moment. The sailors glanced at Pete, but he kept his eyes on Lydia. Alice wondered if he had heard the whole exchange. Pete knew as well as she did that Lydia was lying. Now that the island was "crawling with sailors," as Mrs. Giberson put it, she and Lydia were forbidden to go to the dance hall, though Silas Mitchell kept the place open just about every night, offering beer and pool games.

"This is my brother." Lydia gestured toward him. "Pete."

The sailors nodded at him.

"Well, we better be shoving off," Ricky said. "See you ladies around."

He took his hat from his pocket and, as soon as they were through the door, placed it on his head. The men paused for a moment on the porch, adjusting their caps. Ricky laughed as they climbed into the jeep, but Alice could not hear what they said.

"Ladies?" Pete arched his eyebrows as the jeep started up.

"Yes, ladies," Lydia answered. "What's wrong with that?"

Pete smiled. "I just don't think of you that way. I thought the dance hall was off limits to you *ladies*."

Lydia smoothed the collar of her blouse, feeling to see if it lay flat. "So what if it is?"

"I'm just reminding you. I don't want to see anybody get in trouble —"

"Holy bejesus." Lydia exhaled heavily. "You'd think you were eighty or something, the way you're acting, Pete. I'm going to sign up to do my part for the war just like you. Then see if Mom can stop me from going to the dance hall or anyplace else."

"It's your business what you do then. I'm just reminding you." Pete gave Alice an exasperated look. "Mom wants you to come home, Lydia. She needs to fit your skirt for graduation." Without waiting to see if she would follow, he left, banging the screen.

Lydia crossed the floor slowly. "I don't know what's eating him."

\* \* \*

Alice woke late on graduation day. The air in the attic was hot and musty, and she could smell Will's sneakers on the other side of the blanket. She hurried out of bed. When she had used the outhouse, she unlatched the door of the chicken coop and stepped inside. The hens squawked wildly and flapped their wings as she approached. She moved

quickly from one to the next, feeling for eggs in the straw. The hen she
called Hettie nipped her hand, and the rooster started crowing. "Stop it,"
Alice said. She found four eggs and set them in the basket she had
brought with her.

"All right now, shoo," she said, waving her hands.

The chickens darted ahead of her, out the door into the pen where
they spent the day.

Once she had eaten breakfast and done the dishes, Alice set a basin
in the sink to wash her hair. Unlike Lydia, she did not have a new outfit
to wear for graduation. While she ran the water over her head and
reached for the shampoo, she eyed the blouse and skirt she had ironed
the night before and hung over a chair. The blouse had been new that
fall, and the skirt, though not the length they were wearing them on the
mainland now, as Lydia would be the first to point out, would have to do.
She rinsed her hair and wrapped it in a towel, and changed into her
clothes. She was polishing her shoes when her mother appeared.

"It's hot already," Evelyn said. "I hope we don't have to sit too long
in that sun." She went to a row of pegs on the wall by the door and took
down her straw hat.

Alice removed the towel and twisted the ends of her hair around her
fingers, trying to get it to hold the curl. "You aren't going to wear that
hat, are you?"

"Yes. What's wrong with this hat?"

"It's just a little dowdy."

"Dowdy?" Evelyn sniffed. "This is a perfectly serviceable hat that
keeps the sun off my head."

Alice eyed her mother with misgivings.

"Don't you look at me like that, Alice Daggett. This isn't a fashion
show we're going to." Evelyn set the hat on her head and tied the faded
ribbon under her chin.

Alice checked her hair in the cracked mirror that hung over the sink.
Evelyn stopped her at the door, placing her hands on Alice's shoulders.

"I wish your father could see you today, looking so grown-up and pretty."

"Mom, we're going to be late." Alice stood still while her mother kissed her on the forehead.

By the time they arrived, almost all the islanders were assembled in front of the schoolhouse, seated in the folding chairs Silas Mitchell had brought over from the Improvement Center and set up on the lawn. Alice felt queasy as she made her way up the central aisle and took her place next to Lydia and Pete. She had imagined this day for so long, the beginning of what would be her life, but now that the day had arrived, it stood before her like a chasm with nothing on the other side.

The three graduating seniors sat facing the crowd. The women wore wide-brimmed hats and fanned themselves with the programs the younger children had made. The men stood in clusters at the edge of the lawn. Mrs. Giberson, in the front row, held a camera in her lap.

"You look nice," Alice whispered to Lydia. Her graduation outfit consisted of a pleated skirt and matching jacket, and a striped blouse with a floppy bow tied at the neck.

"So do you," Lydia responded. "Are you wearing lipstick?"

"No." Alice had never worn make-up in her life.

The crowd went silent, and the men took their places as Miss Weeden walked to the podium. Acutely conscious of all the people facing her, Alice crossed her feet at the ankles and smoothed her skirt over her lap. Mrs. Giberson raised the camera and took a picture.

Miss Weeden welcomed everyone and gave a report on the year. All the students were being promoted to the next grade. Mr. Brovelli spoke after Miss Weeden, going on about how the futures of this year's graduates were bright, despite the "specter of war" that hung over them. Then Pete, the senior speaker, rose from his seat. Alice watched the back of his head as he made his way to the podium. His mother had cut his hair for the occasion. He shuffled the pages in his hand nervously and began. "In Robert Frost's poem, 'The Road Not Taken,' he writes: 'Two roads diverged in a wood, and I —/I took the one less traveled by,/And that has made all the difference.'"

Pete looked up, as though checking for confirmation from his audience of the significance of the words. When he glanced back down at the pages he held between his shaking hands, he could not find his place. There was a long pause. Alice saw his eyes darting furiously over the paper. He cleared his throat and continued. The road less traveled was not always obvious at first or easy to find, he explained, but thanks to what they had all learned at the schoolhouse, they would know the road to take when they came to it. This was what the Allies were fighting for, for the freedom to choose which road to take.

The sun beat down on Alice's head. She wished she had a program to use as a fan. Pete went on to talk about the importance of supporting the war effort and remembering why it was necessary to make the sacrifices they had to make, sacrifices like rationing, gas cards, and having favorite radio shows interrupted. He turned and smiled at Lydia on the last example. Someday, he said, they would know without a doubt that it had all been worth it, when everyone in the world was free to choose the road less traveled by.

He rattled his pages and sat down. Mr. and Mrs. Giberson leapt to their feet and applauded with vigor. When the applause died down, Alice and Lydia and Pete walked up to receive their diplomas. Miss Weeden kissed each of them on the cheek. Her lips felt like cold paper. Mrs. Brovelli started up the Victrola, which had been carried out of the schoolhouse onto the lawn for the occasion. The scratchy strains of "Pomp and Circumstance" floated over the crowd, and Alice followed the others down the grassy aisle between the wooden chairs, thinking to herself, it's over, it's over, though she wasn't sure exactly what had come to an end.

In the crowd that surrounded them afterwards, Alice found herself next to Pete. He extended his hand and said, "Congratulations." Glancing quickly around to see if anyone was watching, he leaned over and kissed her on the cheek. "This is for you." He placed a book in her hands, a collection of Robert Frost's poems. "This is the book I took the poem from, for my speech. I want you to have it. I wrote something in it."

He stood there with his hands clasped, looking down at her expectantly. She opened the book. On the front page, he had written: "For Alice, I will always remember our years together at the schoolhouse. Fondly, Pete."

Alice thanked him and slid the book beneath her arm. "That was a great speech. Do you want some iced tea?"

He shook his head, and she turned, skirting the knot of people near the refreshment table. She took the glass Mrs. Brovelli handed her and gulped down the cold liquid. She asked for two more glasses for the Cunninghams and moved across the lawn, glancing in Pete's direction with a certain guilt. He was talking to Miss Weeden. Alice wished she could have said more to him. It had never occurred to her he would give her a present, much less that she might have given one to him.

"I thought you might like some tea." Alice handed the glasses to Martha and her mother.

"Thank you, Alice," Mrs. Cunningham said. "So you're a graduate. Congratulations. Your mother must be very proud."

"Whew, it's hot." Evelyn waved her straw hat in front of her face. "Can you believe my baby's graduated?" she said to Mrs. Cunningham. "I can't believe it. Seventeen years old. Seems like just yesterday I was changing her diapers."

The two women talked about the wonderful speech Pete gave. Alice shifted the book of poems from one hand to the other, half-listening, until she heard Mrs. Cunningham say, "We had a letter from Ethan. Seems that he's gone and gotten married."

Alice felt her skin go cold. What Mrs. Cunningham said could not be true. It was some sort of monstrous joke, Ethan playing games with her over the distance.

"Gotten married? Now who would he have gotten married to?"

Evelyn said, incredulous.

"A girl he used to know from college," Martha said. "He's stationed at Fort Monmouth, down in New Jersey, and I guess he's been going in to the city to see her when he has leave time. She sounds very nice."

Alice heard them speaking with a stunned disbelief. Ethan had never mentioned any women he knew in college. She could only think that she wanted to get away as quickly as possible, that she did not want to hear another word of what they were saying.

"It's a little bit of a relief, you know." Mrs. Cunningham placed her hand on Evelyn's. "I didn't think Ethan would ever get married."

"And they've gotten married already?"

"That's what he says. It was in front of a clerk at City Hall."

"It's a shame you couldn't be there."

"You know how Ethan is. He doesn't like a fuss about anything."

"No, I guess he doesn't. And everyone's rushing off and getting married like that these days, I hear. Well, I hope they're happy."

Alice wished she could clap her hand over her mother's mouth and force her to stop speaking. Instead, she stared at the polished surface of her shoes and gripped the book in her hand until it was damp.

# — CHAPTER 21 —

The days after graduation were marked by the heavy, relentless heat and, for Alice, a sense of aimlessness. She stocked the shelves at the store and reviewed the order forms and drove over to Snow Park, but a feeling of detachment pervaded the daily routine, as though she were observing herself from the lookout tower. The person she saw, moving through her life, was a fool, a fool who had believed that Ethan would return and marry her. She wondered how she had ever come to think such a thing.

The sun was like a hot board, pressing on the top of her skull. She sat beside Lydia in the lookout, staring at the blank, white sky a week after graduation. Years might have passed since that day when she made her way home through the woods with her mother, clutching the wilted diploma and Pete's book in her hand, hearing the name of the woman Ethan had married sound over and over in her mind. Charlotte. This was all Alice knew. Her name was Charlotte, and she was a working girl, as Mrs. Cunningham put it, though no one seemed to know exactly what she did. Ethan promised to send a picture.

"Are you still making those quilts at Mrs. Cunningham's?" Lydia asked.

"No."

"Why not?"

"I'm sick of it." Alice pushed the wet tendrils of hair off her forehead and pulled her knees in to her chest.

"I never knew why you wanted to do it to begin with, spending Sunday nights with those old ladies."

Alice shrugged. "I thought I could help my mother make some money. They sold a quilt to Mrs. Sibley."

"There's a band at the dance hall tonight. Want to go?"

Alice gave Lydia a sidelong glance. "How are we going to manage that?"

"I've got an idea."

Lydia explained while Alice studied the waves of heat that moved through the air like rippling water. They would each tell their mothers they were spending the night at the other's house, and when they came home later, they would say they had gotten sick to their stomachs and decided not to stay. It would work, she was sure, but first they had to get Alice's legs shaved and put some lipstick on her.

Alice gave her a dubious look.

"Oh Alice, come on. This may be our last chance. In another month I could be leaving."

Betty Giberson was already working as a Red Cross volunteer in New York. Alice doubted the Gibersons would allow Lydia to leave along with the rest of the family, but she said she would go to the dance hall and went back to staring at the hazy sky, thinking how her life felt like it was over before it had even begun.

When they were finished with airplane duty, they bicycled over to the inn. Alice found herself standing in the bathtub on the second floor with a razor in her hand, wishing for the first time she could tell Lydia about Ethan. The fact of him and what he had done was like a stone sunk in her chest, but she was too ashamed to admit to the idiocy of her hopes.

"I cut myself again," Alice said. "This thing's dangerous."

Lydia gave her an impatient glance from her place by the door, where she was listening for the approach of Mrs. Giberson's footsteps. "There's hardly any blade left. How can you keep cutting yourself?"

Alice drew Betty Giberson's old razor up her leg. "Am I doing something wrong?"

"Slowly, I told you. In one motion. Don't jerk it. Just go from bottom to top, like this." Lydia drew her hand through the air in a gliding movement.

"That's what I'm doing."

"Make sure you've got enough soap."

Alice finished with her right leg and soaped up her left.

"I'd kill for a pair of those new nylon stockings," Lydia said, ruefully regarding her own shaved legs.

Alice licked her lips and concentrated on pulling the razor slowly up her calf. She made it to the knee without a mishap.

"Hurry up, Alice. My mother's going to be finished in the garden in a minute, and she'll come looking for us."

"You'll have blood all over this tub if I hurry."

Alice started on the back of her leg. The razor caught on her heel, and when she took it away, blood oozed down the skin. "Look."

Lydia rolled her eyes. "I told you, go easy." She pressed her ear to the door and listened. "Okay, do we have our plan straight? Don't tell your mother you're sleeping over until tonight, so she doesn't have time to talk to my mother. If they don't have time to talk to each other, and we both come home early, they'll never catch on. Are you almost finished?"

"Yes. I just have one more section."

Alice left the bony front of her leg for last, afraid of peppering it with cuts as she had the other leg. She brought the razor up lightly, barely touching the skin, and made it over the shin without drawing blood. Handing the razor to Lydia, she wiped her leg with a towel. Lydia made her stand by the toilet, legs together, while she inspected her, front and back. "Not bad," she said. "The cuts won't show by tonight."

\* \* \*

"You've been working awfully hard," Evelyn said when Alice asked if she could spend the night at Lydia's. "Will can help me close up tonight. You go on."

Another time, Alice would have relished how easy it was to slip out of the store. She climbed the hill slowly, listening for jeeps coming down the road. At the top of the path, she met Lydia, who carried a paper bag in her hand.

"What's that?" Alice asked.

"Your dress. Come on."

They hurried up the road to Alice's house and went inside without turning on the lights. In the kitchen, Alice took off her shorts and blouse, and wriggled into the dress Lydia had provided, an old one of Betty's. With a full skirt and belted waist, and white polka dots on blue rayon, Alice had to admit the dress was better than anything in her closet. It was a little long, Lydia said, because of course all the dresses were shorter now, but otherwise the fit wasn't bad. Lydia fastened the buttons up the back and stood back, regarding Alice critically.

"If only we had some stockings." She stared at Alice's saddle shoes and socks for a long moment. "I guess your mother doesn't have any we could borrow."

"Not exactly."

"All right. Come here."

Lydia applied a thick smear of red lipstick to her lips while Alice stood as still as possible. She felt like a doll, like a thing whose arms and legs could be bent in any shape Lydia wanted, but she didn't care. Her body and her heart had ceased to belong to her a long time ago.

* * *

Alice had never seen so many men assembled in one place in her life. They lined the bar and stood in clusters around the pool table, throwing their heads back and opening their mouths to laugh. As she stepped inside the dance hall after Lydia, she glanced from side to side, looking for other females. At first she thought they were the only ones, until she spotted four girls at the bar, circled by a mass of uniformed men.

Lydia nudged her. "Look. Mainland girls."

"How'd they get here?"

"Silas Mitchell. He runs a taxi service in that old boat of his."

The girls from the mainland were perched on the bar stools, wearing brightly patterned dresses cinched in at the waist. Their red lips glistened in the dim light. Alice wondered if her own face looked that strange and garish.

A radio behind the bar blared a swing tune, but no one was dancing, and there was no band up on the stage. A couple of the men around the pool table waved, men Alice recognized from the store. No one else paid them any attention. There were at least fifteen sailors pressed around the mainland girls, all talking and laughing at once. The girls didn't even get a chance to say anything; they just smiled, turning their heads from one to the other as they fluttered their unnaturally thick eyelashes.

"Let's go," Alice said. "There's no band here. This is stupid."

"Go if you want to. I'm staying right here."

Without turning her head to see if Alice would follow, Lydia made her way to the pool table. Alice caught Silas Mitchell's eye behind the bar as she went after Lydia. He nodded and kept on uncapping beer bottles and sliding them toward the sailors. She had been worried that Silas would kick them out of the dance hall or report them to their mothers, but Lydia reassured her. "Silas? All he cares about is making money. He doesn't care how he makes it."

Lydia was almost to the pool table when two sailors separated themselves from the crowd around the bar and came toward them. Alice recognized the men they had met at the store.

"Hey, we were wondering when we'd see you down here," the blond one called. "You remember my friend, Brock, here, and I'm Ricky."

Alice reached for the dress, tugging it down at the waist, afraid that her slip was showing.

"What have you girls been up to?"

"Not much," Lydia answered.

Ricky raised his beer bottle in the air. "Why don't you get these girls a couple of beers, Brock?"

"Okay." Brock gave Alice a quick smile as he turned back toward the bar.

"How old are you girls, anyway?" Ricky asked.

"Eighteen." Lydia did not look at Alice. She answered quickly and held Ricky's gaze. It was not such a lie, Alice thought. In six months, she would turn eighteen, and Lydia would be eighteen in a few weeks.

"Eighteen? I'm nineteen myself, and Brock boy there is twenty. I saw the sign for your chicken supper coming up. You have dancing or anything?"

"Just a square dance," Lydia said.

"I'll bet the food's good. I could use some home cooking. I haven't had home cooking in ages. That mush they dish up down at the base hardly passes for food."

Ricky went on, talking about how he'd give anything for a decent steak with gravy and mashed potatoes and biscuits. His mother made the flakiest biscuits in the state of Illinois.

Brock returned with the beer and handed the bottles to Alice and Lydia. "He doesn't have any glasses," he said apologetically. "This isn't a real high-class place."

"What do you expect on Snow Island? The Ritz?" Ricky laughed. "This is a hell of a place to spend a war. My brother, Sam, he's over there in the Pacific somewhere, on a destroyer. And me? Where am I? Snow Island. My mother couldn't even find it on the map. You're where? she said. It ain't even on the map."

"I thought it was a code word when they told me. I didn't even think it was a real place," Brock said.

"It's on the map." Alice tried not to sound too defensive. The beer

214

bottle was cold in her hand. She had not lifted it to her lips yet.

"What?" Ricky asked.

"The island. It's on the map at the schoolhouse." She realized what she had said and stopped. Lydia was glaring at her.

"You girls spent your whole lives here?" Ricky said.

"Not my whole life," Lydia answered. "We inherited the inn when I was twelve and moved here. I was born in New Haven."

Ricky nodded. He had heard of New Haven.

"But Alice was born on the island. She's a real islander."

"I bet it's a nice place to grow up," Brock said. "It's just a lousy place to spend a war."

"Yeah. Lousy place to spend a war. You can say that again." Ricky raised his beer bottle. "Come on, girls. Drink up so I can get us another round before Mitchell sells out."

Alice held the bottle to her mouth. The golden liquid was bitter and cold going down.

"Snow was attacked in the Revolutionary War," Lydia said. "The British wiped out the whole island. They burned all the houses and killed all the sheep."

"Yeah, well that was the Revolutionary War," Ricky responded. "The Nazis aren't going to make it into the bay, not if we can help it. And if they do, we can kiss it good-bye. We can all start taking German lessons."

"Nobody's going to need German lessons." Brock drained the last of the beer in his bottle. A pink flush had spread across his face.

"Hey, are you empty? I'm empty," Ricky said. "Snag that table, girls. We'll be back with refills."

They sat at a small table against the wall, one of only a few in the place. Alice drained the beer in long gulps. Lydia clinked her bottle against Alice's and did the same.

"Bad news," Ricky said as he set two glasses of light-colored liquid in front of them. "Mitchell's out of beer again. I don't know why he can't get in a bigger order."

"We told him last night he wasn't gonna make it to the end of the week." Brock pulled his chair up next to Alice, so he was seated between her and Lydia. He carried two more glasses that were filled with ginger ale.

"Looks like we gotta go to plan B." Ricky reached inside his shirt and pulled out a silver flask. "This ginger ale's deadly if you drink it straight. Makes your mouth pucker up it's so sweet. But this'll spruce it up." He unscrewed the cap of the flask and held it over Alice's glass. "What do you say?"

"What is it?" Alice asked.

"Whiskey. Slides down smooth as silk. Best stuff we could find last time we were over in Barton. You'll like it." He splashed the gold liquid into both their glasses, filling them to the brim.

Alice brought the glass to her lips. At first she didn't taste anything besides the ginger ale, but then she felt the whiskey, hot inside her chest. The warm, acrid taste spread through her mouth. Not bad, she thought, not nearly as bad as that awful gin she and Lydia found in a cupboard at the inn and drank out of teacups one afternoon when they were fifteen.

Ricky proposed a toast to victory for the Allies, and they all raised their glasses. The liquid in Ricky's glass went sloshing over the edge and onto the table. The men were drunk already, Alice realized. She sipped her drink slowly. The men downed theirs in a few gulps and went back for more.

"Come on, Alice. Don't take forever about it," Lydia said when they were gone. She had emptied her glass and requested another.

Alice took two swallows in rapid succession. A slow, light warmth spread through her skull and made her face feel like it was covered with darting bits of electricity. She couldn't remember why she hadn't liked the gin. This was pleasant in a vague, warm sort of way.

Alice lost count of how many glasses of ginger ale she consumed. Every time her glass was empty, they brought another and added some whiskey from the flask. Her head grew lighter and lighter, until her neck seemed to disappear, and her head was there by itself, floating above her body. She thought it was just the cigarette Brock gave her, taking it from the pack and placing it between her lips and lighting it for her, because she could hardly taste the whiskey. But the dizziness was different from when she and Lydia smoked; there wasn't the sickness of the cigarette, and she felt strangely disconnected from everything around her, a sensation she liked, even welcomed.

Lydia leaned over the table, laughing at whatever Ricky said. Ricky pulled his chair close to hers and put his arm around her. Brock was speaking to Alice, saying something about the place where he was from. Iowa. A city called Des Moines. He said the word *city* self-consciously, ducking his head, and she wanted to laugh for a moment at the pure wonder and stupidity of people. What did the difference between a town and a city mean to her? His lips moved with a slow purposefulness, forming words. She couldn't take her eyes off them; they were so perfectly shaped, they looked like they could have been cut out of glass. She tried to keep track of what he was saying, but as soon as she got hold of one word, it was gone, and others were taking its place, others she couldn't make join up, one to the next. Something about how he went down and enlisted right after Pearl Harbor, the day after Roosevelt declared war, and his mother cried. He was good-looking, Alice realized, in a homely way.

The radio music grew louder, swinging up to the roof and back down. When she glanced toward the bar, she saw that the mainland girls were gone. A group of sailors remained pressed around the pool table, but the bar was empty.

"Want to dance?" Brock asked.

"Sure."

She couldn't remember getting up from the table and crossing the floor. Suddenly she was there, in the center of the room, pressed to his long torso, turning in circles, quick and light as the music itself. He held her hand tight and kept his other hand against the small of her back, and somehow he made her legs move, as if he were pulling on strings attached to the spot behind her knees. She swung one way, then the other, pivoting with his body, coming round at just the moment he seemed to want her to come round. Lydia went past in a rush of warm air and color. The hand Ricky held to Lydia's shoulder appeared unnaturally large, looming out of the half-light and disappearing.

Then the music was gone, and she was still, leaning her head against his chest and feeling the heat flush from her neck into her face. "Outside," she said breathlessly. "I wanna go outside."

He steered her toward the door with one hand on her shoulder, and she was surrounded by blackness wheeling before her eyes, and the air was clean and sharp on her skin. She felt herself breathing, sucking in the air; she turned her head to look at the stars, and there was something damp and hard against her back, and her head hurt like someone had hit her from behind.

"Whooa," he said, bending over her and taking her hands in his. "Lost your balance there."

He laughed, a short, gruff sound like the bark of a fox in the woods over by the sandy beach, and pulled her up so she was seated on the ground, her legs out straight in front of her. She thought he said something, something that came out of the night and went away, about how he didn't have much balance himself either.

"It's . . . cig'rettes," Alice mumbled. "Makes me dizzy."

He laughed again. "Yeah, makes me dizzy, too." He bent forward, kneeling in the grass. The white of his pants legs shone. "But not too dizzy? You aren't too dizzy, are you?"

She shook her head, but thought better of the impulse almost immediately and tried to stop it. Her head seemed to be filled with gallons of water sloshing from side to side. Like a tidal wave, she thought, and then she was getting sick, leaning over the damp grass and letting it all come up. What a terrible thing to do in front of this man, Brock, was that really his name? It seemed like an unlikely name for him.

"Oh jeez," he said. "I'm sorry. I didn't know. We shouldn't have given you that stuff. Are you all right? Here, come on."

He took her by the elbows and helped her across the grass. "I'll be right back. Don't go anywhere, okay? I'll be back in a minute."

He returned a long time later with something in his hand. It looked like a tiny, transparent globe jiggling in the dark until he got closer, and there was something cold against her lips, and she realized it was a glass.

"Here — take some." He tipped the glass forward and let the water trickle into her mouth.

"Now spit it out. Come on." He patted her on the back.

She let the water go onto the ground, on the downhill side of her, and brought the glass to her lips again. The water was like a cold finger, sliding down her throat and through her body, making her clean. He took the glass and stood up, swaying like a tree in the wind. "I'll be right back, okay? Don't go anyplace."

She wondered why he kept saying that. She had no intention of going anywhere. The moon hung over the water down below, making a shiny path she could just see through the trees. Had the troubled face of the moon been there in the sky for hours, watching her, watching every sorry person on earth? It could be midnight, or three in the morning; she wasn't sure. She couldn't even remember what time of year it was. It seemed cold enough to be winter, but she wasn't wearing a sweater, which meant it must be summer. She gazed at her bare arms and wondered why they weren't covered.

The door to the dance hall slammed shut, and someone approached. The door slammed again, and there were more of them.

"Brock boy, what are you up to?" someone called.

"Nothing. Jus' taking this girl home."

Laughter carried across the grass, and the sound of murmuring voices, heading toward the road. "Make sure you get her back in time for school, Evans."

"Aww, eat it, Billings," he muttered. "She's eighteen."

There was more laughter; then silence.

"Come on," he said softly, taking her by the hands and pulling her to her feet. "Let's walk. It'll sober you up some."

"Where's Lydia?"

"I don' know. She's with Ricky — playing pool. They'll be 'long. Come on."

He put his hand on her shoulder and led her down the path toward the shore. The moon wobbled on the water. It made Alice feel shaky to look at it. She tried to concentrate on walking, placing her feet one in front of the other. Beside her the white of his pants legs lifted and fell back, like a flag attempting to raise itself. She felt something on her shoulders. His fingers, pressing into her. He pulled her in, close to him. Her hip bumped against his thigh.

The pebbles slid from under her on the beach. He caught her by the elbow as she pitched forward. "Hey," he said with a laugh, "watch where you're going."

They came to sand, and she felt steadier. She took in deep breaths. The moon stopped moving quite so much on the water.

"Let's sit, huh?" He patted the surface of a large rock.

The stone was cold against the back of her legs. He put his arm around her and bent over, placing his lips on hers. She tried to think why she shouldn't kiss him. She knew she shouldn't, but for a moment she couldn't place the reason, and then she realized that for the first time in weeks she had forgotten Ethan Cunningham. She was struck with the force all over again of what he had done and knew it didn't matter who she kissed now. She could kiss anyone, but she didn't want to.

The sailor's shirt smelled of fresh ironing, and though the scent was nothing like the mingled odor of cigarettes and turpentine Ethan gave off, it made her think of him, of what it was like to smell another person. She kissed him back, clasping her hands around his neck, and wondered if there would come a time when everything she felt and smelled and touched no longer reminded her of Ethan.

He pulled away. "You feel all right now?"

"Yes."

"I'm sorry about the whiskey. That was Ricky's idea."

She reached up, pulling his face back down to hers, and pressed her lips against his. He put his arms around her, holding her close. His body was warm, like a cave where she could hide. She felt almost nothing as he kissed her again and again, nothing but a queasy sensation that started in her stomach and went in and out of her head, but she didn't want the kissing to stop, she didn't want to let go.

"Do you have a boyfriend?" he whispered.

"No."

"I had a girl in high school, but it didn't work out. She married someone else."

She tried to focus on his eyes, but they were so close. His face remained a white, featureless blur. His breath smelled bitter and sweet at the same time, like the whiskey. She wondered how long this would last, this strange watery sensation, her mind detached from itself, all loose and rubbery.

"I better take you home," he said. "It's late."

He helped her off the rock, and they walked down the beach toward the store. She did not want him to see where she lived, the outhouse in back, the missing shingles.

"I just live up the hill," she said when they reached the road. "You don't need to walk me."

He leaned over and kissed her briefly. "Thanks for dancing with me." He ducked his head shyly, the way he had when he told her where he was from.

Alice said good-bye and made her way as quickly up the hill as her wobbly legs would take her, relieved to see that the windows of her house were dark.

# — CHAPTER 22 —

When she woke, there was something thick and numb in her mouth, like a rag pressed behind her teeth. She lay there for a long moment before she realized the parched thing was her tongue. Her head throbbed, and she couldn't imagine what had happened to her. Then she remembered: the whiskey, lurching down the beach with the sailor, sitting on the rock and feeling his lips on hers as though the sensation were occurring far away, across the ocean where the bombs were falling; as though she participated in the touching only by accident, because she happened to be there. She sat up slowly, swung her legs over the side of the bed, and stared out the window. The sun, just risen, made a pink path across the water behind two quahoggers' skiffs. She could tell the day would be a hot one, with the air already breathless and still.

"You don't look good," Evelyn said when Alice came down the stairs. "Was it something you ate?"

Alice said no, she didn't think it was something she ate, and made herself a piece of toast. Evelyn had woken when she came in the night before. Alice stood by the sofa and explained that she was back from Lydia's because she wasn't feeling well. In her sleepy state, Evelyn didn't even turn on the light.

Will was seated at the table, eating a bowl of cereal, his second breakfast of the morning.

"When'd you get home?" he asked between gulped spoonfuls.

"Last night. I got sick."

"Puking sick?"

"No, just sick. Did you check for eggs already?"

"Yes. That speckled hen is laying again."

Alice took the chair beside him and forced herself to chew the dry toast while her mother chattered about the Fourth of July parade. It would be the biggest parade ever in Barton, but how were the islanders going to get there, with the ferry running just once a day?

"I can't bear the idea of missing it," Evelyn said. "They say they'll have ten different bands this year. Don't think you're staying behind this time, Alice. It's your duty, your patriotic duty, to go."

Alice sipped from a glass of water and stared at the front page of the newspaper that had come the day before. The headline ran in block letters across the top of the page: "Germans Gain, Red Armies Hold Intact, Rommel's Forces Thirty Miles From Matruth, Churchill Returns Safely to England."

"You don't have to go to church if you don't feel up to it," Evelyn said.

No, Alice responded, she would go. She set the plate and glass in the sink and checked the state of her hair in the mirror. Frizzy strands framed her head. In the heat, her hair would not lie flat, no matter how many times she wet it down and pulled a comb through. She followed her mother to the door.

Outside, her eyes smarted in the sun. Evelyn told Will to tuck in his shirt, and the three of them went down the hill to the church. Alice was grateful for the darkened interior when she stepped inside. She slipped into the back row.

"What's wrong with you?" her mother hissed, waving her toward a pew at the front.

Alice shook her head and stayed by herself, watching as her mother and Will went forward, and others came through the door, whispering hello. Mr. and Mrs. Giberson arrived with Pete but not Lydia. Alice wondered if they had been found out.

The visiting minister came over on the Saturday ferry and spent the night at the inn. Retired from a Congregational church on the mainland, he was a short, fat little man with wisps of white hair. Lydia said he snored so loudly, they could hear him all the way downstairs at the inn. As he bent over the prayer book, reading in a monotone, his glasses slid down his nose. He pushed them back into place, repeating the gesture every few minutes like a nervous tic. Alice tried to follow the service, but she could not stop watching his glasses, wondering if they would slide right off his sweaty face to the floor.

When the last notes of the final hymn sounded, Alice waited at the back for her mother and ushered her quickly outside, so she would not have a chance to talk with Mrs. Giberson.

"We better get the store open," Alice said. "There's summer people waiting already."

* * *

Alice tried to find things to do behind the counter that did not require much thought or effort. After a while, her head stopped throbbing, and the window no longer vibrated when she looked at it. She felt hunger again, a reassuring sensation. At noon she went up to the house for a sandwich and put on her bathing suit. Owen Pierce was sitting on the porch when she returned to the store. "We're in for a hot spell," he said. "Sky this morning had that haze doesn't lift for days."

Alice sat at the end of the dock in her bathing suit and shorts, feeling the heat on her back. Behind her, a squeal of brakes sounded as Lydia dropped her bicycle in the dirt by the gas pump.

"Hot enough, huh?" Lydia said as she came down the dock, kicking her sneakered feet in front of her.

"Where have you been? I was afraid your mother figured it out."

Lydia took off her shoes and sat next to Alice. "I had to stay home from church because I was sick to my stomach. Where have I been? I should be asking you that question. We came out of the dance hall and you were gone."

"We took a walk down the beach."

Lydia eyed her. "And? Did he kiss you?"

"Yes."

"Well, congratulations, Alice. It's about time you got kissed. Was it a French kiss?"

"Lydia."

"Ricky French-kissed me." Lydia swung her feet back and forth over the water. "My mother gave me the old eagle eyes this morning, but I just played dumb. She's so worried about Hank, she doesn't care about much else anyway. Boy, was I drunk. I nearly got sick, really."

"I did get sick."

"In front of him? Shoot, Alice, that's awful. I had a splitting headache when I woke up. It didn't help to have my mother looking at me cross-eyed. You know Ricky's from Chicago. He says Lake Michigan is as big as the ocean. When he got here, he says the ocean reminded him of Lake Michigan. Isn't that funny? Ricky's all right. He sure kisses better than old Jack Cheaving. He didn't know a thing. Charlie Henderson, too. He wasn't any better."

"When did you kiss Charlie Henderson?"

"Oh, I don't know. At one of the bonfires last summer."

"How come you never told me?"

"It was nothing, believe me."

Alice knew she had no grounds for reproaching Lydia about keeping secrets, but she was hurt anyway.

"I'm frying," Lydia said after a long pause. "Want to go in?"

They pulled off their shorts and tossed them on the dock. Lydia reached for Alice, and they jumped off the end of the dock, hands linked. For a fraction of second, they hung suspended. Alice felt Lydia's hand break away, and she plunged into the coolness of the water with her eyes closed and mouth clenched shut. Her feet came to the sandy bottom, and she pushed off, shooting back toward the surface. She opened her eyes and stretched out her arms, reaching for the light.

When she surfaced, she heard the slow slap of arms against water. Lydia was swimming out, hand over hand. Alice paddled back to the ladder and climbed out. The water was cool, but not cool enough. She could feel the oppressive heat of the air as soon as she lifted herself onto the warm wood of the dock. Lydia turned and waved Alice back into the water. "Come on."

Alice jumped again. The water shot up her nose, and she came to the surface sputtering and laughing, seeing Lydia swim toward her.

\* \* \*

They spent nights all that week playing cards over the store counter, Lydia anxiously turning her head every time the screen door opened, hoping for the men to appear. She talked Alice into letting her help close up, so they could keep the store open as late as possible, but the only person of note to stop in was Phoebe Shattuck, her dress stretched tight over an obviously pregnant stomach.

Since Nate had gone off to the Army, the sound of Phoebe's piano playing carried down the hill for hours at a time. Mrs. Cunningham had guessed she might be pregnant back in May, when she first started to show. Now there was no question. She came into the store with Rachel and asked for milk and eggs. Alice was writing the price of the items in the logbook when Rachel said, "My mother's going to have a baby."

"Rachel," Phoebe said reprovingly, clearly embarrassed.

Alice wasn't sure what to say. Lydia, who sat on a stool shuffling the cards, was no help.

"I bet you'll like having a brother or sister." Alice addressed the words to Rachel.

"A sister," Rachel responded. "I want a sister."

Phoebe took the sack in which Alice had placed the groceries. "We'll be happy with whatever God gives us, Rachel."

Lydia did not speak until Phoebe and Rachel left the store and their murmuring voices moved toward the road. "Does she pay her bill these days?"

"Of course she pays her bill."

"She didn't used to."

"She's got money now. Nate sends her something."

Lydia dealt out the cards. "Where the hell do you think Ricky and Brock are?"

"At the base."

Lydia sighed and scooped up her hand.

When Brock did appear late on Thursday night, Lydia had already gone, and Alice was about to close up. The night was clear and warm. She was sweeping the floor and heard a jeep come droning down the road and pull up out front. Two men got out, but one stayed by the jeep. Brock came through the door, his head bowed. Alice quickly smoothed her hand over her hair, feeling for stray tendrils, and set the broom against the wall.

"I'm sorry we haven't been by," he said. "I wanted to see you, but we've been busy down at the base." His voice had more of a twang than she recalled, and his eyes struck her now as terribly small, set too close together in his face. "I just came to tell you our orders came through."

"Orders?"

"Our orders to ship out. They finally came through. We're leaving before sunrise. There's not much left to do here. Just a few of the men will stay. I thought I should come and tell you. We're not supposed to say anything, but I thought, you know, I could tell you. I'm sorry. I thought I could see you again, but I'm on duty tonight. I have to get back. We're not supposed to be off base, actually."

Alice nodded.

"Well, I'm glad I got to meet you. Ricky said to tell your friend good-bye."

"Lydia."

"Right, Lydia."

He glanced quickly around the store, then leaned over the counter. She stood still and let him kiss her on the lips. A bright blush spread over his face, and Alice felt for a moment that she had tricked him into thinking she was someone other than who she was.

"Maybe I'll see you again some time." He jammed his hands in his front pockets and left, glancing over his shoulder when he got to the door to give her an awkward smile.

"Good luck," she called, realizing the moment the words were out of her mouth that she should have thought of something better to say.

The jeep's tires spun in the gravel, and they started up the hill. A single star flickered above the lamppost up on the road. She watched the jeep move off, until it was only a gray blur.

# — CHAPTER 23 —

Lydia was already perched in the lookout when Alice arrived. "You're late," she called as Alice climbed the stairs.

"My mother's got a headache. I had to leave Will at the store."

Lydia sat cross-legged, her gaze fixed on the sky. "How come it's so quiet? I couldn't see anybody down at the base."

Alice hesitated, wondering if there was some way she could avoid telling Lydia. "They're gone."

Lydia gave her a confused look and went back to watching overhead.

"Brock came by last night, after you left. They shipped out this morning, early. Ricky said to tell you good-bye."

Alice studied the hazy blanket of the sky and waited for Lydia to say something, but she was quiet. "I guess they didn't have much notice."

"Guess not, if Ricky couldn't even say good-bye himself. Well, it's not like I was in love with him or anything. He wasn't all that good-looking even. Shoot, my mother's going to be disappointed about the chicken supper. They were hoping for a big crowd from the base. She and Mrs. Cunningham were set to make thirty pies."

Lydia went on about the food that had already been ordered and what her mother would do. When Alice stole a glance at her, she saw that Lydia had her arms folded over her chest. There was defiance in the gesture and hurt, though Lydia would never let on that Ricky's departure made a difference to her.

The next day, when they boarded the ferry to go over to Barton for the parade, Lydia came running up the gangplank in a blue skirt and red blouse, with a white belt around her waist. She waved to Captain Tony and called to Will, who clutched an American flag in his hand, "Got a flag for me?" She went from group to group on the deck, talking and laughing, making sure everyone took notice of her patriotic outfit.

Alice stood at the railing next to Pete as the ferry pulled away. Captain Tony had skipped coming to the island two days that week, so he could make a special trip over and back to take the islanders to the parade. Over the sound of the ferry's engine, Alice could hear Lydia joking with Owen Pierce. "Have you ever actually seen a hundred-year-old quahog?"

"Lydia's happy today," Alice said to Pete.

"She loves a parade. And any excuse to leave the island."

"Everyone's leaving. Even you're going to leave."

Pete stared in the direction of the mainland. "I wish I wasn't leaving, believe me. Not that I don't want to serve. I do. I just wish . . ." He trailed off, holding his open hands over the water.

The cruelty of so many young men going off to an uncertain fate was too great to take in. Alice did not want any of them to go, but most of all, she realized, she did not want Pete to go. She couldn't imagine Snow without his steady presence.

In Barton, people lined the sidewalks three and four deep, with the children seated on the curb, waving their flags. A somber mood hung over Front Street, where every building was draped with bunting, and yet there was a nervous excitement among the crowds. Alice knew that she and everyone else in Barton that day would always remember it, would tell their children and their grandchildren about the troops marching past, their faces flushed with eagerness and fear.

The islanders stayed together in a spot up the street from the ferry landing, applauding as each new unit of sailors passed. The men had come from the bases in Newport and Davisville to march in the parade. They moved with the precision of a machine, stepping in time, without looking to the left or right.

Suddenly Lydia was clutching Alice's hand. "Is that him?" she said, her voice just audible over the marching drums of a band behind the troops.

Alice followed her gaze. The uniform was the same, and the sailor had blond hair that hugged his head, but he was not Ricky. This man was taller, with wide shoulders and a more serious look. Lydia was about to step forward. "It's not him," Alice said, pulling her back.

"Of course it's not him," Lydia answered. "I was just testing you."

Lydia waved her flag vigorously and cheered at the men going past. Alice searched, too, but she did not see Ricky or Brock, though after a while, all of them looked like the one Lydia was waiting for.

On the ferry ride home, Lydia was quiet. She sat beside her mother on the deck, the flag stuck in her skirt pocket. Alice stood at the railing with Will, watching for the island. Pete came alongside them and gazed out over the water. Alice felt that she knew what he was thinking. He was seeing all those men in uniform and imagining how he would be one of them soon. She wished she could do something to keep him from going.

\* \* \*

A week after the parade, the islanders gathered at the Improvement Center. Mrs. Giberson had canceled the square dance and turned the supper into a birthday party for Pete and Lydia. She had hoped to raise enough for a new fire truck for the volunteer fire department, but there was no chance of that now, with the base nearly deserted.

The islanders and a few summer people filled three long tables. The Improvement Center was quieter than it had ever been, and people talked in restrained voices. Alice joined Lydia and Pete, avoiding the table where her mother sat with Mrs. Cunningham and Martha.

Mrs. Giberson served cake with raspberries for dessert, and they all sang "Happy Birthday." When the polite applause died out, Mr. Giberson stood up and tapped the side of his lemonade glass with a spoon.

"I have an announcement to make," he said, clearing his throat. "These are hard times. We've all had to say good-bye to our boys. Next week we'll say good-bye to another one and to his sister." He raised his glass toward Lydia and Pete. "I'd like to propose a toast to all the brave men and women who are serving our country."

Everyone raised their glasses, and a murmur went around the room. Alice stared at Lydia. People flocked around the table, shaking hands with Pete and Lydia and wishing them well. Alice sat with her half-eaten cake in front of her, continuing to stare at Lydia. She had not believed for a minute that Lydia would actually go, though now she recognized that she should have known.

Owen Pierce and the others went back to their seats to drink their coffee.

"I can't believe it," Alice said.

Lydia smiled proudly. "I could get sent overseas, if I'm lucky."

"Don't push it," Pete said.

"Well, you'll get sent overseas, won't you?"

"Probably."

"So why can't I?"

They were leaving in just five days. "Who's going to do airplane duty with me?" Alice said.

"There's always Will. I almost forgot — I told Mr. Brovelli I'd come relieve him at the lookout tower so he could get something to eat," Pete said.

"Pete, you can't leave. You're the guest of honor." Lydia tossed her rumpled napkin on the table.

"I think the party's about over. Come on, walk me to the lookout." Pete stood up, giving Lydia and then Alice a questioning look.

Lydia agreed to go, and Alice, still stunned by the news, left her plate on the table and went with them. They had reached the door when Mrs. Giberson called Lydia back. Alice was ready to follow her, but Pete grabbed her by the hand. "Come on, just walk me to the lookout."

Before she could refuse, he opened the door and ushered her out into the clean air.

The heat had broken, and the days were still and crisp again. Alice walked at Pete's side down the road.

"I heard Ethan Cunningham got married," Pete said.

When Alice did not respond he asked, "Did his mother tell you?"

"Yes."

"Who'd he marry?"

"Someone he knew before, from college."

"But they hadn't been in touch?"

"I guess not." Alice could not bring herself to look at Pete. She wondered, as she had before, if he somehow knew all about her and Ethan. "I didn't think Lydia would go," she said, trying to change the subject.

"I didn't think my mother would let her, but Lydia's been working on her for months, ever since Betty signed up with the Red Cross. My mother didn't have a chance, really."

At the store, they turned up the road past Alice's house and took the path that wound through the woods across the island to the schoolhouse. It was dark and cool inside the trees.

"You're going to keep working at the store?" Pete asked.

"I guess. My mother needs the help. I can't imagine what it'll be like to have Lydia gone — and you — and everyone else."

"Lydia will miss you, even if she doesn't let on now. I'll miss you, too."

Alice kept her gaze on the ground.

"I've almost got enough saved up for that boat. Remember? When I come back I'm going to build a house and start quahogging."

Alice sensed he was trying to tell her something. "Where will you build your house?"

"I was thinking down near Gooseneck Cove, if I can get the land. Alice —"

He spoke in a serious tone, and she realized, in the moment when she waited for what would come next, that she wanted to hear what he had to say now, that a part of her was pulled toward Pete and his hopes. But just then a long whistle sounded through the trees, and they looked up to see Ernie Brovelli waving at them from the lookout tower.

"Any chicken left?" he shouted.

Pete called back that they had saved a plate for him. He paused in the clearing in the path. Alice stood beside him, waiting for Pete to fin-ish what he had started to say. He glanced up at the tower. Mr. Brovelli continued to peer down at them. "I guess I better get up there," Pete said.

He held her eyes for a moment, turned, and hurried down the path. Alice did not want to walk back with Mr. Brovelli. She quickly retraced her steps, going back into the woods by herself.

# — CHAPTER 24 —

Alice sat on Lydia's bed in her room at the inn, watching her pack.

"You've got to write me, Alice. At least once a week. Even if there's nothing to say. I feel terrible, leaving you here with nobody but Will and your mother and all the old people."

Alice shrugged. "I'll survive."

"Maybe they'll send some more men over to the base."

"Maybe."

"Here. I want you to have this." Lydia handed her a tube of lipstick. "I can get some when I get to the mainland. You keep this in case any more sailors show up down at the base."

Alice rolled the tube between her fingers.

"I'll send you some nylon stockings, too, if I can find any." Lydia lowered the lid to her trunk. "It won't close. Come here and sit on it."

Alice climbed up on the bed and slid onto the bulky trunk. The latch still did not meet.

"God, Alice, you hardly weigh a thing. Try to be heavier."

Alice shifted her weight, and Lydia got the trunk to close.

"Do you think you can carry that?"

"No, but I'll find some man in uniform to help me." Lydia winked.

Alice could see her, standing on a train platform, just waiting for that man to come along.

Lydia placed her hand on Alice's shoulder. "I wish you were coming with me. It's not too late. I bet they would keep us together if we asked."

"I can't go."

"Why not?"

"My mother can't run the store by herself."

Lydia pursed her lips but said nothing.

All of the islanders showed up at boat time the next day. Will skipped back and forth excitedly in front of the porch. His one hope was that the war would last long enough so he could go fight, too.

Lydia gave Alice a quick hug as the ferry pulled in to the dock. "This is it," she said. "Write me."

Pete carried her trunk up the gangplank while Mrs. Giberson put her arms around Lydia and cried. The other islanders lined up to say good-bye. Pete came back through the crowd to where Alice stood, at the edge of the porch.

"Write me, will you?" he asked.

She nodded.

"I'll think of you every day, Alice. You and Snow." He leaned over and hugged her and brushed his lips across her cheek, grasping her hand as he broke away. Alice felt the pressure of his fingers around hers and held his hand tight for a second.

"Pete," his mother called. "It's time."

He let go of her hand and turned toward the dock.

Alice stood with the rest of the islanders, waving, until the ferry pulled out of sight around Gull Island.

\* \* \*

Everyone had gone. The fact surprised Alice again each morning as she made her way to the store and put on coffee for her mother and Miss Weeden and Owen Pierce. She could not have imagined Snow coming to this if she had tried. The island had been swept bare of life so quickly, she could not comprehend the change. It seemed like only weeks since Pete had come charging into the store to tell her about Pearl Harbor.

The Sibleys came to stay for a week, but David and Meg were not with them. Mrs. Henderson planned to spend most of the summer on the island by herself, with her husband coming over on the weekends. The other houses in Snow Park would remain empty, though the Cheavings thought they might be over for Labor Day. Alice kept adjusting the orders for the store, getting less with each passing week.

She spent her time reading old copies of *Movie Mirror* behind the counter and waiting for Will to return from airplane spotting. He and Mr. Brovelli and Owen Pierce divided most of the shifts now, and she filled in when she could, when her mother wasn't up at the house with a headache. It was the heat, Evelyn said, that seized her by the temples and held on for hours at a time. Alice stared at the photos of movie stars in the magazines until they blurred before her eyes.

She was minding the store by herself on the Saturday when the letter came. She saw it the moment she dumped the contents of the mail bag on the counter, an envelope addressed to her, postmarked New Jersey. After staring at the envelope for a long time, she ripped the flap. The letter filled one side of a sheet of lined paper, the words written in a precise hand that made her instantly angry.

"Dear Alice, I am sorry not to have written sooner. I'm sure you wondered why you hadn't heard from me, and then you must have learned my news. I can assure you it was as much a surprise to me as it must have been to you. Charlotte and I cared for each other when we were in college, but neither of us expected to see the other again. The time we spent together was in the past, we thought, and then some old friends brought us together in the city. The rest, as they say, is history. So here I am, a married man. Funny, isn't it? You would like Charlotte. Maybe you'll get to meet her someday — after the war. We seem to have to add that on to the end of every sentence these days — after the war. I'll always remember the time you and I spent together. You made a long winter on Snow less long. Take care of yourself — don't get caught skinny-dipping — and say hello to old Owen Pierce and Miss Weeden and anyone else for me. — Ethan."

Alice threw some kindling wood and crumpled newspaper into the stove and lit a match. Once the pile had caught, she tossed Ethan's letter on top. She left the door open, watching the paper as it curled and blackened. A little smoke billowed out, the letter flamed up, and the Ethan she had known was dead. Another Ethan, one she did not recognize, could go on living if he wanted to.

"Whew, what do you want a fire for?" Evelyn said, slamming the screen behind her.

"I thought you had a headache."

"Of course I have a headache. I've got a headache all the time, don't I? But I can't spend the rest of my life on that blasted sofa. Will you close that stove? I'm going to suffocate."

Alice banged the door shut and turned the latch.

Evelyn held her hands over her ears. "Softly," she said warningly. "Was there any mail?"

"No." Alice eyed the unexamined envelopes uneasily, afraid another would jump out at her.

"Well, are you going to stand there all day?" Her mother gestured toward the pile.

Alice sat behind the counter and slowly made her way through the stack, staring at the names that seemed to go in and out of focus while her mother prattled on about the heat.

"Really, Alice, what in the world made you start a fire?"

Alice shrugged. "I was just burning some trash."

"Mrs. Giberson said to tell you to come over to listen to 'Your Hit Parade' tonight if you want."

Alice shook her head. The thought of sitting in that living room by herself with Mr. and Mrs. Giberson, listening to the top ten hits, was unbearable.

She could not think of anything she would rather do less the next night than go to the Cunninghams', but when the time came, she carried her mother's sewing basket, and they started down the road. The alternative was to sit by herself behind the counter or up at the house, absorbing the silence. Will was over at the Brovellis', playing with Eddie. The fog had rolled in that afternoon, and the wet air clung to their faces as they made their way toward the lighthouse.

A teapot sat in the middle of the kitchen table. The pieces of the new quilt they had started a couple of weeks earlier were spread around it. Alice took a seat beside her mother and opened the sewing box, getting needle and thread for both of them.

"It's so damp, I put on the tea early. Martha, get some cups for the ladies." Mrs. Cunningham gestured toward the shelf above the sink. "How are your headaches, Evelyn?"

"Better, thank you. I don't seem to like the heat, but when it cools off, they're not so bad."

"I don't like the heat, either, though this sort of weather is really worse. My fingers gnarl up."

Martha brought the cups to the table and poured out the tea.

"You must miss Lydia," Mrs. Cunningham said to Alice. She moistened the end of a piece of thread with her lips and pushed it through the eye of her needle. "The island's too quiet, even for me."

Alice nodded. Steam rose from the teacup in front of her, warm and heavy with a scent she couldn't place. She knew it was ordinary black tea, but the aroma suddenly seemed foreign and repellent. Alice reached for the pitcher of milk and poured some into her cup, but the milk did not improve the smell. She peered into the teacup, feeling like she might be sick.

"Have you heard from Ethan?" Evelyn asked.

"I had a letter the other day. He's going to be sent to Gulfport, Mississippi when his training is over. From there we don't know. I'm guessing the Pacific. I hate to think of it. And that poor girl he's married.

Imagine being left alone like that, married such a short time. We had a better start, Mr. Cunningham and I. But these are the times we're living in, I guess. You have to marry when you can. I wrote and told her she was welcome to come live here with us on the island. I had a lovely letter back from her. She works in an office in New York and has her own apartment with another girl, so she'll just stay there. Her people are from up the Hudson. I guess she can get home to see them on the train easy enough."

Alice bit her lip, forcing herself to concentrate on her stitching, wondering why she had come. When she looked up, she found Martha staring at her.

"Are you all right, Alice? You don't have any color in your face."

"I don't?"

"Mother, look at that pallor."

Mrs. Cunningham regarded her for a moment. "Have some tea. That'll make you feel better."

Alice raised the cup to her lips and replaced it in the saucer as quickly as possible, afraid again that she would be sick.

"Do you want to lie down?" Martha said.

Alice shook her head.

"We were hoping Ethan would get enough leave time before his training is over to come visit with his girl," Mrs. Cunningham continued, returning to her stitching. "I guess I should call her his wife, but it seems funny to say that word when I've never laid eyes on her. Anyway, it doesn't look like he'll get enough time to make it up here."

Mrs. Cunningham kept on talking, speculating on whether Ethan's bride would ever want to come to Snow. "She sounds like a city girl, doesn't she, Martha?"

"I guess. We don't actually know a whole lot about her."

"Well, I just mean she's got a job and lives right there in the city and all. She might not take to island life."

"Hasn't Ethan sent a picture?" Evelyn asked.

"Not yet. He said he would next time. I wrote him I wouldn't believe he was married until I saw it with my own eyes."

Alice stared at the small stitches that appeared beneath her hand, raising and lowering the needle mechanically, trying not to listen, but she could not block out the cheerful tone of Mrs. Cunningham's voice. She had nowhere to go these days. When she searched in her mind for a place to hide, she found nothing. Even Gooseneck Cove had deserted her.

In the morning the fog had lifted, but a sticky haze hung over the island. Alice sliced a piece of bread from the loaf and reached for a jar of jam. Before she could finish spreading the jam, she was overcome by nausea. Will was still upstairs getting dressed. She ran to the door, made it across the lawn, and threw up in the bushes. She didn't bring up much, but she kept on heaving for a long time. She put her hand to her head, feeling for a fever. Her forehead was covered with sweat, but she wasn't hot. Instead, she felt cold, filled with the dampness of the fog.

Back in the house, Alice patted her forehead with a dish towel and weakly called Will. She would skip breakfast. Once she reached the store, she would feel better.

"I guess we should go mow some lawns," Evelyn said when Alice and Will arrived at the store.

Mowing lawns used to be Will's business. Now the summer people were writing every week and asking Evelyn to take care of their lawns, since they wouldn't be coming to the island.

"I'll go," Alice offered.

"Are you sure? You weren't feeling well last night." Evelyn gave her a long look.

"I'm all right." Alice brushed past her mother and went to the door.

He had made her sick, Alice thought as she eased the truck up the hill to the road. The news of Ethan's marriage had made her physically ill. She hoped he was satisfied. At the Cheavings', she parked the truck at the edge of the road and unloaded the mower.

The nausea had passed, but she was still weak. She pushed the mower back and forth across the lawn, her arms feeling like they were made of rubber. The grass resisted her. When she was finally done, she let the handle of the mower fall to the ground and lay on her back, staring at the hot sky, wondering if Ethan had planned it all in some perverse way. Is this what you wanted? she longed to ask him. Is this what you intended?

Finally she rose and loaded the mower into the truck. As she drove back to the east side, she thought of the time after her father died, when her feelings of detachment from the world around her were so profound that she hardly recognized herself when she looked in the mirror. During those months of grief, the distance between herself and everything else seemed to serve some purpose. She could see no reason for feeling as she did now.

When Alice pulled the truck alongside the store, Owen Pierce was on the porch, puffing on his pipe and reading a newspaper.

"You over in Snow Park?" he asked.

"Yes."

"Anything going on over there?"

"Not really."

"Not much going on anywhere on this island, is there? Except for the heat. You could swim in this air. You feeling all right?" He folded the newspaper and gave her a close look. "You're kinda pale."

"I am?"

The knowledge hit her then. She had missed her last period. She had missed periods in the past, and when her period didn't come the last month, she had thought nothing of it. Now, submitting to his gaze, she realized maybe this time there was a reason.

"It must be the heat," she said, hurrying inside.

"Alice, you're back," her mother said. "I've been looking everywhere for those ration books. Are you sure the new ones came?"

"Yes. They're under the cash drawer. I told you."

"Oh, of course. Here they are." Evelyn took the books out of the register and waved them in the air. "Now what are we supposed to do with these things?"

Alice tried to think, but she couldn't. Her mind was like a wall she kept running into at full speed. "You put the stamps in the books. You paste them in."

"But how do you know which stamps to put where?"

"It says in the front."

Evelyn went on, complaining about how the ration points never added up right, while Alice tried to remember everything Lydia had ever told her about getting pregnant. When did you start to show? At three months, four months? She had no idea. How did you know for certain you were pregnant in the first place? Did you have to wait for a second missed period before you could be sure? She might have already missed two periods. Usually her mother asked, "Have you had your monthly?" embarrassing her beyond words. This month she had forgotten, too consumed with her headaches.

Alice tried to recall when Phoebe Shattuck was due. Alice thought that Phoebe would not deliver for another couple of months, but she was already huge, her dress stretched so tight across the mound of her belly that she looked hideous. Alice could not imagine herself looking like that, ever.

She counted the weeks since Ethan had gone. If she was pregnant, she was already past two months, though she could not believe this was so. How could you have something growing inside you without knowing it? Alice tried to think where she could go. She recognized instantly she could not stay on the island. She would have to leave, the sooner the better. She stared through the screen, searching the horizon beyond the dock.

"Alice, are you even listening to me?" her mother said.

"Yes, of course I'm listening to you."

"Well, how many stamps is a pound of sugar, then?"

Alice pointed at the chart on the wall. "It's right there."

# — CHAPTER 25 —

The night sky seemed to hug the island. George sat on the porch steps, listening to the cheeping of crickets in the marshes. Down below, the waves broke quietly on the shore, another kind of music.

He would leave soon and go back to that other world, where he lived in a single room and rose to the ring of the alarm clock in the morning. The days at the drugstore were endlessly alike. He stocked the shelves and made deliveries and wrapped packages. He carried Mrs. Foster's parcels home for her and collected a small tip. He ate his meals at the diner up the street from the drugstore; they knew what he wanted each day of the week and had the plate waiting for him when he arrived. It had taken years to get his life to this point, so orderly that he rarely needed to speak to anyone as he went through the day. Now, with the war, the streets and the shops were noisier, a paperboy was on every corner screaming the latest headline. It was hard to hold on to a routine.

On the island, it was quieter. He cringed to think of going back to New Jersey and the radio on all day in the drugstore. George pushed himself up from the porch step and crossed the lawn. Snow Park was so deserted this summer that he was able to walk about at night and even in the day without meeting anyone. There were no lights behind the windows of the houses. Even here blackout curtains were enforced. He passed the large structures, listening for the blare of a radio or the sound of laughter, but silence reigned. He thought of his first memories, when he was no more than three or four. There were only a couple of houses in Snow Park then, so the hillside belonged to them. He and Sarah would stand at the top of the hill to watch for ships heading to Providence and would guess at their cargo. "Toothpicks," Sarah might say. "Nails," George would shout. "String." "Wool." "Flour." "Chocolate." "Tin whistles." They would go on trading guesses, each one more absurd than the one before, laughing at the idea of a whole ship filled with cotton candy and paper airplanes.

They could wander along the shore all afternoon, searching for crabs and mussels, without meeting anyone, even in summer. They could stand at the summit of their hill, hooting and jumping up and down to get the attention of passing ships, and falling on the grass in a heap of laughter. George thought Sarah was happiest then, when he was young enough to share in all her games and odd delights, and they felt they owned everything they could see. Later, after Bertie had sold off the land, and they were confined to the lawn around the twin houses and the woods behind, she lost some of her spirit. She wouldn't wave at the passing ships anymore. "They can't see us, George," she would say, when he tried to coax her into gaiety.

As he grew older, her black days — the days when she couldn't get out of bed — came more often. For a long time, George blamed himself, certain he had failed Sarah in some fundamental way. "I'm sorry," he said one morning.

"For what?"

"Making you feel bad."

She grabbed his hand. "You don't make me feel bad, George. Never. Never, ever."

She sat up and swung her legs out of the bed, as if to show him she really meant it. She didn't have another black day for a long time after that, though George could tell there were days that came close. She would push herself out of bed, giving him a watchful look, and brush her hair with a vigor he knew she didn't feel. He wanted to tell her she didn't have to prove anything to him, but this was one of many things that couldn't be said.

Sarah would have appreciated the quiet that had come over Snow Park now. It was the only good thing about the war. The rest was disruption and anxiety and confusion. George stood at the top of the hill. A slice of moon hung over the water, touching everything with a thin, silver light. He seemed to hear Sarah's voice for a moment, shouting, "Bubble bath. Train sets. Monkeys." He moved on toward the water.

He did not see the girl until he had almost reached the shore. She was seated on a rock, knees pulled in to her chest. He tried to turn away, but his foot slid on the gravel, and she jerked around.

"I thought you were a deer," she said.

"I didn't see you," he explained.

Her bicycle lay on the ground beside her. He had never met the girl from the store over in Snow Park at night. She gestured toward a pile of something on the other side of the rock. "I found this in the water."

He stepped forward uncertainly and peered at the ground. He didn't see anything but a few pieces of broken wood.

"I think it's your boat," she said.

He looked more closely and saw traces of dark red paint. The largest piece was about four feet of gunwale, with an oarlock.

He stooped down and placed his hand on the splintered wood. "I always thought it would wash up on the other side of the channel."

"The tides are funny."

"Do you mind?" He gathered the pieces and carried them up toward the road. She watched him, but did not move from the rock. "I'd like to keep these," he said.

She nodded, as though telling him any explanation was unnecessary.

"I never gave you anything for that day, when you rowed out to get me. And the man, the lighthouse keeper."

"He's serving in the Signal Corps."

"I see." George rummaged in his pocket, wondering if he had any money with him, and what would be appropriate. Was five dollars too much?

Before he could offer her anything, she raised her hand. "I don't want anything. Really. Please."

He removed his hand from his pocket and turned back up the hill, muttering a quick goodnight. George carried the armload of scraps, with the longest piece tucked under his arm and dragging on the ground, back to the twin houses. He glanced over his shoulder to see if the girl watched him, but she continued to sit, staring at the water. He felt a kinship with her he could not explain.

George slid the pieces of wood beneath Sarah's porch, just far enough so that they still showed. At last he had something to tell Sarah, but what would he do now? How would he fill his days? There was nothing left to accomplish on Snow. He would have to leave. He would have to return to that other world and its frantic emptiness.

He went inside and climbed the stairs, glancing into Sarah's room as he went past. He looked at the closet, filled with his small collection of shirts and pants. He would leave soon.

# — CHAPTER 26 —

The sickness came when she least expected it, anytime during the day. She ate little and forced herself to get through it. Alice knew she did not have much time, but she needed to think, and suddenly thinking was harder than it had ever been before.

Lydia had told her once about a friend of her sister Betty's, a girl she worked with at the department store, who became pregnant. There were doctors who could take care of such things, Lydia had said knowingly. Alice paid little attention at the time, but now she tried to recall the story. The girl from the department store went to the doctor and had an operation to get rid of the baby. Where was that doctor? She was sure Lydia had told her. She ransacked her mind, angry at herself for all the times she had not listened to Lydia, all the times she dismissed her for being interested only in clothes and boys. The doctor must have been in Providence, or maybe even Boston. How would Alice ever find such a doctor? It was not the sort of thing they advertised. She considered writing to Lydia and dismissed the idea as impossible. Even if Lydia could remember or somehow get the information, Alice knew she could not tell her she was pregnant. She did not want Lydia to find out, ever. She did not know how to reach her now in any case. Lydia had written to say that she was sailing for England soon, where she would work as a Red Cross volunteer in the clubmobile canteens, delivering food and cigarettes to the Americans based there. She had somehow managed to make the Red Cross believe she was twenty-two, old enough to qualify, and convinced them that she was just the person to send overseas.

Alice supposed the operation would cost a great deal, if she could find a doctor. With business being so slow that summer, the extra money they had saved was rapidly dwindling. Even if there had been enough to pay for the operation, Alice knew she could not take that money. It was all that her mother and Will had to get through the winter. Whatever solution she came up with, she would have to make the money to pay for it herself. This, she recognized repeatedly, would mean leaving Snow, but to go where?

She cursed her own stupidity. Ethan had said they should be careful, that they didn't want "to be making any babies." Alice believed they were taking precaution enough when he pulled out. That last night, she had only wanted to hold him. She had not thought about the possibility of getting pregnant, or she had pushed the thought out of her mind. She had no one to blame but her own stupid self.

The end of July came and went. Alice fell into a routine of minding the store in the mornings and riding her bike aimlessly around the island in the afternoons, or sitting in the lookout tower by herself, searching the sky not for planes but for a plan, something, anything, that could save her. She met George Tibbits on one of her rides around the island, carrying his suitcase. She braked and came to a stop.

"Are you leaving?"

He glanced from side to side, as though assessing whether he had to give her an answer. "Yes. The ferry's coming this afternoon, isn't it?"

"It's supposed to."

"I'll settle my bill before I go."

She nodded, and he picked up his suitcase and moved on. He paid his bill and boarded the ferry that day, without further explanation. Alice felt an inexplicable sense of abandonment as she watched him climb the gangplank. For some reason, she had found it reassuring to know he was over there in Snow Park, to know that he would meander around the island day after day. His predictability had given order to a time that had no order, but now he turned out to be just as unpredictable as everyone and everything else.

The bouts of nausea continued, and her period did not come. She thought that she could see her waistline expanding, ever so slightly. One night, when Will had gone up to bed, Alice poured her mother a cup of coffee and sat across from her at the table.

"I'm going to have to leave the island," she said.

Evelyn stopped rolling a cigarette. "What do you mean, leave the island?"

"I'm pregnant," Alice said.

The paper and tobacco fell to the table, and Evelyn stared at her. "How did that happen?"

"In the usual way, I think." Alice tried not to laugh. Suddenly the whole thing struck her as so ludicrous, it was funny.

"Alice, I've never even seen you with a boy." Her mother continued to stare at her as though she were a wild animal, crouched and ready to spring.

"It was one of the sailors."

"One of the sailors? When were you alone with one of the sailors?"

"Lydia and I went to the dance hall one night. I met him there."

"The dance hall? Didn't I forbid you to go to the dance hall?"

"Yes. I'm sorry. We shouldn't have gone there, and I didn't mean for anything to happen. It just . . . did."

"He took advantage of you?"

"Not exactly."

"What do you mean, not exactly?"

"I don't think he took advantage of me, that's all."

"Alice, you won't even turn eighteen until the fall."

"I know."

"Does this young man plan to marry you?"

"He's gone. I don't know where he went. He shipped out with all the rest of them."

Evelyn continued to give her a stunned look. "Are you sure you're pregnant?"

Alice nodded.

"You haven't had your monthly?"

"No."

"Can you write to this young man?"

"I don't know his last name."

Evelyn's face crumpled, and she burst into tears.

Alice handed her a handkerchief she found between the sofa cushions and sat there watching her mother cry. Pulling a chair around to the other side of the table, she put her arm around her mother.

"I just can't understand how this happened. To you, Alice, such a nice girl." Evelyn blew her nose into the handkerchief. "I never dreamed, I just never dreamed…" She shook her head and blew her nose again.

"You'll give yourself a headache," Alice said quietly.

Evelyn went on sniffling, but her shoulders stopped heaving.

"I wrote to the woman at the hotel in Barton last week and asked her for a job. I figure I can go there and work for a while, and maybe save up enough so I can get a place to stay when I start showing. And then —" Alice paused and took a deep breath. "When the baby's born, I'll give it up."

Hearing herself speak these words, she was surprised at how meager her plans sounded and wondered why it had taken her so long to come up with them.

"You're going to leave?"

"I know it will be hard for you to manage the store alone, but Will can help out more now, and you can send me the orders to review if you want."

"Can't you just stay here, Alice? I don't know what I'll do without you." Evelyn grasped her hand.

"How can I stay? What will you tell people?"

Evelyn looked bewildered.

Alice pulled her hand away. "I don't want anyone to know. Do you understand? No one. You can't tell anyone. Not Mrs. Cunningham or Mrs. Brovelli or Miss Weeden or anyone. Even Will. I don't want him to know, either. Do you understand?"

Evelyn nodded blankly.

"I mean it. You can't tell anyone."

"All right," she said in a near-whisper.

"I don't want you to tell anyone where I've gone at first. We'll just tell people I'm going to get work on the mainland for the winter, and once I've figured everything out, I'll let you know what to say. I don't want anyone to come looking for me at the hotel, you understand?"

Evelyn started crying again. "If only your father were here, he'd know what to do. If he were here, this never would have happened, would it? I blame myself, I do. I did everything I could, but it's just so hard to raise you children all by myself and make a living and see to the store. Sometimes it's too much —"

Alice stood up and grabbed her mother by the wrist, silencing her. She knew she was squeezing her arm too hard, but she couldn't stop herself. "This has nothing to do with you or Dad. It's my mistake." She released her arm. "I'm going to bed." She could hear her mother crying quietly as she climbed the stairs.

* * *

Alice left the island on an overcast morning in August. The small band of islanders who remained on Snow came to see her off, as they had the many others who had gone away in recent months. For the first time, Alice was thankful for the war. No one seemed surprised that she was going to work on the mainland. They accepted her explanation that there would not be much business over the winter at the store, and she needed to help out by finding a job in Barton or Providence, she wasn't sure which. She would stay in one of those boarding houses for young women, she told anyone who asked. More than once during the days before she left, Alice realized she had become adept at lying, adept enough perhaps to fool even Lydia.

Mrs. Cunningham gave her an old suitcase, which she filled with the few clothes she owned, wondering what she would do when they no longer fit. She carried the suitcase down the hill herself the morning of her departure and left it on the store's porch. Inside, Will was seated on the stool behind the counter, ready to mind the place on his own. Alice had spent the time that week when her mother was not crying reviewing the books with her and filling out order forms.

She found Molly asleep beneath the newspaper rack. "I'm leaving," Alice whispered, bending down to plant a kiss on the cat's head.

Molly opened one eye and squinted up at her. Alice took that for good-bye.

"Molly's used to being fed twice a day," Alice said to Will.

"I know."

"Don't forget. You have to remember to bring her something down from the house."

"I'll remember."

"Help out Mom as much as you can."

Will squirmed on the stool. "Okay."

She ran her hand over the top of his head. Will slipped off the stool, rounded the counter, and wrapped his arms around her. "Go see lots of movies for me."

"I will," Alice said, squeezing him hard.

When she reached for her suitcase out on the porch, she saw that the ferry was already in sight. She went to stand with the knot of people at the end of the dock. Her mother was crying again.

Alice put her arms around her mother. "It's going to be okay," she whispered.

Evelyn clutched Alice's hand, holding on to it while the others gathered around, saying good-bye.

Just before she reached for the suitcase and went up the gangplank, Alice turned back to her mother. "Remember, I'll write. Then you can tell everyone where I'm staying."

Evelyn nodded and dabbed at her eyes with a handkerchief. Alice climbed the gangplank and stood at the railing. The horn sounded as the ferry pulled away.

Will jumped up and down, waving wildly. The ferry eased away from the dock. Alice raised her hand, wondering when she would see him again.

The island grew smaller and smaller, becoming nothing more than a green line against the blue water. Alice stared at the slice of green, gripping the railing with both hands, until she could no longer make out the place where it had been.

# PART III

*Place of the Passage of the Waters*

# - 1943 -

A light rain fell over the train platform in Barton. Beneath the awning of the newsstand, a young girl huddled, absently inspecting her nails while the disembarking passengers streamed past. George paused in front of the stand and considered buying a paper. The girl had the face of a child, with small features and pale skin. It was astonishing, he thought, where they had women, girls even, working these days. "Hey, you're blocking traffic," a man muttered as he went past, bumping George roughly on the shoulder. George opened his umbrella, reached for his suitcase, and moved on. The weather forecasters had let him down again.

Earlier in the day, George boarded the train in Trenton under a sky the lightest shade of blue. The weatherman had said it would remain clear for the next three days, long enough for him to wait out the ferry with its erratic schedule, but as the train moved up the coast, the rain began to fall.

On Front Street George passed the tailor's shop where he had stopped to have his suit pressed on the way home from that other war. He passed the greengrocer, the department store, the funeral parlor. The shops remained in the same places he always found them; even many of the names were unchanged, with signs he recognized hanging above the plate glass windows. Yet everything else was different: the anxious, giddy faces of the people on the street; the fast-moving cars; the shrill whistles of boys calling to one another down by the docks. When he had arrived home from his war, the sidewalks were as full as they were now. There was a sense of hope, of purpose and resolution to the crowds of shoppers and sightseers then, but the Barton he found waiting for him today was ruled by something else, a frenzy of perpetual motion, but to what end? No one seemed to know.

A man and woman exited the Priscilla Alden as he approached, walking as quickly and busily as all the others in the street. He was relieved to note that at least the facade of the hotel remained untouched, the bricks still worn and dirty, crumbling imperceptibly bit by bit each year. Inside, he found Mrs. Santos alone at the desk, flipping through a magazine. She glanced up as he made his way across the lobby.

"That time a year already, is it?" she said as she reached beneath the desk. "You got lucky again, Mr. Tibbits." She set the key to room twenty in front of him. "But next time I make no promise. This war keeps up, we're full lots of times. How long you planning on staying?"

George glanced anxiously toward the street. It was still raining. "Two nights," he answered, aware that he made the response sound like a question.

"Okay. Two nights I got for you. It keeps raining, you tell me if you want to stay longer. You got a bag?"

He nodded.

She rang the bell on the desk.

"Oh, Mr. Tibbits. Mrs. Worthington's back. She got the house open. She said to tell you."

The bellhop strode across the lobby and tipped his cap at George as he reached for the suitcase. On the second floor, George followed him down the corridor. The boy, a different one from the year before, opened the door and waited for George to step over the threshold. A luggage rack sat by the dresser. This piece of furniture had been added, but the rest was the same: the iron bedstead, the rocking chair, the dizzying wallpaper. George tipped the bellhop and shut the door behind him. The window was open a crack. He moved the rocking chair next to it.

\* \* \*

Mrs. Worthington opened the door before George knocked. He lowered the umbrella and shook it over the porch steps, and stepped inside. "Mr. Tibbits," she said. "I was expecting you. Mrs. Santos called to let me know, and I rustled up a little something. Potluck, you know. That's what you get if you don't let me know you're coming." She made a clucking sound between her teeth as he followed her into the dining room.

Two children were seated at the table, a boy about ten years old reading the funny papers and a younger girl playing with a doll. "My grandchildren," Mrs. Worthington said, gesturing toward them. "Tommy and Eleanor. They're living with me now. Children, this is Mr. Tibbits."

They glanced up and absently acknowledged him. George took his place at the head of the table. He expected them to leave once he sat down, but they did not. Mrs. Worthington went to the kitchen and returned with plates and silverware, which she set in front of the children.

"My daughter's working at the factory, evening shift," Mrs. Worthington explained while she straightened George's napkin. "And her husband's in England somewhere. That leaves me, doesn't it? Not that I mind, of course." She ran her fingers through the boy's unruly curls.

"I already used up my meat stamps for the week, Mr. Tibbits," she said when she returned with a covered casserole dish. She lifted the lid to reveal a steaming mound of macaroni mixed with chunks of white fish. "I was lucky to get the codfish, to tell you the truth. How's it down your way? Lots of shortages?"

"The same, I guess."

"I'm not complaining. If it helps our boys over there, it's a small sacrifice to pay, isn't it?"

Mrs. Worthington took her place at the opposite end of the table after she had served the four plates. "I hope you don't mind family style,

Mr. Tibbits. With taking care of the children here, I don't have the energy to put supper on the table twice."

George nodded, raising a forkful of the mushy noodles to his mouth.

"I think that munitions factory just plain took it out of me. I was there a whole year, you know. Days, and my daughter worked nights. But I just couldn't take it anymore. I told her to come here and live with me. I'll take care of the children, and you can keep on working. It's the only thing that made sense, to tell you the truth."

"When can we turn on the radio?" the boy asked.

"When supper's over. Completely over," Mrs. Worthington answered.

"At home we listen to 'Pot O' Gold' during supper," the girl said.

"Yes, well you're not at home. You're —"

"At Grandma's house," the boy finished.

Mrs. Worthington glared at him and went to get the dessert, a pudding with the metallic flavor of artificial vanilla. The children gulped theirs down and hurried from the table.

"I won't have that radio playing all through supper," she said when they were gone. "So you've got rain again?"

"Yes," George answered. "Not what they forecast."

"Forecast?" She laughed. "Oh, they can't forecast the weather around here. Never could. The '38 hurricane? They said it was going to be clear and warm that day. Just goes to show you. Well, I'll expect you tomorrow if the rain hasn't let up."

Mrs. Worthington kept glancing toward the living room, where the children were sprawled on the floor with a pile of pencils and paper. George folded his napkin, set it next to the dessert bowl, and followed her to the front door.

"I'll look for you tomorrow, then," she said, handing him the umbrella.

The rain had turned to a fine mist, obscuring the fronts of the houses and the shrouded storefronts he passed. George could not think where to go. The dining room at the hotel would be full of diners for another

264

hour at least. He could not bear the idea of sitting in his room, listening to the clink of silverware and the murmur of voices down below. He paused as he came abreast of the theater and went inside.

The newsreel was already on, and most of the seats were taken. He made his way down front until he found a row with some vacant seats on the end. He only attended movies if he could sit with an empty seat on either side. He would not spend two hours in the dark with a stranger brushing his elbow. His eyes had not yet fully adjusted to the muted light, but as he lowered himself into the seat, he saw that the nearest person was three seats away, someone small and slight, a girl.

The newsreel was about the war. They all were these days. "Allied bombers and fighters based in North Africa are sweeping in waves over the Central Mediterranean to deliver the most devastating blows yet visited on Axis docks, communications, and airfields in Italy and her island outposts," the announcer intoned. George set his hat on the seat next to him and placed his umbrella on the floor, glancing at the other occupant of the row. The girl's profile was oddly familiar, but he didn't know anyone in Barton, not these days. Then he realized she was the girl from the store on Snow, the one who had helped to rescue him. Aware of his glance, she turned her head. Their eyes met, and he looked away.

After the newsreel came the short subjects, then the movie. It was a musical with those big dance numbers that made him dizzy. George left halfway through. The girl remained in her seat, eyes fixed on the screen.

\* \* \*

George watched for the stars all night from his place by the window. He listened to the church bell mark the slow passing of each hour and waited for it to clear, but the rain kept falling, lightly, teasingly. Perhaps it would not be the next day that he followed his ritual of stepping from the ferry and making his way around the island to the west side, or the day after that. Perhaps he would have to wait. This year he would make the walk around the island, and spend a night at the inn, and return to Barton. There was nothing left for him to do on Snow, now that he had taken the long-planned boat trip and placed the broken remains of that trip for safekeeping under the house. It was better to follow the old pattern he had held to for so many years.

There were still times when he let himself wonder what might have happened if the telegram had never come. George would have circled the island on that bright morning and found Sarah waiting for him, changed after Bertie's death, but not so altered he would not have known her, could not have helped her resume the life they led before the war. He saw himself there already, opening the door to Sarah's house and stepping into the musty darkness, searching the living room. Each year he made his mind a blank, pretending that he didn't know. He climbed the stairs to Sarah's room and saw her in his mind's eye, hair strewn over the pillow. He took the telegram from the table and read it again, as he had that day, a telegram informing him of his own death. In a way, the telegram was right. He had died that day, a worse death than in some muddy trench in France.

The impersonality of it struck him again each year when he returned and read the message over. Headed "Report of Death," it read: "On the night of October 14, Tibbits volunteered to go out in front of our trenches and carry in some wounded. He had returned with a group of other men carrying the wounded when a machine gun opened fire and Tibbits was hit. He was dead when we reached him. He was buried in Le Cateau." The cause of death was listed as shellfire.

It was true that he had gone out to bring in the wounded, that he had been hit by shellfire. How the rest of the story became fact, he could not say. When the telegram arrived on the ferry, Ernie Brovelli circled the island and delivered it to Sarah. George could only imagine her confused, frightened state. She did not let Mr. Brovelli in or tell him of Bertie's death. She slipped the telegram into her apron pocket without removing the flap that concealed its contents and shut the door.

Though he had searched both the twin houses thoroughly, he had found nothing in Sarah's hand, no letter of farewell or explanation. She had left a will and the rest of her papers in a box on the dining room table, receipts for seed orders and fabric ordered through the mail. There were no outstanding bills, nothing left for him to attend to besides the funeral and burials. Over the years, the telegram had become Sarah's final message, until, returning to read it again each year, George had nearly convinced himself that she had written the words herself.

In the stiff formality of the brief explanation, he heard her voice, asking him to understand, telling him she was sorry, pleading with him not to blame her. As he watched the workers through the window, pouring out of the factory and emerging into the gray light, George wished he could tell her that he never had.

# — CHAPTER 27 —

Alice did not see George Tibbits leave the theater. She looked for him at
the end of the movie, but he was gone. She sat with the empty popcorn
container in her lap, watching an army of blondes in red, white, and blue
dance across the screen. The musicals were her favorites. She didn't even
try to follow the plot, just sat there and let the spectacle and the music
wash over her. Tonight she rose to go before the lights came up. Outside,
a light rain fell. She went quickly past the storefronts and ducked into
the Priscilla Alden.

"How's the movie?" Mrs. Santos asked.

"Good. It's the new one with Gene Kelly."

"Oh, I want to see that one. Maybe tomorrow night I go."

Mrs. Santos crossed the lobby to lock the front door. Alice called
goodnight and made her way down the hall behind the front desk, where
the help stayed and the Santos had their rooms.

After a few minutes, the gap beneath Alice's closed door went dark.
She sat on the bed in her clothes without turning on the light. If she left
the light on, Mrs. Santos would come rap on the door and ask if she was
all right. Alice knew she should go to sleep, but she didn't feel like it. She
didn't feel much like sleeping these days. Sometimes she sat up in bed for
hours. She could make out the shapes of things — the foot of the bed,
the dresser across the room — but in the dark the pieces of furniture took

on a bloated appearance, like caricatures of themselves.

Tonight the quiet hush of the rain beyond the window kept her company. She folded her hands on top of the blankets, thinking how even her skin still seemed foreign, like it belonged to someone else. For so long she had been dragging herself through the days, her body huge and misshapen, leaving her constantly off balance. Now her stomach was slack, the wrinkled skin settling back into place, but she continued to feel awkward and cumbersome.

As far as she could tell, there was no one who suspected what had befallen her now that it was over, besides Fred, the bellhop at the Priscilla Alden. Once her confinement (as Mrs. Santos called it) was past, Fred had taken to following her around, asking questions like, "Where is your husband stationed?"

"The Pacific," she would answer vaguely.

She knew he didn't believe her.

When Alice arrived at the hotel in August, asking for work, she had folded before Mrs. Santos's kindly inquiries and told her everything. Mrs. Santos immediately took the situation in hand. She explained to Fred and the women who waited tables in the dining room that Alice was the wife of her nephew from down in New York, and she was going to spend her confinement at the hotel, since her husband was away in the service. Through the long months, she kept Alice hidden in a room behind the front desk, where she did the hotel's ironing, and did not let on to anyone connected with Snow that she was there. The islanders believed Alice worked in a factory in Providence.

Mrs. Santos paid her for doing the ironing and gave her room and board at the hotel. For months before the baby came, Alice had not left the Priscilla Alden, except a few times late at night, when she walked down by the docks and stared across the water at the place where she knew the island to be, though she could not see it. She had wanted to go home from the moment she arrived. Day after day, she stood at the ironing board and imagined she was on her bicycle, slowly making her way around Snow. She would start at the store and bicycle toward the lighthouse. She would wave at Mrs. Giberson as she went past the inn and turn up Schoolhouse Road, watching for deer. She would take the time to see every inch of the shoreline in her mind and each house overlooking the water. She could remember things, like the shape of Owen Pierce's old cap, that she never knew she had noticed before. In the time it took to bicycle all the way to Gooseneck Cove and back, she could iron two sheets. Reaching for the next sheet, she would start her tour of the island again.

She missed almost everything about Snow. She even missed having Will on the other side of the blanket in the attic, rustling in his sleep. He had written three times, short, messily scrawled notes. "School is boring," he said. "It snowed but it all melted the next day." Alice searched his notes for signs that he suspected the real reason for her absence, but there were none. As the months passed, she began to believe that her mother had not betrayed her. Mrs. Santos had supplied an address in Providence, the boarding house of her friend Mrs. Dunn, where Will and the others wrote to her. Mrs. Dunn sent the letters for Alice on to Mrs. Santos.

The room where Alice ironed was separated from the front desk by a heavy curtain, and she could hear whatever went on out front, if she cared to listen. For the first months, she paused in her ironing every time a new guest checked in, straining to catch a familiar voice. Anyone from Snow could come to the mainland, and if they did, they would stay at the Priscilla Alden. After weeks of disappointment, she stopped listening. She focused on the radio Mrs. Santos left playing all day, pushed the iron over the surface of the cloth, and saw the island in her mind. One night a voice broke through. It was the middle of December. Alice had stayed late at her post, though her legs and back ached. She was nearly finished when she heard someone speaking out front. He was registering, taking a room for the night. There were no trains until morning. Yes, he said in response to Mrs. Santos's question, he was on leave from the Army. He was stationed at Pine Camp in western New York. He would be sent to a base in California soon.

From the moment she heard his voice, Alice longed to see Pete. She simply wanted to look at his face, she told herself, nothing more. She did not want to speak to him. She did not want him to know she was there, or worse, to see her. She listened as Mrs. Santos gave him a key. Did he need supper? she asked. No, he replied, he had already eaten. He should be up early to catch the first train, so he'd turn in soon.

Mrs. Santos came through the curtain when he was gone. "That was a boy from the island," she said.

"Oh? What's his name?"

"Giberson. You know him?"

Alice nodded.

"I figure you know him. Nice-looking boy."

Alice paused with the iron hovering over a pillowcase. "What room is he in?"

"Room five, down the hall. You want to see him?"

"No. No, I just wondered."

When she heard a knock on her door later that night, Alice assumed it was Mrs. Santos, coming to check on her, the way she did sometimes. She put down the letter she was writing to her mother and tied the belt of her bathrobe over her bulging stomach. She found Pete waiting in the hall. She tried to close the door before he could get a look at her, but he jammed his foot between the door and the frame.

"Alice, please let me see you, just for a minute."

She peered around the edge of the door, keeping her body hidden.

"Please," he said. "I want to see you."

"No, you don't."

"Look, I heard you behind the desk. I came back to ask that woman a question, and I heard you talking. I knew it was you, Alice. Please just let me talk to you for a minute."

"How'd you find out what room I was in?"

"I waited for you to leave and watched from down the hall."

"You didn't ask Mrs. Santos? She didn't tell you?"

"No. I just want to talk to you, Alice. We can sit in the lobby if you want."

"No. Come in." She stepped back, letting the door swing open, and watched his face for signs of horror as he took in her body, bloated and huge, a walking monument to her own folly.

He glanced at her belly, then raised his eyes. "Why didn't you tell me or Lydia or someone?"

"I couldn't."

They stood gazing at each other for a long moment. "I suppose you want to know how I got this way," she said.

"Only if you want to tell me."

She realized suddenly that she did want to tell him, that she wanted him to know the truth. "Ethan. Ethan Cunningham."

"The bastard."

Tears slid down her face. She did not want to cry. She wiped her eyes with the back of her hand, and he put his arms around her, pushing the door closed behind him. She pressed her face against his shoulder while he stroked her hair.

"I'm getting your uniform wet," she said finally, raising her head.

He took a handkerchief from his pocket and handed it to her. She blew her nose. "Does he know?"

She shook her head. "By the time I knew, he was married."

"And you're not going to tell him?"

"No. I'm going to give the baby up." Alice felt tears running down her face again. "I'm sorry. I haven't seen anyone from home in such a long time."

"How long have you been here?"

"Since the summer. Since I left Snow."

"You were never in Providence?"

She shook her head.

Alice felt her breath come more evenly and realized she was standing inches from Pete in her nightgown and bathrobe. She went to the bed and sat against the pile of pillows Mrs. Santos had given her, pulling the spread over her legs. Pete stood beside the bed, gazing down at her. She was afraid to meet his eyes.

"You must think I'm an idiot," she said.

"No, I think Ethan Cunningham is a goddamned bastard, and if I ever get the chance, I'll kill him."

"It wasn't like that. I wanted to be with him."

Alice saw the hurt on Pete's face and instantly regretted her words. He stared at the floor, his hands clasped loosely together, as though he could not bear to consider the idea that she had chosen Ethan.

Pete cleared his throat and raised his head. "Do you still . . . care for him?"

"No. I hated him for a long time. Now I don't feel much of anything when I think about him."

"I hated him, too." Pete lowered himself into the chair by the bed. Neither of them spoke for a long moment. "I wanted to do something, Alice, but I couldn't think what. I wanted to talk to you so badly. I should have. I should have spoken to you before I left. I tried, but I could see you didn't want that."

Alice felt suddenly ashamed. "I shouldn't have made you feel that way." She wanted to touch him, but she stopped herself.

Pete shifted in the chair. "I was going to come find you in Providence, but I've only got seventy-two hours leave. I was thinking of trying to get a bus up to Providence tonight and going to find you in that rooming house. I asked your mother, but she said you probably wouldn't be there, that you were working double shifts."

"Was she convincing?"

"I didn't think anything of it."

"I was sure she'd tell everyone." Alice glanced down at her stomach. "She's not great at keeping a secret."

Pete reached out tentatively and took her hand. She wrapped her fingers around his. "I've always cared for you, Alice. For as long as I can remember."

She nodded, afraid that if she tried to speak, she would cry again.

"Back when we first came to Snow, I felt this way. I was just a kid then, but now . . ."

He did not finish the sentence, but she understood. They weren't children anymore.

"I know this isn't the right time." Pete stopped. "What am I saying? There's never going to be a right time, is there? I guess I've been waiting too long for the right time."

Alice held his fingers tight.

"I don't have a speech. I just want to know if you'll marry me."

She heard his question and realized that she was not surprised, that she had been expecting this question for a long time, that she had even expected Pete to be the one to ask. She did not have to think for more than a moment before answering. "Yes," she whispered.

He leaned over the edge of the bed, and they kissed, the meeting of their lips tentative at first. Then he pulled her to him and kissed her fully, holding her close. His mouth was soft and full on hers. When he broke away, his face shone with a clear and simple happiness, the way she had remembered him in the months since he had left Snow.

"Tomorrow," he said. "We'll go to Town Hall, first thing in the morning."

"You have to get your train."

"I'll take the next one. So I'm late. What can they do, court-martial me?"

"I don't want you to marry me because of this."

"I'm not marrying you because of this. I'm marrying you because I want to. If we get married, you won't have to give the baby up."

Alice felt how tempting it was. She did not want to let the baby go. She had grown to love the child that stirred inside her, but she could not ask Pete to accept Ethan's child as his own.

"It's not right," she said softly.

"This isn't right, either." He gestured toward the mound of her stomach and wrapped both his hands around hers. "Don't say no this time."

She felt the sting of his words, thinking of all the times she had turned away from him in the past. "I don't want to start this way. I would always think of Ethan when I looked at the baby."

Pete grimaced.

"I was so stupid. I know that now. I don't want a life with you to be founded on that stupidity."

Pete touched her cheek. "I don't care. I want to make it right."

Alice shook her head.

"But you'll marry me?"

"Yes."

"When? Tomorrow?"

"No, when you come home, and we can do it the right way. After... the baby."

Pete ran his fingers through her hair. "I want you to be happy."

"I am, happier than I've ever been." Alice felt the truth of these words and wrapped her arms around Pete, pressing her lips to his.

Through the hours of that night they sat side by side, talking and kissing, holding each other quietly. They spoke of returning to Snow and laughed to imagine how surprised Lydia would be. They thought of how others would react, too — Alice's mother, Pete's parents, even Miss Weeden — but what anyone else thought did not matter. The certainty of what they had found belonged to them and them alone.

In the early hours of the morning, they fell asleep in each other's arms with the swell of her stomach between them.

# — CHAPTER 28 —

Alice was seated behind the desk, minding the lobby while Mrs. Santos ate breakfast, when George Tibbits appeared on the staircase. He did not seem to age from one year to the next. His face remained the same, neither young nor old. He wore his brown suit and worn hat, and his skin had the pale look of someone who does not go outside often. Alice watched him cross the lobby, wondering if he had recognized her in the theater the night before. As he passed the desk, he glanced up and said hello.

Mary came from the dining room. "What's with him?" she asked, watching him go out into the street.

"He's a little strange."

"A little strange? Mrs. Santos says he won't go anywhere if it's raining. He stays here till the sun comes out."

Alice thought of the stories she could tell about George Tibbits, but said nothing.

When Mrs. Santos returned from breakfast, Alice and Mary carried stacks of sheets and towels upstairs and went from room to room, making the beds, emptying wastebaskets, dusting dressers. Mary sang while they worked, going through her repertoire of Andrews Sisters songs. Alice hummed along as she smoothed the sheets flat and tucked in the ends. Now that she was no longer pregnant, she went out in the rest of the hotel. She had become friendly with the girls who worked in the dining room. They didn't ask questions the way Fred did.

Alice set folded towels at the end of a bed and paused at the window in the empty room. Rain streaked the glass, and the hum of machinery carried from the factory. Over the rooftops, she could just make out the ferry at the dock. In another month, when she had saved enough money, she would be going home.

Her baby would be eleven weeks old now. Mrs. Santos had told everyone at the hotel that the baby had died. A stillbirth, she called it. When Alice returned from the hospital, the girls spoke in hushed tones, saying they were so sorry. It was a fitting lie. She could still see his perfect body as the doctor lifted him into the air and told her he was a boy. Alice watched the doctor carry him over to the basin to be washed, memorizing the tiny hands and feet, and the red skin. Though the labor was short, she was exhausted, every drop of feeling wrung from her body. She just wanted to touch him. "Please," she said to the nurse, "let me hold him."

The nurse wiped a damp washcloth over Alice's face and shook her head. "It's better this way," she said.

Moments later he was whisked away, wrapped in a white blanket. Alice lay on the gurney, racked by sobs.

While she smoothed the bedspread and arranged the pile of towels, Alice spoke to her baby in her mind. She called him Bill, after her father. She imagined he was being loved by some other woman, who held him and fed him and rocked him to sleep. The nuns who ran the adoption agency had reassured her. There were plenty of people looking to adopt. He would have a good home.

Gathering up her pile of clean linens and a pail full of rags, Alice went down the hall, passing the door to room twenty. She knew not to knock and ask if George Tibbits wanted his sheets changed. She moved on to a room that had been vacated that morning. On the dresser she found a movie stub and a comb missing most of its teeth, which she tossed in a trash bag. The odd personal items she discovered in the rooms made her think of Pete. Somewhere he was living in strange quarters, too.

"I have a picture of us from graduation," he had written in his last letter. "You, me, and Lydia sitting by the podium. My mother took it. I carry it in my wallet and look at it every night before I go to sleep. You keep getting prettier."

She had received that letter at the end of April, from the embarkation base in California where Pete had been sent. "I wish you could meet some of the men," he had written. "I've become good friends with one from Indianapolis. He's always asking for stories about Snow. He loves the idea of living on an island. I see now how lucky we are to be from a place where everyone knows everyone. Cities are so different. I wouldn't want to live somewhere so impersonal. Of course, if you wanted to leave Snow, I would consider it. You know I would be happy anywhere with you, don't you? But I think you feel the way I do, that the island is home."

He called her "dearest" in his letters and "my love." She read the words with which he carefully filled the V-mail and felt how she had misjudged Pete, thinking that someone with his quiet steadiness could not feel passion.

Finished with the rooms on the second floor, she followed Mary upstairs. "Will you look at this?" Mary called.

Alice went down the hall and found Mary on her knees, scraping something from the floor with a rag.

"Gum," she said with disgust. "These people don't have any manners. I'm sick of cleaning up after people who are just plain rude. Hell with it. I can't get this up without a knife." Mary tossed the rag in her bucket.

Alice went into the next room and stripped the sheets from the bed, listening as Mary started singing again. She and Pete had not told anyone of their plans yet. Alice wanted the pregnancy to be safely past, and she did not want to write the news in letters. Now, as the time when she could tell people drew closer, she imagined how she would make the announcement. She saw the islanders standing around her at the store, surprised but happy, offering their congratulations.

Alice and Mary finished cleaning the last of the rooms and carried their supplies down to the lobby. The kitchen, where the hotel's help ate, was a hot, noisy place smelling of fried onions and fish. Ricky, the cook, stood over the stove with a spatula in his hand. "Alice," he called when they entered, "look what I got for you today — your favorite. Minestrone."

Mrs. Santos said she would have preferred a Portuguese cook, but these days, she was lucky to get any cook at all. She had to make do with an Italian who over-spiced the food and insisted on making his mother's lasagna, which none of the customers ordered.

"You're looking too skinny again," Ricky said as he handed Alice a bowl of soup. "Ain't she too skinny, Mary? Look at this – nothing to grab hold of." Ricky pinched her cheek between his fingers and whispered, "I'm giving you extra bread."

Alice shook her head. "Keep it for yourself."

"I know, you don't want me to fatten you up. You're thinking what you're gonna look like in a bathing suit. All you American girls are too skinny."

Alice carried her soup to a long table at the rear of the kitchen, away from the prep area. She had actually gained weight since the pregnancy, but Ricky could not be convinced of this fact.

Ricky kept up a running monologue while he fried the fish fillets and dished up potatoes. "Look what these people order. The most boring food on the menu. I make them a beautiful red sauce, but do they want it? No. What do they want? Just to fill their stomachs. They don't care."

He darted a glance at Alice and Mary, tossing the spatula in the air with one hand and catching it behind his back with the other. The girls laughed in spite of themselves. While they ate, the waitresses came and went through the swinging door, shouting orders and picking up plates.

They balanced trays on their shoulders and pushed the door open with their hips. They had a certain glamour in their uniform dresses with the little lace aprons tied round their waists. There were moments when Alice wished she could join them out on the dining room floor, scooping up tips.

"Hey Ricky," one of the waitresses called, "customer's complaining that the food's not hot."

"Not hot? Bring me that plate. I don't serve anything's not hot enough." He rolled his eyes at Alice. "They sit there talking for twenty minutes, and then they complain the food's not hot. You know what I think? I have to go out there and feed them myself."

Alice finished her soup and took the bowl to the sink, where the dishwasher was scrubbing pots. She told Mary she would see her later and made her way down the hall to the back room. A stack of tablecloths and napkins and wrinkled sheets waited for her on the ironing board. She sprinkled water on the linens while the iron heated up.

When the noon-time crowd had cleared out and the waitresses had gone home, Mrs. Santos came into the back room and took a seat beside the ironing board. "You're looking good, Alice. Not so pale anymore. I wish you'd stay here with me. You're the best girl I ever had."

Alice shrugged off the compliment and unfolded a tablecloth. Mrs. Santos went on, talking about how if the war kept up, she would need all the help she could find. Everybody was going somewhere these days.

Mrs. Santos was saying she might have to advertise all the way to Boston if any more of her girls left to go work in the factory or volunteer with the Red Cross, when the bell sounded out at the desk. She stubbed out her cigarette in the ashtray on the arm of the chair and pulled the curtain aside. Alice listened to the exchange of conversation, but she could not tell who was out there. Moments later, Mrs. Santos returned. "The mailman," she said.

She flipped through a pile of letters, extracting an oversized envelope with a return address from Providence. She slit the envelope open and two letters fell out. "Here's something for you."

Alice checked the return addresses and slipped them in her pocket. One was from Lydia, the other from her mother.

"You can take a break," Mrs. Santos said. "Go on — read your letters."

Alice shook her head. She liked to savor the letters, to read them in private. She ran the iron over the tablecloth and said she would wait until later.

* * *

For supper that night, Ricky made codfish Portuguese-style, baked with tomatoes and peppers. The recipe was his one concession to Mrs. Santos, proof that he could cook Portuguese if he had to. He served the fish with rice and made a show of putting a sprig of parsley on each girl's plate. "For good luck," he said, winking at Alice.

The waitresses ate early, before their shifts started, but they took breaks back in the kitchen, stopping for a minute to smoke or have a couple of bites of pie. "Hey," one of them called to Mary, "we're going to the movies tonight. Want to come?"

"What's showing?"

"I don't know. Some new picture."

Mary said okay, she'd meet them out front later. "You want to go?" she asked Alice.

"I went last night."

"So?"

It was true that now she was no longer pregnant, Alice went to the theater night after night, seeing the same movie three or four times. "Maybe tomorrow," she told Mary.

When she was finished eating, Alice rose from the table and took her plate to the sink. She said goodnight to Mary and Ricky, and made her way down the hall to her room. Closing the door behind her, she switched on the lamp by the bed. She opened Lydia's letter first, a thin aerogram all the way from England.

Lydia did not write often, but when they did come, her letters were full of news. She worked from early in the morning until late at night nearly every day, making donuts to serve the Americans stationed at the airfields and bases. She said that the smell of dough never left her skin, but she didn't mind. She was too busy and tired to care, putting in such long days. This time she had written: "Dear Alice, It sure would be great to have you here with me. I miss you and everyone else from home, but I'm having a terrific time. The other girls are a great bunch. We get to laughing so hard when we're making the donuts we cry. But then a plane flies over and we remember what we're doing here. God, the war is just awful. When will it ever end? You should see the American G.I.s lined up in the lobby when we come back to our hotel at night. I could have a different date every night if I wanted, but I'm being careful. Our captain says the men are so lonely, it's not right to take advantage of them. I've only heard from Pete a couple of times, but he sounds okay. Maybe he's written you. I bet the mail gets through better and faster over there in the States. How is that stinky factory of yours? I hope you're making lots of money and buying yourself some new clothes. Don't send all the money you make back to Snow. Really, Alice. Well, you know I can't wait to see you. We'll both have stories to tell. Until then, lots of love, Lydia."

When Alice read Lydia's letters, she felt that she had traveled across the ocean for a moment herself. She could hear the planes overhead and smell the donuts. Her mother's letters were less exciting, though they brought news of the islanders. Alice slit open the envelope and pulled out a single page.

"Dear Alice," it read. "We are getting along. It looks like business will be slow this summer, so I'm not placing too many orders. Will says hello. I can leave him alone to mind the store now and he does pretty good. We had some sad news last week. Pete Giberson was killed in action on the island of Attu, up near Alaska. I guess there's a whole string of islands up there that the Japanese have taken. Will showed me on the map. Pete was part of an attack on the Japanese. The American boys went in to take the island, and they were ambushed. Mrs. Giberson was so overcome, she didn't leave the house for three days. I took them some cookies I made. They're planning to have the funeral and bury him on Snow once Lydia gets home. She's taking the first ship she can get back. He was such a nice boy. It doesn't seem fair. I'll let you know when the service is in case you want to be here. I'm sure the Gibersons would appreciate that. Let me know when you think you can come home. We miss you. Love, Mom."

Alice set the letter on the table by the bed and stared at the sheet of paper. She would not believe it. She reached for Lydia's aerogram, examining it again. It was dated the middle of April. Lydia couldn't have known anything then, though clearly she did now. Alice took up her mother's letter and read it over. The words had not changed.

She walked from one side of the room to the other with the letter in her hand. Tears slid down her face, but she was barely aware of them. She wanted to leave, to go someplace where the news could not be true. She threw the piece of paper on the floor and tugged on her jacket.

Mrs. Santos was busy with a customer at the desk. Alice went quickly past her and out of the hotel. The streets were blessedly dark and wet with rain. She turned down Church Street to the docks. There was only one thing to do, she realized. She had to go home. She would sail the ferry herself if she had to.

Alice walked the length of the dock. The ferry waited at the end. She thought of somehow trying to climb aboard. She sank to her knees and leaned over the edge of the dock. The tears ran down her face, into the rippled water below. She wanted to enter that cold darkness. She wanted to pass beyond feeling, to a place where she could not be touched.

The rain fell on her back, but she did not experience being wet or cold. She remained there at the end of the dock for minutes or hours, she could not say which, until she felt a hand on her shoulder and raised her head. George Tibbits was bending over her.

"I'm sorry," he said. "I don't mean to intrude, but I saw you walking away from the hotel. I was out myself …"

He kept his hand on her shoulder. When she didn't respond, he said, "I know I have no business intruding on you, but you were so kind to me on Snow."

Alice gazed at him blankly and heard herself whisper Pete's name.

George nodded, as though he understood. He bent down. "Do you think you could stand up?"

He held Alice's arm and helped her to her feet. Holding on to her arm, he turned and guided her down the dock. In her senseless state, Alice went with him, without questioning where he was leading her or why.

He took her down the back street by the docks and asked if there was another entrance to the hotel. Yes, she answered automatically, the kitchen. She pointed to the back door of the hotel. George kept his hand on her arm and led her through the door. The kitchen was empty. Ricky had gone home, leaving behind the smell of cigarettes and fish.

Alice went down the hall with George beside her. When they came to her room, she stopped. "This is where I stay," she said.

George opened the door and stepped aside to let her enter. She expected him to leave then, but he did not. He followed her inside.

He sat in the room's only chair and did not look at her. Alice lay on the bed, knees pulled in to her chest. She did not see how she could ever get up out of the bed, how she could speak or walk or eat again.

The clock in the church tower chimed midnight. Alice heard the tolling of the bell and cried silently. George did not talk to her. He did not touch her or try to get her to stop crying. He simply sat there. When Alice woke in the morning, he was still seated in the chair. She saw that he had taken the blanket from the foot of the bed and placed it over her.

He turned toward her when she sat up. "I'm going to the island today," he said.

Alice realized then that she would be going to Snow, too.

\* \* \*

Alice sat on the deck of the ferry, on a bench by the wheelhouse, with the sun pouring over her. Captain Tony sounded two long blasts of the horn as the ferry slipped away from the dock. She watched the shore-line recede, the ferry leaving behind the flat roof of the factory, the church steeple, and the tangle of fishing shacks along the water. She could pick out the windows across the top floor of the Priscilla Alden when the boat pulled into the open water.

She took in the rooftops of Barton, and Captain Tony's profile, and the scrubbed deck of the ferry as if for the first time. Everything had a raw, unpolished look. It was not that the world was changed by Pete's death. What she saw around her was the same, but every face, every new object, had a power to hurt her that it did not have before.

George Tibbits stood at the railing with his back to her, gazing at the place across the water where Snow would appear. After a while, the green hump of the island came into sight. Alice went to the railing. The island looked so small in the distance, hardly large enough to hold a handful of people.

She unbuttoned her sweater and took in a deep breath of the salt-laced air. The smell was different here from the scent hanging over Barton. Out on the water, the air remained open, full of the sea, without the damp closeness of town. Alice knew this air, the air of the island.

George turned toward her. "You will always remember the boy who has died," he said quietly.

"Yes," she answered. "I will."

He gave a small nod of his head and faced the water again.

As they grew closer to Snow, the tops of the trees became visible, distinct from the shore, and the island took on form. They passed

Gooseneck Cove and the far end of the island. There was no one in sight along the road by the dump. Tony's assistant strode across the deck and leaned on the railing next to Alice, ready to throw the line over the pilings. A small group of people stood clustered by the dock.

They slowly assumed features: her mother in the old straw hat, and Will tossing stones in the water, and Owen Pierce with his pipe clamped between his teeth, Miss Weeden beside him. Phoebe Shattuck held a baby in her arms while the other children ran in circles around her. Mr. and Mrs. Giberson stood off to the side by themselves.

Up the hill, the windows of the houses shone in the sunlight. The islanders who for generations had shaped lives from so little were present in the still, bright scene, and the ones who had come before them, calling this slip of land "place of the passage of the waters." There was nothing more to honor the memory of the dead but what Alice saw before her — a small band of islanders waiting on muddy ground, the store where every morning she would start a pot of coffee, the rowboats bobbing along the shore. She studied each of the faces turned expectantly toward the dock. She saw other faces, the ones not present, their absence a piece of the land and the water and the sky, making those who stepped forward to greet her now all the more precious. The shrill note of the ferry's horn pierced the air. Alice gazed up at the white shape of a gull coasting overhead and waited for the ferry to pull alongside the dock.

# ACKNOWLEDGMENTS

The first chapter of *Snow Island* was published in *Garden Lane*, in a somewhat different form. I am grateful to the editors for this early affirmation. I am thankful as well for the time and space given to me by Yaddo and the Virginia Center for the Creative Arts.

I began work on this book the year I held the George Bennett Fellowship at Phillips Exeter Academy. The support of the fellowship and the Exeter community were crucial in helping this work take shape, and the friendship of the Bennett Fellows over the years has been important to my journey as a writer.

A number of readers looked at early drafts of this work and provided valuable feedback. I would like to thank Carrie Sherman, Ann Ott, Kelly Harrison, David Hadas, Brian Rogers, Meryl Schwartz, Leela and David Towler Kausch, Sat Charan Khalsa, Jim Vescovi, Jeanne Heifetz, and Ilya Kaminsky. I could not have kept writing without the generous encouragement of many friends, especially Sandell Morse, Deborah Hodge, Anne Welch, Jim Hill, Hildred Crill, Mimi White, Tom Gervat, and the editors at *The Mars Hill Review* — Stuart Hancock, Gina Bria, Caroline Langston, Judith Kunst, Sheryl Cornett, and Joey Earl Horstman. The junior high and high school students from schools in New Hampshire and Maine who listened to me read from this work and cheered me on were another invaluable source of encouragement.

In writing this book, I was assisted with research on everything from the Model T to the business of quahogging. I would like to thank all those who answered my questions and pointed me in new directions, including James K. Sparrell, Michael Huxtable of the Portsmouth Public Library, Steve Seymour, Terry Whiting, and Flora and Howard Sparrell.

Finally, I would like to give special thanks to my parents, Jane Kellogg and Lewis Towler, for their support and memories of the war years; my agent, Deborah Schneider, for staying with me; Jennie Camp for being the first to give this book a chance; my editor, Pat Walsh, for his encouragement and expert guidance; Jeanne Schinto and Manette Ansay for crucial advice; and Ned Bradford and others for giving me places to work in the years when I wandered around New England without a car. Most of all, I am grateful to Jim Sparrell for his patient and constant love, and for making a life with me as I wrote this book.